Highland Sparks

LOGAN & GWYNETH

KEIRA MONTCLAIR

Copyright © 2014 by Keira Montclair

All rights reserved under International and Pan-American Copyright Conventions

By payment of required fees, you have been granted the *non-exclusive*, *non*-transferable right to access and read the text of this book. No part of this text may be reproduced, transmitted, downloaded, decompiled, reverse engineered, or stored in or introduced into any information storage and retrieval system, in any form or by any means, whether electronic or mechanical, now known or hereinafter invented without the express written permission of copyright owner.

Please Note

The reverse engineering, uploading, and/or distributing of this book via the internet or via any other means without the permission of the copyright owner is illegal and punishable by law. Please purchase only authorized electronic editions, and do not participate in or encourage electronic piracy of copyrighted materials. Your support of the author's rights is appreciated.

No part of this book may be reproduced or transmitted in any form or by any electronic or mechanical means, including photocopying, recording or by any information storage and retrieval system, without the written permission of the publisher, except where permitted by law.

Thank you.

Cover Design and Interior format by The Killion Group
http://thekilliongroupinc.com

NOTE TO THE READER

PLEASE READ IF YOU HAVE READ JOURNEY TO THE HIGHLANDS!

As you begin to read this novel, you may notice some similarities. You may even think you have read it before. If so, you're not wrong. There are parts of this novel in which the dialogue is exactly the same as in Robbie and Caralyn's story in JOURNEY TO THE HIGHLANDS.

Logan and Gwyneth met in JOURNEY TO THE HIGHLANDS when Logan left the Grant keep in search of Robbie Grant. This scene was in Robbie's story from Robbie's point-of-view. I needed you to see the same scene from Logan and Gwyneth's point-of-view. This means the dialogue will be the same, but the descriptions and thoughts will be different.

I apologize and hope this doesn't make the story drag for you, but I felt it was imperative to see how these scenes played out and how they affected their relationship. It wouldn't be an accurate representation of their connection without a closer look at when they met and how it affected each of them. Take note that this is true of the first scenes only.

Enjoy! I hope you love Logan and Gwyneth's journey.

Keira Montclair

CHAPTER ONE

October, 1263
South Ayrshire, Scotland

Gwyneth of the Cunningham smiled as she thought about how well she had done at the butts. Her father, who'd first taught her how to nock, draw, and release an arrow, would have been so proud. How she missed her da and her brother Gordon. They had held such fierce competitions, and even though she'd lost most of the time, it had improved her skills as an archer. She picked up her pace so she could find her younger brother, Father Rab, to tell him of her good fortune for the day.

As she approached the back door to the Kirk, a rustling in the bushes startled her a few seconds before two sets of strong arms picked her up and pinned her to the ground. She tried to scream, but a gag was stuffed in her mouth, stifling the words she wished to shout: *Help me, please! Someone help me. Who are you?*

She kicked and squirmed with everything she had, but to no avail. One vile brute held her arms while the other pinned her legs. The smell of fish invaded her nostrils.

She prayed for her brother to step outside or for anyone in the area to assist her. But it was dusk, and the men wore dark clothes. Bystanders would have to be close to realize what was afoot. Even Gwyneth could barely make out the looks of them. The lout at her feet tied her legs together.

"Och, 'tis a feisty one, is she no'? I'd like a wee taste of this one." The smelly one at her head spoke first.

"Keep your shaft between your legs. Duff will skin you alive if you touch her. He says she still has her maidenhead." The name made her buck and kick even harder. Seven long years ago, she had watched her father and brother die at the hands of Duff Erskine. He was her one sworn enemy.

Smelly guffawed. "Well, I would no' mind checking for him."

The second attacker finished tying her legs before nodding to his partner. "Shut up before someone hears you, fool. Tie her hands together so we can get moving. The boat leaves shortly."

Gwyneth panicked. The boat? As in a boat to send her off from the docks? Where were they sending her? Her heartbeat sped up as her vision dimmed.

"You know Duff makes ten times the coin for a lass whose maidenhead is intact." He grinned at her as she continued to fight against her bindings. "Whoever buys this one in the East will have a challenge taming her."

Her maidenhead? The East? What were they talking about?

A chill ran up her spine as cold sweat drenched her body. All the possibilities—one worse than the next—raced through her mind as her eyes searched the area for someone, anyone, to help her. Not paying any heed to the desperation, the two men tossed her in a horse-drawn cart like she was a sack of flour and covered her with a scratchy blanket. At the last minute, her bow landed beside her.

"Why'd you do that?" Smelly asked the second man.

"Duff says he can sell any weapon. He'll make coin off her bow and quiver."

Screaming through the gag, she bucked with all her might, but no one came to her rescue. Angry tears slid down her cheeks at her own powerlessness. All the training in the world with her bow and arrow would not help her now.

Papa, help me. Lord, help me. The words repeated themselves over and over in her head as she was bounced along in the cart. It seemed as though she had been moving forever, but in truth she knew it had only been about an hour before the horses finally slowed.

The smell of the firth reached her and she closed her eyes, not wanting to accept what would happen next.

Nay, nay, nay.

She bucked again in an attempt to throw herself over the side of the cart, but failed. A few minutes after the horses stopped, Duff Erskine's hated voice reached her ears.

"There she is." He removed the blanket and her gag and stroked her cheek. "Och, you did grow up to be a beauty, didn't you? And those blue eyes. I never noticed them before." He broke out in a huge grin. "You will fetch me a large number of coins. How are that bow and arrow working for you? I'm glad the lads brought them along. I'll sell them in the East as well."

Gwyneth screamed and Erskine slapped her. "Close your mouth." She screamed again, and he wrenched her up by her hair. "No one will help you. I send women abroad whenever I please, and no one ever helps them. Why? Because no one dares face me, not even the sheriff. But have no fear, you won't be alone," he said with a smirk. "Several women will be going with you." As soon as he was close enough, she clawed her fingernails across his hand. "Bitch!" Flinging her head back down, he cursed again at her, checking his skin where she'd scratched him.

Duff Erskine had changed. No longer looking like he lived by the water and just came off a boat, he wore finery like any nobleman in England. A sickish smell emanated from him, some type of scent much like a lady would wear lavender. Gwyneth's nose wrinkled, but then she grinned, noticing a small trail of blood sliding down his arm. It was a shallow wound, but each drop of blood was a small victory.

He turned to one of his comrades—the one she knew as Smelly—and said, "Rodney, hold her head down."

The brute pinned her head to the cart. No matter how she fought, she couldn't escape his grip. Erskine leaned over and pinched her nose. "Open up."

Gwyneth refused to open her mouth and held tight for as long as she could, flailing and kicking at the same time.

The other brute pinched her thigh and said, "Open up, bitch. I gotta get home."

She couldn't hold on any longer. Her mouth opened as she gasped for air and Erskine forced a vile liquid into her mouth. She fought to spit it out, but gagged on it, swallowing much of it.

Fight, Gwyneth! Fight! A persistent voice cried out in the back of the head, but darkness overpowered her as her squirming weakened, whatever liquid he gave her taking over.

***

Gwyneth had to clear her mind and find her bow and arrow. If she didn't, she would never be able to accomplish her one purpose in life—killing Duff Erskine. She struggled to lift her head but could not. The muted echo of Erskine's laughter set off a fire inside her, and she willed herself to get up just so she could hurt him, kill him, anything.

She couldn't move. What had been in that liquid? She made out bits and pieces of what he was saying to his lackeys. "Once you get to the East...highest price for ...the dark-haired one. They'll pay lots of coin for blue eyes."

Finally, the fingers of her left hand wiggled as she commanded, prompting her to grab for something nearby, anything that would help her hoist her body up and fight. She gripped the handle of a wooden chest, scraping the raw skin of her hand across the rough wood, but she ignored the pain, pulling with every muscle in her arm to lift her torso off the ground. Suddenly, her entire body rolled along with the floor beneath her. *Fie, a boat. I'm on a ship.*

"Aye, the others are young enough to get good coin, but you should get the most for Gwyneth. Besides, she scratched me like a bobcat. She owes me."

She rolled onto her side, bracing her bound hands on the floor, hoping to stop the movement. She searched the closest area, taking in the other prone bodies strewn across the oak planks of the ship. Women. Who knew how many? Duff stood at the bow talking to several men, chuckling as he handed them coin before he left the ship. Hoisting her head up, Gwyneth continued to assess her surroundings until the ship caught another wave, and she fell back again, striking her head on a wooden plank. The last thing she saw was Duff's cruel eyes staring straight at her, a big grin on his face. He tugged on his clothing as if he were a member of nobility, every dark hair in place while he fidgeted with the heavy gold adorning his hands.

He tipped his hat at her with a wink before he stepped off the boat. "Have a nice trip, Gwyneth."

She would kill Duff Erskine if it was the last thing she did.

***

The next time Gwyneth awakened, women's screams and men's shouts echoed all around her. She tried to focus, to hold her eyes open, but whatever Duff had given her held fast. Drugged into slow motion, she attempted to lift her head again, but to no avail. Right away, she knew. The smell of the air and the movement of the swaying oak planks underneath told her all she needed to know. They were afloat.

Her guess was they sailed on the Firth of Clyde. She

fought to clear her mind and remember exactly how she had come to be here. She had been attacked on her way from the archery butts to the Kirk where she lived with her brother, Father Rab.

Moving her head, she caught sight of a large galley ship bobbing next to theirs. Thank God, someone would rescue them, for she had yet to find her bow. Squinting to see who was boarding the boat, she groaned and fell back against the rough hewn planks. More bad news. The boat was flying the raven banner of King Haakon, the king of the Norse, who was rumored to have brought thousands of his men to pillage and plunder Arran and Ayrshire in order to keep control of the Western Isles away from the Scots.

Lying in the corner of the ship's deck, she attempted to stay as unobtrusive as possible as she worked to free her bindings while hiding under a slip of canvas. Hoots and hollers from the invaders sent the crew of her ship scrambling in different directions, and then a group of filthy Norsemen came aboard, pushing past the lasses in pursuit of the crew. Moments later, she heard fists pound against flesh, accompanied by the sound of breaking bones. Men yelled, begged, and threatened, but to no avail. Dissonant sounds rent the air—clashing metal, screams, and men falling overboard. Who survived, the crew or the Norse, she didn't know. She feigned sleep in case they returned.

Moments later, relative quiet descended. Gwyneth opened one eye to see if she could determine who had won. She had to survive no matter what, for Rab, her only family member left, and to finish Duff. The Norse returned from the bow of the ship with shouts of exhilaration, each man grabbing a lass and tossing her on her back, sometimes two to one. She managed to struggle out of her bindings to locate her dagger inside her clothing, praying that Duff hadn't removed it, and sighed when she found it. No one would get her without a fight.

A meaty hand gripped her by the front of her tunic. The warrior's clothing she favored had not confused the man in front of her. The brute tossed her flat onto her back, then landed on top of her with a shout of jubilation. His hand reached down to fondle her breast, and she brought her head up with a snap, knocking her forehead against his hard enough to stun the lout for a moment. He slapped her twice before pinning her to the ground. Furious and fueled with new purpose, he continued by ripping through her clothes and fondling her private area. A jolt spread through her as a hard piece of flesh met her entrance. The last haze of the drug wore away instantly.

Naught could have brought a stronger reaction from her. A fierce growl wrenched from her gut as she reached into the fold of her clothing and pulled out her knife, aiming directly between the blackguard's legs. When she connected with his flesh, he bellowed and screeched as blood spurted out before he could reach for his bollocks. She had found her mark. Swinging his fist, he caught the side of her head before she managed to roll away from him.

Another Norseman bellowed out a warning, and the fool she had speared glanced back to look at his comrade, who was pointing up the firth. More ships headed in their direction. She could tell from the expressions on their faces that they were worried. Norse or Scots? After a quick murmured conversation, the invaders scrambled back onto their longboat and rowed away. Gwyneth pulled herself into a sitting position, not bothering to hold her ripped clothing together. She surveyed the deck, fighting to stay awake and think clearly. At least five other women were moving; two weren't. Dead? Could they be dead already? Scanning the area again, she couldn't find one male on board.

She put her hand on the nearest woman. "Are you unhurt? Can I help?"

The woman shook her head, pushing her hand away and sobbing. Gwyneth looked around the boat again, but her first impression had been correct. There were no men. A small sliver of hope sprung inside her. Perhaps they wouldn't be sent to the East. The Norse had done them a small favor.

Every last member of Erskine's crew had been thrown overboard.

CHAPTER TWO

Logan Ramsay spurred his horse forward, ignoring the voice in his head. *You can stop now. You don't need to protect everyone. Your niece and nephew are better now that Brenna Grant has healed them...*

His brother Quade's two children, Lily and Torrian, had both developed a sickness that had made them so ill they could not even get off their pallets. Torrian had barely been able to lift his head off his soft pillow, and he had been in too much pain to move. Logan, who loved the children as if they were his own, had been beside himself. Quade and his mother had stayed by the weans' sides year after year. But he couldn't handle it, choosing instead to wander whenever he felt overwhelmed by the failure of not being able to cure what ailed the wee ones.

Then he had kidnapped Brenna Grant, renowned as the best healer in the Highlands, and brought her to his home. She had not only healed both children, but also fallen in love with his brother and married him. Brenna, Quade's wife, was quite simply the best thing to happen to his family. So he would now do anything for her. It was, he told himself, the reason he still rode.

Robbie Grant, the captain of the Grant warriors, was the reason he was on this journey. Robbie was Brenna's brother, and he was determined to find him and bring him back to the Highlands. The Grant clan hadn't heard from him since the Scots' battle with the

Norse at Largs, which had ended in a decisive victory for the Scots. Logan had taken it upon himself to ease the Grants' minds, out of gratitude for all they had done for his own clan... And, perhaps, because Logan did not know what to do with himself when he was not on a mission.

Nudging his horse, Paz, he organized his plan in his head. Robbie Grant had just secured a powerful victory at Largs. There had been around four hundred Grant warriors in the field at one point. There had to be a group of them still in camp near Ayr. Even if Robbie had been sent south again after the battle, he must have left some clansmen in the royal burgh, close enough for Logan to discover more information.

King Alexander was unlikely to allow Logan into the royal castle, so he would have to dig up his information in the town of Ayr.

A couple more days and he should be close to Robbie Grant.

***

When he entered the royal burgh, Logan caught up with a couple of warriors dressed in the well-known Grant plaid. It didn't take him long to determine Captain Robbie Grant's location from them, though he wondered at their news. Robbie was apparently back at the royal castle, but word around the burgh was that the skirmish was over. The Scots had sent the Norse running home.

He sidled up to the castle gate and waited there for an hour or so, smiling as soon as his quarry exited the castle. "Grant, would you make haste?" he called out. "I need to speak to you."

Robbie Grant squinted at him but didn't speak. Hell, the man appeared dazed.

"Will you stop your staring? Can you not recognize one of your sister's family members?"

Robbie peered at him before breaking out into a broad smile. "Logan? Logan Ramsay? What in hellfire brings you here, you hedge-born halfwit?" He hurried out of the gate with his friend Tomas fast behind him.

Logan grasped Robbie by both shoulders once they met on the cobblestones. "Halfwit, is it? We'll see what your brothers call you when you get home. They're vexed over your disappearance and sent me to find you."

Robbie cocked his head at him. "Somehow, I doubt my brothers sent you to find me."

Logan couldn't contain his smirk. Grant knew him well enough to correctly assess the situation. Most people in his close circle were aware of his need to wander.

Robbie continued. "You couldn't stay in one place, so you came here on your own. Dundonald informed my brother of what I was doing, and I already sent one group of warriors home. My brothers couldn't have been overly concerned about my welfare."

Logan chuckled. "Middling bastard. Does it make a difference? Mayhap not your brothers, but the women are all worried about you, thinking you'll never return. You broke too many hearts in the Grant clan." The lasses' broken hearts were not what worried him, but the happiness of his brother's wife. If she had concerns, he would do aught that he could to settle them.

Robbie chuckled. "Now can we hear the truth? You just wanted to be in the thick of things, Ramsay. You just can't settle for long."

Logan laughed. "Och, aye, that, too. Enough about my reasons for coming, though. What are you still doing at the king's castle, and where are you headed?"

Robbie paused. "You're here at just the right time. I need a couple more warriors for my next assignment. Will you join me?"

"Of course, 'twas my intention all along. Lead the way."

***

Gwyneth bound her large breasts as best she could, cursing at the fact that all the binding she had done over the years hadn't forced them to shrink. It wasn't the most comfortable practice, but it did keep them out of the way when she was shooting. She hurried to finish before another boat reached theirs. When she was appropriately covered again, she wove her way through the prone bodies on the deck, assessing the women's injuries and trying to find anyone who was well enough to assist her in rowing the ship toward shore in case enemies approached instead of friends. She offered kind words and encouragement, but was unable find any of the battered women equipped to help. Most of them were in far worse shape than she.

The sound of the advancing ship grew louder, so she did her best to stand and determine the identity of the vessel. A sigh of relief escaped her lips as she searched for the raven banner of King Haakon's ships and didn't find one.

As the ship drew close, a Scotsman yelled at her. "Lass, is anyone alive but you?"

"Aye," she yelled back, nodding.

"Where are you from and where were you sailing?"

"We came from near Glasgow. We were forced on the boat against our will and were being taken East. 'Tis all I know." Her hands settled on her hips as the longboat pulled up starboard.

"And your crew?"

"I was drugged and fuzzy, but I think the Norse threw them overboard."

"Dead or alive when they were thrown?" The captain of the ship's gaze searched the surrounding waters for survivors.

"I can't answer that." Gwyneth held tight on the side of the boat to keep from falling overboard as the other ship came close, sending waves through the water.

As soon as the two crafts were close enough, the

captain jumped onto the deck, landing near her. Shock registered on his face. "Lass, the Norse do that or your captors?" He nodded toward her battered face.

"The Norse."

The man tied a rope to their boat and signaled to his crew to head toward shore. He turned and announced to Gwyneth and the rest of the victims. "We'll tow you back to South Ayrshire, the closest land from here. There's a Kirk not far from the beach."

Once she knew they were headed to shore, she sat next to the woman nearest her and placed her arm over her shoulder, rubbing her back to try to calm her. Gwyneth didn't recognize her, but what the Norse had done to her and the others made her ill.

Their rescuer inclined his head toward the other women. "The rest look the same?"

"Worse."

***

Logan heard sobs as they came near the Kirk south of the royal burgh. Robbie had informed him their mission wouldn't be pleasant. Apparently, the Norse had attacked a ship full of women in the Firth of Clyde—women who'd been kidnapped and were being sent East to be sold as slaves. Logan had to admit he had trouble believing such a travesty would take place just outside the royal burgh.

Robbie had been told the women were not in good shape, so Logan prepared himself for the worst. He couldn't handle seeing defenseless lassies beaten, though he knew it happened often enough. It didn't happen in front of him.

He and Tomas hung back while Robbie knocked on the locked door of the Kirk, night having settled in around them. The door swung open just a touch and a man of the cloth stared out at them. "State your purpose."

Once Robbie convinced the priest they had been sent by Dundonald, he beckoned to them and led them through the front door while the other Grant warriors waited out front. Robbie followed the priest into the back, and Logan and Tomas waited in the chapel, both pacing in anticipation of the job they had ahead of them. The two exchanged glances as the cries of women in pain reached their ears. He vowed to make it his business to search for the bastard who had kidnapped the young lassies.

Robbie stuck his head out of the back room and beckoned for them to come forward, so they followed. Inside the chamber, several women rested atop small pallets, groaning and crying. Logan had to struggle not to react as he wished, by pounding his fist into the wall.

Robbie turned to the priest, his expression a question. Logan knew what he wished to ask—he was concerned about how to transport women with injuries. Grant had been wise to bring more warriors to aid with the escort.

Father MacLaren spoke in a soft whisper. "Probably better to move them tonight, lads. There is naught more we can do for them here. They need to be tended by women, and we just don't have the supplies for bandaging or the healers to set their broken bones to rights."

Robbie frowned. "How shall we move them, Father?"

"There are two carts. I believe we can get them comfortable for the most part. There are several mounds of hay in the back. My fear is if you wait until daylight, you'll draw more attention to the women. If you leave soon, you should be able to make it to the priory by morning. At least you'll travel through the royal burgh in the dark."

Logan peered around the room and froze when his gaze rested on a dark-haired lass with light blue eyes, a color he had never before seen except in the crystal clear skies of summer. She stared directly at him, her bronzed skin darker than most women's, and everything about her was so beautiful he couldn't tear his gaze away.

When he moved closer, he noticed the bruises that marred her beauty, and his mind created a satisfying fantasy of killing the bastard that had dared to touch her. He reminded himself of what the priest had told their group about the ordeal these women had faced, how they'd been attacked by foreigners after being taken captive by their own countrymen. Approaching her made the tragedy that much more real. Few women would survive such a thing with their spirit intact. The fire in this lass's light eyes marked her as a fighter.

Her eyes were both haunting and challenging, probably in an attempt to mask the pain and humiliation she had just endured. He was drawn to the lass like a moth to a flame, even though every ounce of her warned him off.

The woman hissed, "Touch me, and I will rip your bollocks in two, you rutting bastard."

Father MacLaren pivoted toward the young lass, who looked to be around twenty summers in age. "Gwyneth, these men are here to help. They aren't the enemy. Their mission is to transport you to the priory. Please be agreeable. We'll get you back to your brother's Kirk in Glasgow."

The lass named Gwyneth lifted her head into the light so she could survey the rest of the group. The slight movement brought more attention to the bruising of her delicate features. She looked as if she had been slapped and punched, which only fueled Logan's fury. He could hardly fault her for wanting to blame every man in her vicinity. He would allow her to direct her ire at him, for he knew how difficult it was to be a strong person with no control over your circumstances. He had felt the same way when his wee niece and nephew were near death.

Dressed in warrior's clothing, including leggings

and a clinging tunic, she ignored him and continued to fidget with her torn clothing. Logan moved over to stand in front of her. She hoisted herself up, standing tall enough to almost look him in the eye. He was still a mite bit above her, but she was close to his height. Long limbs supported her, and she clutched a small plaid to her torso.

She never took her eyes off Logan, but she directed her comment to Robbie. "Take me back to Glasgow, and I will be eternally grateful, but I won't go to the priory. I'm going to my brother's Kirk. Fair warning for any of you, if you try to touch me, I'll stick a knife between your ribs when your head is turned."

Father MacLaren said, "Gwyneth, these are the men who fight for the Scottish crown. They aren't here to hurt you."

"Your pardon, Father. Other than you and my brother, all men are the same to me right now. Three kidnapped me and threw me on a boat, and another tried to rape me. So don't expect me to be grateful. Get me to Glasgow, and you'll never have to see me again. Just give me my bow and arrows and my knife, and I will leave a happy lass. And don't try to tell me they aren't here, because I know the rotten bastard intended to sell my weapons, too."

Logan celebrated inwardly; she was a fighter and an archer. There were not many lassies able to use a bow and arrow correctly; this he would beg to see. The more he learned about her, the more he wanted to know. He smiled at her when her gaze caught his.

"Do that again, and 'twill be the last thing you do, warrior or not." She leaned in, so she was nose to nose with Logan. "You don't frighten me. I could kill you easily."

He had to give the lass credit. He could see in her eyes how close she was to falling apart. Somehow, he knew she would hold it together. He would not do anything to make it more difficult for her. "I have nae doubt you could, lass," he said. "I'll keep my hands to myself until you request otherwise."

The two stared at each other for a long moment, complete silence as everyone else in the room waited to see what would happen next. He let her set the pace, something he rarely did for a woman. Even the way she wore her hair, pulled straight back and plaited from a spot high on the back of her head, enticed him. Something about the glossy sheen made it look stronger, cleaner, and more beautiful than that of any other lass. Much to his delight, the lass held strong under his gaze. Logan had found a woman who would stand up to him. The urge to kill the bastard who'd put her in this position raced through his body again, unstoppable as flames through a field of wheat.

Finally, Father MacLaren cleared his throat and said, "Come, lass, I'll give you your things as long as you promise not to use any of your weapons on these men. And please give my regards to your brother."

Gwyneth limped along behind the priest. "Father, I intend to get back to my home in Glasgow, but if anyone tries to prevent that, I'll do what I need to do. As long as no one touches me, you have my word. If a man dares to lay a hand on me, believe me, his life will be in *my* hands."

CHAPTER THREE

Gwyneth climbed into the cart after helping the other victims get settled. Still restless from all that had transpired, she was even more ill at ease from the looks the braw warrior, Logan, was sending her way. True, she couldn't deny his good looks, but she didn't care at this point. She needed to get to Glasgow, talk to her brother, and seek out the bastard, Duff Erskine.

She had begged to ride a horse, but there were only enough horses to pull a cart and one for each warrior. Logan had offered for her to ride with him, but she had rejected him in a hurry. After all that had occurred, she couldn't deal with any part of a man's body touching hers for now. She attempted to rest, but each time she closed her eyes, the wild Norsemen took over her thoughts.

Bolting upright, she decided to forego any sleep. Probably better to stay alert. Who knew what would happen when they passed through the burgh?

Logan pulled his horse up next to the cart and tossed a blue plaid over to her. "Here, lass, rest your head on this."

Gwyneth caught it and tossed it back. "No need, warrior. Keep it."

Logan sighed. "I know where your head is right now. You're thinking of ten different ways to kill the bastard who did this to you."

"Aye." She stared straight ahead, refusing to make

eye contact with him. For some reason, he unsettled her, and she didn't like it.

He grinned. "And what is your preference? What would serve justice best?"

She glanced at him before bringing her gaze back to the front. "An arrow right between the eyes."

"You know him?"

"Aye."

"And you know where to find him?"

"Well enough, though he often moves. I'll take care of him, make no mistake." Peering at him, she had to admit he was impressive atop his stallion. Light brown hair, a strong jaw line, and massive muscles rippled through his tunic. "Your name again, warrior?"

"Logan Ramsay, and I would be mighty pleased to help you, lass." He smiled at her.

"I can handle him by myself." She looked away again as a bolt of warmth shot through her limbs, not wanting to scrutinize her body's reaction to him.

"Are you capable of placing an arrow between his eyes? Because if you can't guarantee his death with the first arrow, you may require some assistance."

"My arrow goes wherever I choose." She returned her gaze to him, lifting her chin as a challenge.

"Truly? I look forward to seeing that," Logan chuckled.

"You don't believe me? I challenge you at first light. We'll see if your aim is as sharp as your tongue."

"Gwyneth, if I heard your name correctly, I am not out to beat you. I have other games in mind. But if it would please you to challenge me, I welcome it."

Logan's grin riled her. "Aye, my name is Gwyneth of the Cunninghams, the best shooter in the Lowlands, do not doubt my claim. And just to be clear, I'm not interested in rutting with any beasts, even one who fights for the Crown."

"Understood. The only way to beat the bastard who hurt you is with food in your belly and proper sleep to make your aim true." He tossed the plaid back to her. "Take your rest and build your strength. Killing him ten different ways in your mind won't make you any stronger, lass. I know."

Gwyneth caught the plaid and stared at him. His words were similar to her brother Rab's. He was right; she hated to admit it, but she did need to save her strength. "My thanks, beast." She rolled away from him and tucked the cloth under her head.

Aye, this man unsettled her. Ever since her father and brother had died in front of her eyes, she had lived a sheltered life. She and her brother, Rab, had gone to live with her Uncle Innis at the Kirk. They had made do and survived, her brother turning to the church while Gwyneth turned to revenge, focusing her efforts on mastering archery. Her goal was in reach and she was more driven than ever. She would kill her family's murderer. Now she had more reason than ever.

The result was she hadn't spent much time with others her own age. Her mother had died giving birth to Rab, a year younger than her, and Gwyneth had grown up with her father and two brothers. Moving to the Kirk had surrounded her with religious men. She didn't know how to deal with men outside the church, at least not kind men. She hadn't met many, and she didn't know much about interacting with other women either.

She found herself unable to fall asleep as her imagination spun images of a brawny warrior who actually supported her at her side instead of trying to kill her.

***

As soon as they arrived at the priory, Gwyneth hopped out of the cart, and stumbled on her weak leg before righting herself, cursing. She helped the other women out and guided the men as to which of the wounded needed the most assistance. After she located her things in the back of the cart, she turned to glance down the street and found herself swept into the arms of a grinning warrior.

"Put me down, Logan Ramsay. I told you that you were never to touch me. How dare you assume I need help when I don't. And I'm not staying here either."

Logan grinned all the way down the stairs and into the chamber in the base of the priory, not loosening his grip a bit. "Just following orders, my lady. Want to make sure you have no serious injuries." Logan plopped her down on the nearest pallet, and she landed with a string of curses.

Gwyneth swung at Logan, but he sidestepped with a chuckle before he turned to leave. The foolish brute should have to listen to a few more choice words, but she was in a priory. Out of respect for her brother's profession, she cut off her cursing as soon as Logan left her side. The sound of her name caught her, and she spun her head around, searching for the source.

Caralyn Crauford hobbled across the room in her direction, limping and in pain, but with a smile on her face and her arms wide open. "Gwyneth? Blessed saints, 'tis really you?"

"Caralyn? Hellfire! How I have missed you." She stood, moving as fast as she could toward her friend. The two lasses threw themselves at each other, hugging as if they hadn't seen each other in years.

Caralyn stepped back and stroked Gwyneth's arm. "I was afraid I would never see you again. It has been months, hasn't it? Where have you been? Are you unhurt?" She ushered Gwyneth back onto the bed, then sat down next to her.

"I wouldn't sit here for anyone but you, Caralyn Crauford, especially not for this lout!" She waved her arm toward Logan, who had not gone very far at all and was now leaning against the wall by her pallet, his arms crossed and a smile on his face. With a huff, she turned away from him, giving him her back. "Caralyn, I am so happy to see you. Where are your sweet lassies? Wee Gracie must be so big by now."

Caralyn's expression turned to a frown, and she shook her head. "I don't know. Please, may we talk about this later?" She glanced up just as Robbie strode over to the bed. Gwyneth watched as her friend met the Highlander's gaze and he shook his head.

He whispered so no one else could hear him but Logan, Caralyn, and Gwyneth. "Sorry, lass. We haven't yet found your wee ones."

As soon as Logan and Robbie left, Gwyneth grasped her arm. "Where are your daughters?"

Caralyn's expression on her face crumpled. "I don't know. Malcolm has taken them from me and will only allow me to see them when he gives me permission. 'Twas supposed to be every sennight, but now he is angry and said only once a moon." Tears misted in her eyes. "You know how much I love them. I miss them so, and I have no idea who is caring for them or if they are hurt."

"Is Captain Grant going to help you?" Gwyneth asked. "He appears of sound character. Surely he would help you find the weans. I would trust the captain, and he has knowledge that others cannot obtain." How she had fallen in love with Caralyn's two daughters during their visits to her brother's Kirk in the royal burgh. They hadn't come often, but she and Caralyn had become fast friends. After a time, Caralyn had revealed the truth of her situation with Malcolm, how he forced her to be his mistress and worse by threatening her daughters. It was yet another example of the cruelty of men. Gwyneth and her brother had discussed the matter, but they hadn't come up with a solution.

"Aye, he said he would find them for me, and then come rescue me. I only hope he can find them. They are too young to be alone with two brutes. They are only two and eight." She clasped Gwyneth's hands in hers. "Gwyneth, you look tired. I am sure you have had a terrible ordeal. Why don't you rest? I'm going to help the sisters with the other women. I won't leave without saying good-bye."

Gwyneth had to admit she was tired—tired of fighting Duff Erskine, tired of worrying about her friend. Her brother shared her feelings about Duff since he had also been a witness to his cruelty, but when she had gone to Rab about Caralyn, they hadn't come up with any solutions to her problem.

Gwyneth had been forced to act on her own. After several years observing Duff Erskine, she had decided to seek help. How could a man like Duff get away with all his crimes? How could someone like Malcolm treat Caralyn the way he did and not be forced to stop?

Wealth. Duff Erskine had grown his merchant business over time and therefore, had increased his fortune. She guessed he used his fortune to pay off the local sheriff and other government officials. Apparently, Malcolm Murray did the same. So she had gone to someone for help, someone very high up in the Scottish government and presented her evidence.

Now she worked for the Scottish government covertly. She needed to notify her supervisor of what she had seen. It had been a long time since Duff Erskine had sold slaves. She knew he would go back to it eventually, but she hadn't expected to be one of his potential victims.

Gwyneth rested her head on the pillow. "Aye, I am a bit weary. 'Twas a long night and I couldn't sleep on the wretched cart. Wake me before you go." Her eyes closed, though her hands still clung to Caralyn, her only close female friend. She would help her find her wee ones if Robbie Grant didn't, and if he did search for them, she would be right behind him, whether he wanted her help or not.

Gwyneth opened her eyes, wanting to see Caralyn's smiling face once more. How she treasured their friendship. When she had traveled to the Kirk in Ayr with her brother, she had been sitting in the back during a service when Caralyn had come in and sat next to her with her two lassies. Ashlyn had stared at her cautiously, but Gracie, sitting on her mother's lap, had held her arms up to Gwyneth right away.

Living in a man's world, Gwyneth had never held a bairn before, but Caralyn handed her over without a word, settling her on Gwyneth's lap. Gracie had plopped her thumb in her mouth and leaned back against her, falling asleep to the lulling voice of Father Rab. After service, Caralyn had said, "She doesn't go to others easily."

Ashlyn had nodded. "You must be special."

Gwyneth had never forgotten how special she felt that day, and how her friendship with the trio had grown since then.

She needed to see her brother, see her boss, and find two bairns. She would do this for Caralyn, Gracie, and Ashlyn. Tomorrow would be a busy day.

CHAPTER FOUR

Logan followed Robbie up the priory staircase. As soon as they stepped outside, he peppered him with questions. "Who's the woman, Grant, and what is she to you?"

"She's naught to me. Caralyn is a woman I found on the coastline south of Ayr. A Norseman was dragging her to his galley, and battered her along the way."

"Hellfire, good thing you were there to stop it. Had to be enjoyable taking the Norse on. How do men beat defenseless women like that?"

"Caralyn wasn't defenseless. She fought hard and got a few blows in, but he overtook her."

"And now?"

"Now he's a dead man." Robbie glanced at his friend, a smirk on his face.

"And the two lassies?"

"They were hiding in the rocks. Their mama trained them well. I found them the next day after I brought Caralyn back to my camp. Since we were almost ready to skirmish and their home was destroyed by the Norse, I brought them to the priory here. A man who says he's her husband took the three of them out of the priory back to his keep and has now hidden her girls to control her. I promised to help."

Logan quirked his brow at his friend. "And?"

"And naught. That's it. I don't like the man, and I cringe when I think of where the wee lassies could be.

The youngest, Gracie, reminds me of Lily." He paused, watching Logan for his reaction. "You don't have to follow if you have other plans. Tomas and I can handle it."

"Aye, I'll go along. What do you know of the one in leggings? What is the relationship between Caralyn and Gwyneth?"

"I have no idea. I met Gwyneth for the first time when you did. Caught your eye, I see."

Logan scowled. "I suppose she has. She's got spirit, but I can't help but want to help a battered woman."

"Doesn't look like she wants your help."

"True, but she has a sweet arse." Logan smiled. "And she's plotting revenge on her captor. I think she might need some help there. You know I'm all about helping defenseless lassies."

"She doesn't look defenseless to me." Robbie gave Tomas a knowing look. "Where were you headed? Back home?"

"I was searching for you. Hadn't made any further plans. Do you want help finding the lassies?"

"We could use your help. Do you know Glasgow?"

"Nay, not well. You'll need someone as guidance. 'Tis a big town."

Logan stared at Robbie. "You are going after the wee ones now, are you not? You can't ignore where the lassies could be."

Robbie nodded. "We need a plan."

"Aye. Do you have any idea where to start?" Logan asked.

"Nay. I don't know Glasgow any more than you or Tomas. I suppose we'll start by questioning people, or spending time in the market talking to local vendors. What ideas do you two have?"

A fourth person joined the group without a word of greeting. "I'll go with you," Gwyneth announced, hands on her hips as if daring someone to disagree.

Robbie asked, "Do you know Glasgow?"

Gwyneth nodded. "I know Glasgow and I'll find the lassies. I have a hunch as to where Murray would hide them within town."

"Then I welcome your assistance," Robbie said.

Logan glanced between Robbie and Gwyneth. "What? Are you daft, lass? You belong on the pallet resting."

Gwyneth retorted, "Like hell I do. You think just because I'm a lass, I'm not strong enough to join you?"

Logan argued. "Nay, I think someone did an exceptional job beating you, and you're bruised from head to toe." He checked her over as he spoke, though he knew she wouldn't like it. What a fine specimen of a woman she was—the very sight of her almost took his breath away. But at the same time, seeing all her bruises fired him up in an entirely different way.

Gwyneth didn't slow for a second. "That has naught to do with it. Those lassies need to be found, and I'm the one to find them. Or is your cock so small you fear women just because they might find out the size?"

Logan smiled as he grabbed his crotch. He would banter with her; there was naught he would enjoy more at this point. "Would you like to see my cock and judge for yourself?" He judged that her sense of pride was not far different from his brothers'. Piss her off, and she wouldn't have time to think about her bruises or what had happened to her on that boat. He'd keep her focused on this new mission...and he would enjoy every moment of it.

Fire burned in Gwyneth's gaze. "Aye, bring it out, but let me grab my dagger first. I'll take one of your sacs as a trophy. The last one I cut off, I flung into the firth."

Dead silence hung in the air. Logan waited to see if anyone else would approach that comment. He thought his comrades' thoughts no doubt echoed his own. Was she telling the truth? Someday, he would ask her. The rotten bastard who'd attacked her had picked the wrong victim. He stifled his grin so as not to antagonize her any more. She was already good and fired up.

Logan whispered, "I don't doubt your strength on a good day, lass. But the Norse knocked the wind out of you. I can see the fine tremor in your hand. The only thing you need is rest."

Gwyneth took a step closer to Logan. "Fortunately, what you say doesn't mean anything to me. I do as I please, not what some man orders me to do."

Robbie held his hands up. "Och, lass. No one is trying to order you. You came to us, remember?"

"Aye," she said, her gaze never leaving Logan's. "And I'm going with you."

Logan's hands settled on his hips as he continued to meet her stare. No way would he allow her to go. She needed rest and food to keep herself healthy and whole. "Give me one good reason why we should take you with us. I see you as a detriment to our mission. You'll be slow, and we'll have to cater to your needs." He wouldn't be able to handle it if she were hurt on their travels. As strong as he guessed she was, he could see she wasn't at her best. He didn't want her to risk her life. They could—and would—find Caralyn's bairns on their own.

Gwyneth moved her face a few inches closer to Logan's—the threat obvious, and strangely enticing. "I won't be slow, and you won't have to cater to my needs."

Returning her stare, Logan said to Robbie, "Hmmph. Did you hear a reason for us to take her, Grant? Because I surely did not." Could Grant not see she would be at risk herself if she joined them? Or was he too desperate to help Caralyn to judge the situation impartially?

Gwyneth crossed her arms in front of her. "Because the lassies know me. They'll never go with you. And I don't think any of you wish to deal with a two-year-old's rags once you find them."

Logan had cared for his niece and nephew through rags and vomit. He had forced himself to remain strong because his brother had needed him. The memories of how ill they had been were painful to him. He didn't need them fresh in his head during this mission.

Stepping back, Logan peered at Tomas and Robbie for a long moment, a frown on his face. Then he finally dropped his hands from his hips and stalked away. "Guess she goes with us. Saddle up and let's move."

From behind him, he heard Robbie say, "Let's go before sundown." With that, Gwyneth traipsed in front of him and jumped onto his horse before he had the chance.

Logan growled, "Lass, find your own horse."

"I did." She smiled and took off down the path.

Turning to his friends, who were both holding back smiles, Logan mounted Tomas's horse in a flash and headed down the path after her. God's teeth, but this woman was going to give him a worthy ride. He loved the fire in her. Watching her bum in breeks bounce on his saddle was worth every moment of aggravation. Hell, he would *have* to have this lass someday.

When he was close enough, he grabbed the reins, winked at Gwyneth and said, "You better hang on." With that, he whistled, and his horse came to a screeching halt. Gwyneth almost flew off the front, though she somehow managed to hang on.

Gwyneth yelled. "Och, stop! I'll get off. Have your foolish horse."

Hellfire, he smiled again. She'd held on. He tossed his reins over a nearby branch and hopped off Tomas's horse. When was the last time he had seen a lass handle Paz the way she just had? A horsewoman and an archer—he definitely would have to get to know Gwyneth better.

She started to dismount, but he caught her around

her waist, tossing her back up in the saddle, then climbed behind her. A string of curses flew out of her lips. "Lass, didn't you say your brother was a priest? My dear, I hope you don't talk like that around him."

She whirled in the saddle and clubbed his arm with her fist. "Let me go."

"Lass, there are only three horses. You want to fight with me, do it later. I relish the battle. But for now, we need to find the bairns, so stay where you are."

By that time, Tomas and Robbie had caught up with them. Tomas jumped off and grabbed his horse. Robbie's face let Gwyneth know he wasn't in any mood for arguing, so she settled. Gwyneth whispered and slapped his hand. "Don't touch me, you brute."

Logan chuckled and took off, whispering in her ear. "Should have thought of that before you stole my horse. Now you ride with me." He held her back against him in a death grip while he yelled over his shoulder. "Move on, Grant."

Hellfire, but her curves fit him just right. This was the best ride he'd had in a long time.

CHAPTER FIVE

Gwyneth took the lead since she was quite sure she knew where they might find the lassies. The surprising thing was that Logan did not raise an objection. He was such a beast she hadn't expected him to listen to her. Originally furious she'd been forced to ride with him, she was grateful for it at present because his heat warmed her insides. She probably should have eaten something before joining them outside the priory, but she'd worried they would leave without her. Her brother had warned her many times of the importance of keeping yourself strong. How in hell had Logan noticed her tremors?

She knew Glasgow very well after searching for Erskine for seven years. Unfortunately, she had always been a bit behind him. The scum moved quickly. After they had ridden for a bit, they found themselves in an area that looked a bit suspicious; tight rows of unkempt huts filling the area with no one visible because the townspeople preferred to stay hidden. Once Dougal Hamilton had officially hired her as a spy for the Scottish Crown, she had made it her business to know all of Glasgow. This area was the most likely area for Malcolm to hide his lackeys. The area was very poor and no one would pay attention to them here.

Gwyneth signaled for the group to stop and investigate. This had been an early haunt for Duff

Erskine, but now that his wealth had grown, he would never be caught in a section of town like this. Her nose wrinkled at the odor of sewage and waste piled in front of the huts. A creek ran behind the rows of ramshackle shelters, probably their only source of water. Given the amount of sewage nearby, it was a wonder anyone managed to live here. This section of town was just the area she had guessed they would find the two lowlifes who held Ashlyn and Gracie.

Logan dismounted, sliding Gwyneth slowly down his body, his grin heating Gwyneth's anger. Fie, but the beast must learn to keep his hands to himself. He would pay for touching her. As soon as her feet hit the ground, she swung and clobbered Logan in the side of his head with her fist. To her surprise, Logan spun her around immediately, as if expecting her attack, and held her in a vise grip in front of him. Gwyneth struggled to free herself but couldn't move the brute. Logan was big, broad-shouldered, and built with solid muscle. Robbie stood to the side with Tomas, watching the two of them battle without moving to stop them. No need for them to interfere, she would handle the animal herself.

"Leave me be, you rutting bull." Gwyneth tried to kick him, but he held her fast. Powerless. Hellfire, but she was powerless again, just as she had been with Erskine. Just as she'd been on that boat until the Norsemen boarded it. Duff had drugged her enough so she couldn't fight. This was worse because she was completely alert, yet she was still powerless against Ramsay. It was not to be borne.

Logan squeezed her back against his chest and spoke into her ear. "Now, do I have complete control of you, lass?"

"Aye, leave off, you surly brute!" She fought until her face was beet red, spitting and kicking at anything she could.

"Remember that. I have complete control over you.

You have no power over me without your weapons. Agreed?"

"Aye," she hissed.

"Then learn something. I will never hurt you or force you. If I wanted to, I could throw you down on that ground and rut all I wanted. But I won't. Do you know why?"

The only sound from Gwyneth was a low growl as she fought to free herself from Logan's grip.

"Verra well, I'll tell you though you're not inclined to listen, please hear me and heed me."

Gwyneth managed one kick to his shin as she squirmed in place.

"Lass, I will never hurt you. I don't hurt women. 'Tis not part of me nor is it in my friends. You need to accept that. There are two kinds of men, those who hit lassies and those who don't. 'Tis unfortunate the only men you have met are rutting snipes, but I'm not. I like my lassies willing and I never hit."

He continued his soft whispers into her ear, and she feigned acceptance, though she was determined she would repay him—come what may. Perhaps he wouldn't hit her or rut with her against her will, but he still did not have the right to imprison her. She hoped someday he would know how it felt to be powerless. There was not a worse feeling in the world, and she'd promised herself she would never experience it again. Now she'd been its victim twice in a matter of days. She held back her tears, not wanting to give him the satisfaction of knowing how much it hurt to be overpowered, both body and spirit.

"But I will protect myself. Can you promise not to hit me or my friends? I won't let you go until you agree."

His words fell on deaf ears because her mind raged with all the atrocities of the past two days. She fought to calm her rage—at her captors, at her enemy, against this man's confining grip. She thought of her brother's calming nature and how she missed him, forcing her to again cover up her feelings and deal with what she had to for the moment. If she didn't do as Logan asked, he would never release her. Still, she couldn't just give in to him. And somehow, she knew he wouldn't hurt her.

Logan continued. "I am here to save the wee lassies. I have a niece named Lily whom I adore, and she is a bit older than Gracie. I would kill any man who dared to hurt her. So you need to decide. Will you join us to help retrieve the lassies or will you continue to try to make me pay for whatever atrocities you have been forced to endure which will slow down our rescue considerably?"

He had to mention the one thing that would calm her on the spot—Gracie. A tear slid down her cheek before she nodded.

"I am going to let you go, and I swear on the saints above, if you swing at me, I will tie you to that tree while we search for the lassies. We didn't bring you along for you to attack us." Logan relaxed his arms, and she shoved away from him.

Gwyneth swallowed three times before she spoke. Much as she wanted to retaliate, much as she hated to admit it, he was right. Caralyn's daughters were what mattered right now. She could exact her revenge later.

Robbie finally broke his silence. "Think hard, Gwyneth. I'll help him tie you to that tree if need be. I am here for Ashlyn and Gracie. Are you?"

She conceded for now, but vowed the beast would still pay later. "Aye. Tell me what to do. I can kill Logan while he sleeps tonight." Not fully trusting herself, she clasped her hands behind her back.

"Is this the most likely area, Gwyneth?" Robbie asked.

"Aye, some are just poor, but many are questionable."

Robbie noticed she refused to look at Logan.

"Any particular row?" Tomas asked.

"Nay, they could be anywhere. We need to look closer."

Robbie gave instructions for his plan. "I want each of you to search around both rows of cottages and see if you see any sign of weans. Mayhap we'll hear voices or crying, anything. 'Tis an area with many cottages because of the creek. If you look in that direction, I think you'll find another row around the bend in the creek. Meet back here in the next hour."

Gwyneth took off toward the stream. She didn't need any man behind her; she could find the lassies without them. Carefully checking each cottage, she searched for any clues that a bairn was inside. After passing several cottages, she finally found what she had been looking for—a pile of wean's rags.

She turned and ran back to find Captain Grant. Though she would love to save the girls herself, she was not willing to take chances. The Highlanders could help her get inside the cottage.

"What is it, Gwyneth?" Robbie asked as she headed straight for him.

She paused to catch her breath. "Rags," she panted.

"What?" Robbie asked, his face a puzzle.

"Raggies. A wean's rags." She pointed to the cottage. "A whole pile of urine drenched rags are in front of that hut."

Robbie made his bird call to summon the others, and Tomas and Logan rushed to his side. "I think we may have them if Gwyneth is correct." He pointed to the hut in question. "Gwyneth, you go to the door to see if the lasses are there and how many guards are watching them. Ask for the nearest tavern and act as if you are lost. I promise to guard you while Tomas and Logan go around back."

Gwyneth stumbled up the front path, making a ruckus while Robbie got in place, and the other two ran around the back.

A slim woman opened the door, a wee bairn on each hip. Gwyneth stood there staring, realizing they had chosen the wrong house. Her gaze searched the inside, but there were no other weans in sight. "Mistress, I seem to have made a mistake. Are there any other bairns in the area? Two wee lassies? I came to visit my friend."

The woman shook her head and started to close the door, then paused. "Aye, I did see two lassies outside taking care of their needs yesterday. One was brown-haired and the other blonde. They be at the end of the path." Her finger pointed down toward the creek.

"My thanks." Gwyneth nodded and the door closed. She turned to Robbie and he whistled for his friends to join them out front.

As soon as Logan and Tomas returned, Tomas said, "Nay? Wrong place?"

Robbie said, "Aye, but she directed us to the cottage we need. Same plan, down the path."

Gwyneth stumbled up the path again as Logan and Tomas snuck around back. The front door swung open, just as they'd planned, and an overweight dolt appeared in the doorway.

"Fingal, look what I found." His eyes lit up as he reached for Gwyneth. "A plaything. We have something to entertain us."

Gwyneth glared at the fool, barely managing to stifle the urge to swing at him and stomp on his foot. She had to get inside the room to determine if the girls were there. She brushed her breasts across his arm invitingly, and he stilled, staring at her with wide eyes. Grabbing her by the arm, he tugged her inside, chuckling as he closed the door behind him.

The dolt's friend sat in a chair by the back door, stuffing his face with food. Much younger than the dolt, he was slim with spittle all over his face as he licked his fingers. A small dagger sat on the table, but well away from his grasp. "I'd rather eat. Do as you wish." He barely gave her a glance.

Gwyneth squelched her urge to snort. Ignoring her could cost someone their life, but he was too stupid to know it.

"Fingal, no wonder mama liked you better. All you ever think of is feeding your belly."

Fingal countered, "Well, apparently I never fed my belly the way you did." He gave his brother's girth a pointed look.

Searching the room once her eyes adjusted to the light, Gwyneth finally located the two girls huddled together in the corner. She also caught the light of recognition in Ashlyn's eyes so she gave the lass a pointed look and shook her head just a bit to get the message to her not to speak. Gracie started toward her, but her elder sister held her back.

The big man who'd pulled her inside was reaching for her, his eyes full of lust, when Tomas burst through the back door, Logan directly behind him. Not missing a beat, the dolt yanked Gwyneth back against him and held a knife to her throat. The one named Fingal reached for the girls, but Tomas twirled him around and backed him up against the wall with his sword at his throat.

Robbie crept in behind her, "Let her go, and my friend will release your comrade."

Gwyneth wasn't helpless. She had to do something, but the putrid smell of the brute who'd attacked her—the odor of a man who hadn't bathed in weeks—suddenly assaulted her and her vision clouded in response. Her stomach clenched so strongly in reaction to the smell that she couldn't move. Powerless, it was happening to her again. How could a mere odor control her? But she knew. It was the same odor she had smelled on Duff Erskine seven years ago and the same odor as the Norseman. It would never leave her. Now Duff covered it with a sickening smell.

The big lout shook with fear, though his grip stayed

tight. "Nay, let Fingal go and we'll leave. You can have the lassies. Let him go, or I'll cut her throat."

Logan strode farther into the room, moving until he was almost within reach of Gwyneth and the dolt. What in hell was he thinking? Gwyneth stared at Logan, hoping to send him the message to stand back. She didn't want this lout to lose it and kill her. Sweat beaded across her brow as she sensed the tremor in the fool's hand.

Hot stinking breath huffed into her ear, and she cringed in response. "One more step and I'll kill her. Let us go, and you can have all three bitches."

Gwyneth glanced at the lassies in the corner, at Fingal held in place by Tomas, and at Logan Ramsay. How would they get out of this without anyone being hurt? The edge of the knife cut her skin directly in front of her windpipe. One small move and she wouldn't be able to take a breath again. She fought to clear her head and not weaken at her circumstances.

Logan's voice called to her as he spoke to the man holding her captive. "That would be impossible." A smirk crossed Logan's face. "That's my lass you have your hands on."

Logan glanced at her for just a moment, and she drew strength from his gaze. One look empowered her, because with one look she knew he would always be there for her, to protect her as no one else had been able to do. Gwyneth struggled not to react to his declaration because it confused her. Would she want his protection?

She took her gaze from him and glanced at Ashlyn, huddled with her sister. Hoping to give the girl strength, she smiled at her before returning her focus to her captor.

"We don't want any trouble," the big man said. "You can have her. Let us go."

"Can't do it," Logan said.

"Why not?" His gaze darted back and forth between

Logan and Tomas.

"Because you touched my lass, and no one touches her."

Logan flung his knife and Gwyneth's heart stopped, hoping his aim was true. She didn't feel so much as a rush of wind from the weapon before she heard a thud and bubbling sound. She let her breath out as soon as she saw the knife had landed between the dolt's ribs. He released her and crumpled to the ground, his own knife dropping from his fingers. Gwyneth headed straight for the girls in the corner, her legs almost buckling underneath her.

Fingal screamed, "You killed my brother." Gwyneth turned in time to see him pull out his own knife and attempt to stab Tomas, but Robbie's knife landed in his body at the same time as Tomas pierced his neck.

Fingal fell to the ground, dead.

The girls were safe.

CHAPTER SIX

Ashlyn yelled, "Gwyneth!" and rushed forward and jumped into her arms.

Gwyneth leaned down to grab Gracie too, but the wee one ran right past her straight into Robbie's arms. He picked her up, and much to Gwyneth's amazement, she wrapped her arms around his neck.

Gwyneth's nose wrinkled and Ashlyn burst into tears. "We smell, Gwyneth. Other than changing Gracie's raggies once a day, they wouldn't allow us to clean ourselves. We are dirty. Mama would be so upset."

Robbie said, "We don't have time to clean you now, Ashlyn. We must leave."

As if he hadn't heard the other Highlander's words, Logan passed a jug to Tomas and said, "Grab some water from the creek."

"What in hellfire are you doing, Ramsay?" Robbie barked, his hands on his hips.

"My guess is you're sending them north, aye? To your clan?"

"Aye. So how does that change the situation?"

"Weans do not like to be dirty and we have a long trip. The further we travel, the colder it will be for them. 'Tis better here near the creek." Logan winked at Gwyneth, whose arms were still wrapped around Ashlyn.

Robbie finally agreed and set Gracie down. He said

to Gracie, "We need to clean you before we go. Then I promise to take you both away from here."

Not long after, Tomas came in with the water. Gwyneth stared at the ewer, unsure of what to do next. She had been around Caralyn's girls, but she had never bathed them...or any other weans, for that matter. Scratching her head in thought, she accepted the ewer when Tomas gave it to her so he and Robbie could drag the two bodies into the other room, out of the girls' sight. She might be the only woman in the group, but what the devil did she know about washing weans?

She glanced at Logan, hoping for guidance. Ashlyn's eyes misted and she whispered to Gwyneth. "Please? You don't mind? Gracie doesn't like to be dirty, and Mama hates it when we smell."

Logan grabbed a big basin and took the water from Gwyneth to dump it inside. After Tomas and Robbie returned, he handed the three of them bowls and buckets and said. "More."

Gwyneth ran out to the creek, happy to have a task she knew how to accomplish, one that didn't involve washing the lassies. Robbie looked as relieved as she did as he stood next to her at the creek bank, leaning over to fill his jug.

By the time they returned, Logan had ripped strips of linen from Ashlyn's shift and both girls were scrubbing their faces with his sliver of soap. He dumped the buckets of cool water into a large bowl, took Gracie's gown and rag off, picked her up under her arms and said, "Ready, lass?" Gracie nodded, and Logan dipped her bottom into the water and swirled her around in it. She yelped and giggled as they all stared at her.

Gwyneth had never heard Gracie laugh or talk before, yet here she was giggling with Ramsay. The little one trusted these Highlanders...more than Gwyneth was yet willing to do. When Logan finished bathing Gracie, he took her out of the water and handed her to Gwyneth with another linen strip. "Dry her." Then he turned his back, held his plaid out to the side, and said to Ashlyn, "There's another basin of fresh water. Go ahead and do what you need to, lass. We won't watch. Gwyneth can help if you need."

Gwyneth was speechless. The beast was wonderful with the bairns. And they both seemed to like him. She stared at the brawny Highlander in shock. Men usually did not have the patience to be good with bairns.

Logan glanced at her. "What?"

Robbie laughed. "You have talents even I didn't expect, Ramsay."

"I told you I have a niece, but I also have a nephew, and both were sickly with no mother. I learned how to care for them. 'Tis not so difficult." He glanced at Gwyneth as he spoke.

When Ashlyn finished, they headed out to the horses. Ashlyn rode with Tomas and Gracie with Robbie. Gwyneth climbed on the horse with Ramsay again, but this time she didn't object. The brute had proven trustworthy thus far. They headed north and outside of town.

Gwyneth leaned back against Logan. He didn't seem to mind and tugged her tighter to him. She should have eaten before leaving the priory so she wouldn't have weakened as she had. Going from one trying experience to the next had exhausted her. She closed her eyes, visions of a brawny Highlander filling her mind. Had he meant what he said? Did he consider her to be his?

Having been so sheltered at the Kirk with her brother, she had never given any thought to a relationship with a man. All her time had been spent working as a spy for Dougal Hamilton and focusing on vengeance for her father and brother. The thought of a relationship with a man never occurred to her. Since her mother had died young, she had naught to guide her.

The next thing she knew, Logan was shaking her arm.

"Lass, wake up." His breath warmed her ear and a foreign heat washed through her.

She sat forward and glanced over her shoulder at him. "My apologies, brute."

"No need to apologize. I don't know how you held up in the cottage after all you've been through."

"Where are we?" Gwyneth scanned the area, but didn't recognize it.

"We need to regroup and decide what our next step is. Robbie found a hidden clearing. We aren't far from the town." Logan dismounted and helped her off the horse. Ashlyn ran to her and grabbed her hand as they gathered on a group of logs.

"Hellfire, Grant. I thought we'd go back to the priory to find Caralyn," Gwyneth said.

"Nay, 'tis after dark and she would be with Murray by now. He still controls her." He pulled both girls over to him and spoke directly to them. "Lassies, I know you wish to see your mama, but 'twould not be safe for now."

Ashlyn's head fell, and her shoulders slumped. "Can you get her away from Malcolm, Captain Grant?" She swiped at the tears on her cheeks. "We don't like him."

Two wee faces stared up at him, and Gwyneth's heart broke at the mere sight of them. Somehow, she believed without a doubt Robbie Grant would save her friend, but how did you convince two weans they had to go away from their mother to be out of danger?

"That is exactly what I plan to do, Ashlyn, but I need to make sure you two are safe so he can't come and steal you away again. Your mama is forced to do what he wants when he holds you away from her. Do you understand?"

Ashlyn nodded. "I think so. I always hear him tell

mama he will hurt us, and he did paddle us both once while mama screamed and cried. She told him she would do whatever he wanted as long as he stopped hurting us. I don't want to go back with him ever again. Where will you hide us?"

"I am going to send you to a wonderful place, but 'twill take a while for you to get there, so I need you both to be strong. And you won't see your mama for a wee bit, but everyone there will love you both and take care of you, and I promise we'll join you soon. There will be other weans for you to play with, but most of all, I know you will be safe."

"Where is that?" Ashlyn stared at him, wide-eyed. "We have never played with other weans."

"I am sending you to my clan. You're going into the Highlands to the Grant keep, a big castle with lots of nice people to love and care for you."

God bless him, but Captain Robbie Grant was going to take care of Caralyn and her daughters. Gwyneth almost got teary-eyed at the realization that dear Caralyn's nightmares would finally be over. In a way, she wished the same could happen to her. Grant was a good man.

"Will Mama come, too?" Ashlyn asked.

"Aye, as soon as I rescue your mama, I'll bring her to you."

"Can we not wait for you?" Ashlyn whispered.

"Nay, Malcolm will try to find you again. I need you away from here. I'm sorry, lass, but 'tis the only way." He patted her on the back, and Ashlyn gave him a brief smile.

Ashlyn pondered what he'd said, then nodded. She grabbed Gracie's hand. "As long as we go together."

"Aye, you'll go together."

"How will we get there?" She chewed her lip as she glanced at the group around her.

"Logan and Gwyneth will take you. Tomas and I will find your mama."

Gwyneth made a strangling sound in her throat. Holy heaven! What was he thinking? No way could she travel through the Highlands with Logan Ramsay. Besides, she had a mission to complete...one that required her to stay right where she was. But she refused to say anything in front of the girls. She didn't want them to think her refusal was because of *them*.

Ashlyn peered up at her. "Gwyneth, you'll go with us? Please?"

Gwyneth nodded. At the same time, she gave Robbie a hard look to get his attention. He clearly noticed, because a moment later, he said, "Tomas, take the girls and find them some oatcakes. Lassies? You're hungry, are you not?" Both nodded and followed Tomas over to the horses.

As soon as they were out of ear shot, Gwyneth edged up to him, not stopping until she was a mere inch from his nose. "You can't mean it. I will *not* travel with that lout."

"Gwyneth, I am trying to do what is the best for the lassies. I need people I trust to travel with them through the Highlands, which is not going to be an easy trip this time of the year. I have four other guards I'll send with you as protection."

It would force her to wait to wreak her revenge, but she wanted the wee ones safe as much as he did. She pondered what he said and decided it was a sacrifice she was willing to make.

"Fine, then send Tomas with us. Logan can stay here." Anyone, anyone but Logan would be acceptable. The man was exhausting. And she didn't like the way he made her feel.

Robbie glanced over her shoulder, and when Gwyneth turned to follow his gaze, she saw Logan standing there, his arms crossed and a smirk on his face.

"Nay, Logan knows the Highlands the best of anyone I know, and he's the foremost tracker, too. I would feel better if he was with you. He won't just lead the group, but also track ahead and make sure no one is in the area. Traveling with two bairns is too much of a risk. There are wild boars and wolves. You will protect the lasses while Logan leads, tracks, and kills when necessary."

"But I have never been to the Highlands. I don't want to go that far north. 'Tis freezing up there." She swung her arms wide as she rambled, frantic to find a different solution, even though she knew this was the right thing to do for the girls.

"Didn't you tell me you are good with a bow and arrows?" Robbie asked.

"Aye, I am, but..."

"Then you can help find food, too. See how thin Ashlyn is? Surely they haven't been fed much, and Ashlyn gives Gracie her share of whatever food they are given. I need you to go and watch over both of them. 'Twill not be an easy journey, and the girls need you. And I think Caralyn will feel better if she knows you're with them. I am asking you to put your problems with Logan aside for the lassies. Once there, you can do whatever you like, but I am sure Caralyn would appreciate it if you wait until she arrives before you take your leave, and I think the girls will feel safer with you around."

Everything he said made sense, and she could brook no argument. She looked back at Logan again, her hands on her hips.

Robbie tried his best to convince her. "Lass, I think you might like the Highlands. 'Tis beautiful land, and you may stay as long as you like at the Grant clan. We'll reward you when I arrive. Take a trip to our armory, find new weapons for your arsenal. I'll pay you in wool garments for the winter. Whatever your needs, let me know."

Logan sighed, the smirk leaving his face. "Lass, I have pledged it before, and I'll do so again—you have my word of honor on the Ramsay clan that I won't touch you unless you ask. I will control my banter for the girls' sake. I think Ashlyn will feel more comfortable riding with you."

He then strode over to his horse and pulled out one of his plaids. "Here, you can wear this when you get cold, and it *will* be cold, especially at night."

She stared at Logan, and then walked over to take the plaid he offered, throwing it over her shoulders and tying it in a tangled mess around her waist. "Lord, give me strength. Grant, I need to borrow your horse for a bit before we go to alert my family of my plans." She strode into the trees before she yelled over her shoulder. "I'll need my own horse, and I'm not your lass, Ramsay."

She heard Logan's previous comment.

"You are now, with my plaid on you."

He could think what he wanted. She was *not* his lass, regardless of the Highland custom of claiming a lass by giving her your plaid. She had heard his declaration before he had stabbed her captor, but she was sure he had been saying it for effect. Gwyneth chuckled. She accepted his plaid because she knew it would keep her warm during their journey, not for any other reason. He could believe whatever he wanted.

***

She had two important stops before she could leave—she had to see her brother and she had to see her boss, Dougal Hamilton.

She stopped at the Kirk first, and her brother threw his arms around her in a fierce hug, so relieved to see she was safe that he cried. He'd feared her dead when she disappeared without a trace.

He tugged her into their small living area in the back of the church and sat down with her at the table. Gwyneth's story flew out, and he quietly listened, making a comment every now and again, mopping his brow as she spoke, but allowing her to share her story.

When she neared the end, he apparently couldn't contain himself any longer and jumped out of his chair. "Duff? Duff Erskine kidnapped you? And he put you on a boat? Why?"

"For the same reason, Rab."

"What same reason?"

"You recall when he shot Da and Gordon? He had a cargo of women in his cart."

"For what? What were his plans for you?" Rab's eyes grew wide as he spoke.

"His plan was to send me to the East, along with several other women."

Rab sat down and placed his head in his hands. "Good Lord. How could he do such a thing? My Gwynie..."

She finished her story, and he promptly begged her not to travel.

"Rab, please. I need to do this for my friend, Caralyn."

"Gwyneth, how can you consider traveling all the way to the Highlands with several men? 'Tis unseemly, not to mention dangerous. I fear for you." Rab fingered the cross around his neck as he spoke, glancing at the cross on his wall for comfort. He closed his eyes and prayed, as Gwyneth knew he so often did.

"I will be much safer with Logan Ramsay and the Grant warriors than I was here," she said gently. "Look at what happened to me right outside your door. I was kidnapped from the side of the Kirk."

"I know, Gwyneth, and this whole time I have been sick with worry. I cannot lose you, too. Please don't go. Stay here with me."

"And what if Erskine still searches for me?" While she hated the forlorn expression on her brother's face, she was not about to sit here waiting for Erskine to strike again. If she stayed, it would be to go after him.

Rab mopped his brow with a linen square and paused for a moment, sighing. "You could be right.

Gwynie, you look terrible, all bruised and beaten. I will say many prayers for you. Perhaps it would be best if you went away to heal. I hear the Grant warriors are strong and honorable. I don't think even Duff Erskine would dare to tangle with them." He wrapped his arms around her again, then stood back, holding her at arm's length. "Stay for a bit first? I would love to talk to you. You have no idea how worried I have been."

"Rab, I'm sorry, but I must go now. Two lassies are depending on me. I cannot, in good conscience, send them off alone with the men. I go to protect them and ease their journey. I love you and I will let you know as soon as I return."

With that, she departed, in part because she couldn't stand to see her brother so tormented.

Her next stop was to visit her supervisor, Dougal Hamilton, assistant to the steward Alexander of Dundonald, whose job it was to ferret out important information for the Scottish Crown. Gwyneth had spied for him for the past year, covertly following men of interest to see whether or not they were loyal to the Crown. Her position had been arranged through the priests at the Kirk, though her brother had only agreed because of Hamilton's importance and persistence.

When Hamilton had first approached her, he had been hesitant. Word had reached him about her prowess as an archer and he had been searching for another spy. Word of unrest among the Western Isles and the King of Norway had spread through the land like wildfire, but the information was rumor, at best. He had wanted someone he could trust to sneak covertly into areas of interest around certain people.

Her first assignment had sent her to the royal burgh at Ayr in search of a traitor selling information. Gwyneth had discovered his identity within a sennight. He had been arrested and hung by the sheriff of the burgh.

Hamilton had smiled when she returned to him in Glasgow. She had passed her test because no one had suspected her role due to the fact she was a woman. Gwyneth had just shrugged her shoulders as he chuckled in delight.

Her final test had been to demonstrate her prowess at the butts, Hamilton claiming to want to guarantee she was capable of protecting herself in the field. Dougal had guffawed in delight every time she struck her target and hired her without hesitation.

With the Norse fleet coming closer, she had been on continuous assignment. One of her ongoing tasks was to find Duff Erskine and discover his activities. Hamilton had encouraged her to follow him along with three others. Gwyneth had been successful in uncovering the underhanded actions of the other three traitors, but Erskine was as elusive as ever.

Her latest assignment had been to follow Duff Erskine and to learn his current pursuits. The government had known of the previous doings with women, but was unaware of any recent activities. No missing women had been reported. He was a primary suspect in selling information to the Norse, but they had been unable to prove it.

Dougal Hamilton would be shocked to learn what she had discovered...and that she had been part of Duff's cargo.

As soon as he noticed Gwyneth in the castle, Dougal Hamilton motioned her into his solar. "Tell me everything. Rab had contacted me about your disappearance and I have men searching for you. Where did you get those bruises?"

Gwyneth filled him in on the details.

"My apologies. Erskine needs to be stopped. I had wanted to catch him selling information, but selling women to the East is beyond heinous. We need to take him out now. You will finish your mission?"

"Nay. I have something I must do for a friend first." She panted, out of breath from tearing across the countryside. Somehow, she would have to convince him how important this task was to her. The lassies needed her and she wouldn't desert them, even if it cost her time she could have spent pursuing Erskine. Robbie had been right. The weasel could wait. "I am to escort two wee lassies to the Highlands with Captain Robbie Grant of the Grant warriors and Logan Ramsay of Lothian. If I don't go, there may be trouble for the bairns. And Ramsay is overbearing and stubborn; he would be slow to let it go. I will be back to complete the assignment as soon as possible."

"Gwyneth, I can see the marks on your face. You have much that needs tending and that is the only reason I am agreeing to this journey. You also look exhausted. Please go slow so you can heal. I will assign two others to him in your absence, but I suspect this issue will not be settled by your return. Erskine is now aware of your activities. I'll feel better knowing you are healing away from the area. I hope you are headed out of Glasgow."

"We travel to the Highlands guarding two wee lassies."

"Do what you must. But I want this completed within a moon. You understand the need better than anyone, Gwyneth." He nodded to her. "Remember, time is of the essence."

Gwyneth heaved a sigh of relief. She had to do this first.

Little did she know that Logan Ramsay had just been by to update Dougal Hamilton with the same exact information.

CHAPTER SEVEN

Tomas walked into the clearing with the two girls in tow, a stunned expression on his face. "Did I just see Gwyneth with your plaid on, Ramsay?"

"Aye, but she apparently doesn't know what it means, so be quiet about it. 'Twill be a cold ride and you know it." Logan said, stooping to pick up wee Gracie.

Robbie chuckled. "I doubt you gave Gwyneth your plaid just to protect her from the cold. Didn't think I'd see the day, but I am enjoying the two of you together. Gwyneth is indeed unique and your response to her is even better. Always wondered what kind of woman would catch your eye."

Logan bounced Gracie in his arms until she smiled. "Had to be someone special, didn't it, Gracie? Gwyneth will definitely light up this journey."

Robbie sent Tomas back to town with instructions while Gwyneth headed home. "I don't want to wait long, Tomas. Find some provisions and the guards fast and get back. We probably only have a few hours until Murray discovers the girls missing. He may send guards out right away."

Logan said, "Don't worry. We'll lose them if they do." Since Malcolm Murray used the girls to blackmail Caralyn into being submissive, he wouldn't be happy when he discovered the lassies missing. Bastard needed to be stopped. He wondered what Robbie's intent was toward the lass.

After Tomas left, Robbie smirked again at Logan. "Quade will love to hear this."

"Aye, I meant what I said in the cottage. She's mine and no one touches her. The plaid will guarantee that your guards know their bounds." Then he snickered. "Just don't inform her of its meaning. I don't understand why she doesn't know, but mayhap they don't do this in the Lowlands to the west of Glasgow. And I'll tell my brother when he needs to know." He mounted his horse and yelled, "Grant, I'll be back shortly. One errand to do before we leave."

Logan knew Robbie could handle the weans by himself. He had to see Dougal Hamilton and inform him of his pending journey.

A few hours later, he managed to make it back to the clearing before Gwyneth. Tomas had returned and they waited for her. As soon as she arrived, Logan strode over to help her dismount. "Where'd you have to travel to that was so important?"

"'Tis no concern of yours, Ramsay. I have to travel with you, but I don't have to like it or answer to you. Do your job, and I'll do mine."

Hell, but she looked mighty nice with his plaid over her shoulder. The blue was a nice match with her blue eyes, though her eyes were a bit lighter. She also could sit a horse well, too. He found himself wondering about her background—he'd never met a lass anything like her, and he wanted to know what made her so unique and strong. He watched her bum as she strolled over to the two lassies. *One sweet bum, you have, lass.* Aye, he was looking forward to this trip.

In a short time, the group was saddled and ready to go. Right before Gwyneth was about to mount, a somber-faced Gracie ran over to Robbie and held her arms up to him. Robbie picked her up and she whispered in his ear, "Pweez save my mama." She cradled his face in her wee hands and gave him a kiss before hopping down and running back to Gwyneth.

Logan had never heard Gracie speak a word before today. Captain Grant had a tough road ahead of him.

***

Logan searched the hills but saw nothing. He had to admit that protecting three lassies did force him to be more on the alert than usual, if such a thing were possible. They didn't linger at all since Logan and his four men were worried about being followed by Murray. He sent two ahead and the other two brought up the rear, just to be safe.

Autumn was definitely in the air for their journey. Logan took a deep breath just to enjoy the crispness of the Highland day. How he loved the outdoors, especially playing outside with Lily and Torrian. Now that they were well, he could chase them about—a game all three of them enjoyed. The leaves were just starting to turn. Fortunately, they hadn't had a hard frost yet, so the ground was still soft, there were still plenty of leaves on the trees, and there was still food available for picking and digging. The squirrels were busy hiding their winter stores, and the rabbits hadn't yet gone into hibernation, so at least their trip should be fruitful. The lassies were too thin, and could use some meat on their bones.

Since they were all on horseback, they made good time the first day, which made him relax a bit. He had taken a couple of different turns off the main path to confuse anyone who might be following them, and he often sent one of his men behind to clean up their tracks. It was a good sign that they'd made it through the first day without any sign of pursuit.

He found a clearing and signaled for the group to stop around dusk, hoping there would be enough light to hunt. He was ravenous after consuming a strict diet of oatcakes during the day, so the others must be as well. After he helped the bairns down, he reached for Gwyneth, but she shoved his hands away.

She hopped down with a short, "I can handle myself, Ramsay."

"I see you can," he said with a grin. "I was just offering a kindness."

Gwyneth snorted, and he laughed. She was quite entertaining, though he had to contain his attraction to her around the lassies. Logan sent two men out to watch and two to hunt. "Lass, do you wish to hunt or stay with the girls?"

Gwyneth grabbed her bow and headed out after the two hunters, yelling over her shoulder, "Hunt. Can't count on a man to get enough."

Logan chuckled, eager to see what she could do with her bow and arrows. He knew one of Robbie's men to be a good archer, so the challenge was on. "Ashlyn, will you and Gracie gather some sticks for me so I can get a fire going? 'Twill be chilly tonight."

Gracie raced outside the clearing just as Logan whistled. "Not too far, wean. I want to be able to see you." They collected branches and twigs enough to get the fire going. Watching Gracie at work was definitely entertaining. She would find one twig, then come back and carefully place it on top of the growing pile before racing off to find another. He laughed as he watched her, but rather than suggest that she try to carry more than one at once, he said, "Good lass, you're a great helper." Must be she had some energy to burn from being on the horse all day. At least her rags gave her some padding to keep her bottom from getting sore. Naught seemed to bother her.

He started the fire and waved the flames to build it up, throwing Gracie's kindling in to get it roaring, when Neil and Gilroy each returned with one rabbit each.

"What the hell, Gilroy." Logan stared at him as he spoke. "Do you think two wee rabbits will feed eight of us? I thought you were supposed to be an accomplished bowman."

Gilroy gave him a sheepish look. "Och, the lassies won't eat much."

Neil stood beside his comrade. "There aren't many rabbits out there this time of year, Ramsay. You try your luck."

A rustling in the trees made them all turn in time to see Gwyneth stride into the clearing with four rabbits hanging from her belt. She tossed them near the fire and said, "Do you want more?"

Logan quirked an eyebrow at her. "Well done, lass." He turned to Neil and said, "Not enough rabbits out there?"

Neil's brow furrowed. "Aye, she got them all."

Giving them each a rabbit to skin, Logan took one to work on himself. "Six should be enough. Get cleaning. I'm starved."

Ashlyn turned her head as soon as they started slicing, but Gracie stood right next to him, her eyes on the rabbit, a wee hand on his leg. She pointed to the rabbit. "Eat?"

Logan smiled at her. "Are you hungry, lass?"

Gracie nodded. "I hungry." Then she patted her belly before patting Logan's belly. "You hungry?"

Logan laughed. "Aye, I am, but I will save you some. Can you be careful with the bones?"

She nodded, her gaze catching his before it returned to the rabbit.

Poor lass was hungry. Probably hadn't been fed much by the fools who'd held them captive. Both girls needed fattening since their cheeks showed dark hollows. Hellfire, but he would give the girls his portion. The wee one was almost salivating, and though Ashlyn wouldn't look at the gore of the rabbits, he could tell she was just as starved. Logan directed his question to Ashlyn, "Did they feed you at the cottage?"

Ashlyn stared at the dirt while she shook her head. Poor thing was embarrassed to be so hungry. "Not much. Only stale bread. I had to give mine to Gracie because she was so hungry."

Logan raised an eyebrow at Gwyneth, nodding at her bow. Hellfire, how long had it been since Ashlyn had eaten if she kept giving her food to her sister?

With a return nod, Gwyneth stood and stalked back out of the clearing. A few minutes later she returned with several apples, some with her arrows still in them. She sat on a log and pulled them off, offering one to Ashlyn. Gracie ran over and folded her hands in front of her, asking, "Pweez?" before she leaned on Gwyneth's leg and grabbed a piece of fruit, her wee hands gripping her tightly.

Gwyneth glanced over her head to Logan and said, "If you hadn't killed the two louts, I'd go back and kill them with my bare hands right now. Neither one of the brutes looked like they'd ever missed a meal."

As soon as they finished cooking the rabbits, Logan handed meat to Gwyneth to dole out to Gracie and gave some to Ashlyn as well. He then left the clearing with an empty sack he pulled out of his satchel. "I'll be back. Don't kill the fire."

"Where are you going?"

He glanced over his shoulder. "To find dessert."

Gracie clapped her hands.

***

The girls had eaten everything they could get their hands on. Logan couldn't stand to see wee ones go hungry. He remembered all too well the same haunted look in his nephew's eyes that had come from going without eating for so long. Food had made him vomit, so the poor lad had given up all but the thinnest gruel until Brenna came along and realized the problem— the boy and his sister could not stomach wheat.

Hungry bairns were something he could not handle. He'd find supplies for them to carry on their trip...enough so that the wee ones would never go without food again. Wandering through the thick forest, he searched in cracks and crevices and climbed tress to see what was available for foraging. A few moments later, he smiled. He had found just what he had been looking for—hazelnuts. He filled his sack and continued to look in the usual hiding places. He found mushrooms, the perfect kind for eating, and some pea vines. He cut down as many as he could and took them back along with some of the wild kale. He sent a blessing to Brenna—not only had she cured his brother's bairns, but she'd taught him enough of the vegetables that grew in the wild that he'd be able to fill the lassies' tummies.

When he came back into the clearing, Gracie ran over to him, her gaze hopeful.

"Hold out your hands, lassie." Logan beckoned Ashlyn over as well. Gwyneth came up behind them to see what he had found. As soon as he saw two wee sets of cupped palms, he filled them with peapods and a couple of hazelnuts each. Gracie's face lit up and Ashlyn said, "Gracie, peas. Your favorite," a smile lighting up her gaunt face.

Gwyneth said, "Well done, beast." She gave him a nod and a smile.

Logan smirked and held his hand out to her with an innocent look on his face. "Nut, Gwyneth?"

Gwyneth coughed and said, "Nay, my thanks, beast."

The two little ones sat near the fire and opened their pods, chewing their treats carefully. To his surprise, after Gracie ate the sweet peas from inside the pods, she chewed on the fibrous outsides too, crunching away as if she hadn't been fed for days. Logan smashed the hazelnuts so they could dig the sweet meat out of the shells.

"Are you sure you don't want one, Gwyneth?" Logan asked.

"Nay, beast."

"Gwyneth, why do you call Logan a beast?" Ashlyn

peered up at her.

Gwyneth scowled and turned away, not knowing how to answer that. He answered for her. "That's her endearing term for me, Ashlyn. It means the opposite."

She swung around to face him, her eyes in a fury as she glowered at him.

He held his hands up. "Sorry. I promised, didn't I? It won't happen again."

Gwyneth stomped off into the bushes, a low growl coming from her.

Logan laughed.

"I think she really likes you, Logan. Don't feel bad," Ashlyn said.

"I think you're right," he whispered.

A squeal came from the trees not far away. Logan laughed again. "Not my words, Gwyneth. Just a bairn's observations."

After eating her treasures, Gracie walked over to Logan and kissed him on the cheek after patting her belly. What better reward could one ask for?

His biggest challenge in keeping the lasses safe and comfortable would be the cold nights in the Highlands. He had a couple of furs and two plaids, but the air would soon be quite chilly. All three of the lasses were too thin to stay warm, another reason for him to speed up their journey. He had to get them to the Grants without delay.

He decided to settle in for the night and check on Gwyneth. As soon as he laid his plaid on the ground, Gracie waddled toward him with her arms raised and a big smile on her face. "You wish to sleep with me, lassie?"

Gracie nodded and plopped down into his lap. She peeked up at him and said, "He save my mama?"

Logan nodded. "Aye, Captain Grant will save your mama. We'll wait for her at the Grant's castle. You'll see."

Gracie pointed to the opposite side of the clearing

and then put her finger up to her lips. "Shhh."

Looking around, he saw the two guards who were off-duty snoozing at one side of the clearing, one of them already snoring. In the middle of the night, they would trade places with the two guards who were now on watch. Gwyneth, who had clearly waited for the guards to settle before returning just now to choose a sleeping spot, was as far away from the sleeping guards as possible. Ashlyn held Gwyneth's hand while she arranged a fur on the ground not far from Logan and the fire.

"Ashlyn, you would probably be warmer over here with Gracie and me. 'Twill get mighty cold tonight."

Ashlyn shook her head and clutched Gwyneth's hands tight, her knuckles going white.

Hellfire, he would like to kill the bastard who had put that fear into a lassie's eyes. His niece, Lily, wouldn't hesitate to sleep near any warm person she knew. He understood her hesitancy with the strange guards, but he'd hoped she would trust him by now.

"Ramsay, go to sleep. We'll be fine." Gwyneth positioned herself with Ashlyn tucked beside her and wrapped the plaid around both of them.

"Suit yourself. I'll be here if you change your mind." He winked at Gwyneth. "My plaid is always open."

Gwyneth snorted. "I'll bet."

"No reason to get nasty, Gwyneth. That is quite an unladylike sound you made, by the way." Her face was out of sight now that both of them were lying down, but how dearly he wished he could see it to catch her reaction to his comment. She was fun to goad. He was trying his best since he had promised her to behave, but hellfire, she left herself open to teasing. How he loved a lass with spirit, and Gwyneth had plenty.

She snorted again for effect. He chuckled and nestled into his plaid, tucking Gracie up close to his heat.

Logan woke up when the guards were switching

posts. He was about to close his eyes again when he noticed a wee figure standing in front of him shivering. "Ashlyn, do you wish to join us?"

She nodded. "I'm cold."

Logan opened his plaid and shifted Gracie to make room for her sister. When he had both lassies repositioned, he wrapped his arms around them and covered all of them with his plaid. "Och, lassie, you're a piece of ice." He set one of his warm hands against her cold cheek and she sighed with relief. It took a few minutes to stop her shivering, but eventually she calmed.

"Gwyneth, you should join us. Logan is warm." Her voice squeaked out through the plaid.

"I'm glad you are warm, Ashlyn. I am fine. Go to sleep."

Logan could swear her voice trembled. About an hour later, he felt her cold back press up against his. She had moved her fur. He whispered over his shoulder, "'Tis much warmer in front. The girls are nice and toasty now."

Silence. The lass was ice cold, but too stubborn to move. "You have my word of honor as a Ramsay. I promised Grant I would behave and there are two bairns next to me. What do you believe I would do, Gwyneth?" A few more moments of silence before he heard her slide the fur over to the front of him.

Her blue eyes bore into him. "Promise?"

"Aye."

"Because I couldn't handle it after the ship incident. 'Twas bad." He heard the tremor in her voice as she stared at the ground, and he knew how hard it was for her to say those words.

"Aye, you have my word." He held his plaid up.

"How can we possibly do this with three of us?" she whispered.

"Gracie needs my heat most. I'm taller than you, so she can squeeze between your shoulders and me.

Ashlyn can fit in front of you and my arms are plenty big enough to wrap around all three of you."

She nodded and climbed behind Ashlyn, who hardly stirred in her sleep. As soon as he had everyone comfortable, he tossed the plaid over them and tugged them close. Why were women always so cold? Gwyneth shivered against him for a few minutes and must have started to fall asleep, because she let out a moan that went straight to his groin. She must have felt his hardness, because she froze and held her breath.

"I promised. I can't help being a man. Let it go, and I will, too."

God's teeth, though, she felt like heaven in his arms.

CHAPTER EIGHT

That first night set a pattern for the rest, and Logan was pleased that the girls continued to eat whatever food he found for them. Further up the trail, he found some wild carrots and turnips in the ground. Once he scrubbed the dirt off them, wee Gracie would spend the entire day gnawing on a carrot as she rode in front of him. One evening Gwyneth and Ashlyn had broken into peals of laughter when they finally stopped—Gracie's face was orange from all the carrot smeared over her cheeks. Gwyneth's laughter was a sweet sound, he had to admit. The lass was much too serious and had dealt with so much tragedy in her short life. The sound of her enjoyment was wonderful to behold.

After they ate a small meal, he returned to his horse and put the leftovers in his sack.

"Ramsay, are you willing to share your skills?" Gwyneth stood on the far side of the clearing, her bow hooked over her shoulder.

He grinned. "Aye. I can think of many skills I would share with such a fine lass as yourself, Gwyneth."

She glared at him. "Just remember, I'm close enough to you at night to use that dagger as I promised."

Ashlyn's head spun around to stare at Gwyneth. "What? What would you do?" Her eyes were wide with alarm.

Shrugging her shoulders, Gwyneth let out a deep

sigh. "Naught. I was teasing him, Ashlyn. I promise not to hurt Logan."

"What skill would you like me to share with you?" Logan sneaked over and whispered in her ear.

She took a step back. "Tracking. I would like to track our trail so I can find my way back on my own."

"You don't need to do that, lass. I'll lead you back myself." Logan's wry grin did not sway her to smile. He'd try a little harder to earn a smile from her—it was all he wanted. "Just you and me." He glanced at her. Nothing, not even a twitch of her mouth. In fact, her eyes had become narrow slits.

"I don't need help. I'll find my own way back. Will you teach me or not?"

He picked up Gracie and said, "Come, I'll show you a few things. Ashlyn? Stay with us. And you can learn, too. Girls need to be smart."

Gracie patted his shoulder and he grinned at her. "You, too, wean?"

Gwyneth quirked her brow and he finally detected a small smile at the corner of her mouth. Now he knew how to make her smile.

"What are you showing us, Logan?" Ashley asked.

"I'm going to show you what you can learn from the outdoors, about tracking other people, foraging for foods, about animals, and how to remember your way back."

"Why?"

"Because lassies need to be strong, too. Don't you want to be strong and be an archer like Gwyneth?"

"Don't most women use bow and arrows? Although I know my mama doesn't." Ashlyn kept her hand clasped tight in Gwyneth's.

"Nay, most women do not use bow and arrows. Gwyneth is indeed a special lass." He glanced at her and smiled. He absolutely meant what he said. There weren't many like her.

"I want to be like Gwyneth when I get bigger. Will

you teach me Gwyneth?" Ashlyn looked up at Gwyneth with a look of wonder.

Gwyneth nodded. "Of course, Ashlyn." She glanced at him out of the corner of her eye, a small sense of appreciation flitting in her gaze.

Aye, the wooing had begun.

***

It was just past dark a few days later when they finally made it to the Grant Castle. Gracie didn't move on Logan's lap, so she had to be asleep, but Ashlyn sat up straight in front of Gwyneth, taking it all in.

"Gwyneth, I have never seen anything so big. Have you?" She turned to look at Gwyneth, her eyes big as saucers.

"Nay, I haven't. 'Tis quite a place." Rows and rows of cottages sat outside the walls of the keep. There were towers in each of the four corners of the enormous building's stone walls, tall enough to keep most invaders away. Men crossed the battlements and there was a flurry of activity as the group approached the keep.

They moved through the outer bailey and were greeted by a few scattered clan members, but word of the approaching visitors traveled fast and a group of warriors rushed to greet them in a short time. Once they realized four of their clan rode with them, the men relaxed.

The horn sounded as they came up to the portcullis. Ashlyn stared at all the torches atop the gates and the parapets. "It looks magical, does it not?"

"Aye, the torches at night give it a special appearance. It is a huge place."

"Gwyneth, I was worried they wouldn't have a place for us to sleep. I think they'll manage to find room."

She laughed. "I would guess they have room for many to sleep here. The castle is three stories high, plus look at all the cottages in the bailey. 'Tis almost a town of its own."

They rode to the stables, leaving the guards at the gate, where a very large man approached to help them down. "Ladies, I am Laird Alexander Grant. Welcome to my home."

Alex Grant was quite an impressive figure, taller than anyone Gwyneth had ever seen. He had long dark hair, gray eyes, and massive shoulders, but a smile that promised he meant what he said.

"Logan Ramsay," he clasped his shoulder. "Good to see you again. I presume you have located Robbie and have news?"

"Aye, Robbie sent us ahead. He'll be following with the lasses' mother."

Ashlyn just stared up at him. "Captain Grant is saving our mama. Are you Captain Grant, too?"

"Nay, lass," he tousled her hair, "I'm Laird Grant. Are you hungry?"

Gracie nodded her head so fiercely that Alex laughed. "Come, we'll find you something to eat. My wife will fill your bellies."

"Laird Grant, do you have enough room for us to sleep inside tonight? 'Tis verra cold sleeping on the ground." Ashlyn held her sister's hand. "May we sleep inside?"

"We'll take good care of you until your mama arrives. I promise. You can sleep in the lassies' room tonight."

Gwyneth wondered briefly where she would fit in.

He turned to speak to Logan and led them across the courtyard and up the steps to the great hall, asking questions about Robbie as they went. At the top of the steps, another man who looked like Robbie stood smiling at them.

"Greetings, I am Brodie, Robbie's brother." He held the door for them to enter the keep.

Once inside, they met Alex's wife, Maddie; Logan's brother, Quade; and his wife, Brenna. After exchanging warm greetings, they beckoned them to sit at a long table surrounded by playing bairns. Servants brought food and ale and before long a lad and a lassie ran over to Logan shouting, "Uncle Logan!"

Logan introduced his niece and nephew, Lily and Torrian. They also met Jennie, Robbie's sister; Celestina, Brodie's wife; Loki, Brodie's son; and Avelina, Logan's sister. Lily held her hand out to Gracie. "Come play with me."

Gracie peered up at her sister and Ashlyn nodded her head. "Go ahead, Gracie." Avelina and Jennie came over to talk to Ashlyn.

Gwyneth was so confused by all the names and faces that after she stumbled into her chair, she just stared at all the people in the room, all laughing and trading stories. She watched Logan with his niece and nephew, amazed at how much love he showed the bairns. His brother didn't look at all like him, except for their eyes. Quade seemed much calmer than Logan.

Eventually, the girls returned to the table to eat. Gracie ate everything she could and Ashlyn picked at her food, more concerned with Gracie than herself.

After they were fed, Lily came over and grabbed Gracie's hand. "Come, you can sleep with us."

Maddie stopped her. "Lily, please wait." She turned to Gwyneth and said, "Would you like your own chamber, or would you prefer for the girls to sleep with you?"

Gwyneth just stared at her for a moment, uncertain of what to say.

"If you would rather sleep on your own, they can stay in the girls' chamber. Jennie, Avelina, and Lily sleep there together in a verra large bed. My maid sleeps in her own pallet in the same room. I'll make sure to introduce you to Alice."

Wee Gracie turned to look at her sister, as if leaving it to her to make the decision. Lily, who still stood in front of them, started to hop in place in excitement. "Sleep with us. Please? 'Tis fun to sleep together."

Ashlyn glanced up at Gwyneth, as if for permission. "Go ahead, lass," she said with a smile. "Sleep with the lassies and know that I will no' be far away. If you change your mind, you can come to me later."

"Why don't we all go look at it now," Maddie said with a smile.

The bairns tore up the staircase, excited to show the newcomers the girls' chamber. Gwyneth trudged behind with Maddie, uncertain of what to think.

She had never been around this many girls in her entire life.

When they reached the girls' chamber, Maddie followed the laughing lassies inside and Gwyneth stuck her head in the room to make sure they would all fit.

Ashlyn turned to face her. "Look how big the bed is, and how many furs are on it."

A voice from behind her caught her attention. "Come, Gwyneth, I'll take you to your chamber." Brenna led her down the passageway carrying her daughter, wee Bethia, who was about a half a year old.

"How was your journey?"

"Not too bad, though 'twas a bit cold for the bairns."

Brenna stepped inside the room, holding the door open for Gwyneth. A fire had been started in the hearth and the bed was covered with warm furs. "Will this chamber suit you?"

Gwyneth nodded, rubbing her arms at the chill and moving toward the flames in the hearth. She had to admit the bed looked very inviting, though she usually didn't mind sleeping on the ground.

"The cold didn't bother you sleeping outside?"

"Nay, I prefer the outdoors." She gestured to her clothing. "'Tis why I dress this way mostly."

"Logan is my husband's brother. I hope he wasn't too difficult on the trip." Brenna motioned her over to a nearby chair.

"Nay, he was helpful, but he can be a bit stubborn

at times."

Brenna sat down next to her in front of the hearth, settling Bethia in her lap. "How did you two meet?"

"We met when..." Gwyneth made a quick decision to trust Brenna. "Well, he was with Robbie when they came to Ayr to escort a group of us to Glasgow."

"I don't mean to pry, but you don't look like someone who would need an escort anywhere. You seem self-sufficient to me." Her eyes sparkled and a wry grin spread across her face. The wean on her lap gave Gwyneth a smile as well, as if she could sense her mother's good mood.

"I am. We were attacked by the Norse. Most of us were wounded."

Brenna's brow furrowed. "I'm so sorry. That must have been terrible for you. I'm a healer. If you ever need my help, please ask. You are well now?"

"Aye. I keep telling Logan I am fine and can take care of myself, but he doesn't believe me."

"Then there must have been some sparks flying on your trip between the two of you. He's a strong minded man, and I can tell you are a strong minded woman. I couldn't help but notice his gaze followed you downstairs. I'm sure after your ordeal you are wary of men, but you can trust Logan."

"Aye, he is stubborn, but I do find him trustworthy."

"One more question, if you don't mind. I haven't seen my brother in a while. Robbie has an interest in Caralyn? Is that why he sent her daughters here?"

"Aye, I think the feeling is mutual, but Caralyn's situation is unique. I'll let them explain it to you. Caralyn is verra nice and a good friend to me." Gwyneth folded her hands in her lap, unsure of what else to say. "Captain Grant was verra helpful."

"Again, welcome to Clan Grant. None of us here will mind that you wear warrior's clothing." Brenna smiled at her as she bounced Bethia on her lap. "There can never be too many warriors. Usually we reside in

Lothian, but my husband and brother both wanted us here for the duration of the battles with the Norse. If you need anything, just ask."

"My thanks." Gwyneth nodded then glanced at the door. "Am I able to bar the door from the inside?"

"Aye." Brenna paused for a moment. "Do you have any sisters or family?"

"Nay, just a brother."

"So you aren't used to being around so many girls."

Gwyneth shook her head.

"I would be happy to bring you clean clothes, but I don't know if we have warriors' clothes that will fit you. There's a bathing room down the passageway you are welcome to use." She stood and moved over to the door, Bethia on her hip. "If you need anything at all, or if you just wish to talk, please come find me anytime." She went on to explain where her room was.

For some reason, Gwyneth liked Brenna Grant. "I'm fine, and my thanks for your hospitality. I won't be staying long, just until Caralyn and Robbie arrive."

As soon as Brenna left, she barred the door. She hoped the others would get here soon. She was used to spending time on her own and didn't know how to handle herself in this huge keep filled with all these people.

After a trip to the bathing room, she felt much better. On the morrow, she would clean her clothes. She climbed into the pile of furs and luxuriated in the feel of the soft material on her skin. But something was missing. She was loathe to admit it, but she had become accustomed to sleeping near Logan's warmth. His glance in the cottage in Glasgow had told her he would protect her, so she had slept hard, not worrying about Duff Erskine. She had not had any nightmares when she was wrapped in Logan's arms.

She wondered where he slept tonight. Would he even think of her?

***

The next morn, everyone sat at the family table in their great hall, enjoying a feast while they all talked at once. Logan was pleased to have been able to tell the Grants—Brenna in particular—that Robbie would arrive in just a few days.

Since the night before had been chaotic, this was the first chance they would all have to get acquainted. Lady Madeline had told Cook to prepare a feast and had specifically requested pastries for the two girls.

Gracie and Ashlyn ate in sheer delight. The wean had started with porridge, then moved on to freshly baked brown bread with coddled eggs, and was presently devouring goat's milk and boar stew. Ashlyn hadn't eaten quite as much, but she'd definitely filled her belly. It was a pleasure to see them this way.

Lily sat on his lap, chattering with Gracie on one side of him and Ashlyn on the other, and Gwyneth sat across the table from them, taking everything in without comment. He thought she still looked tired, but better.

Lily's excitement overflowed. What spirit she had. "Uncle Logan, I am so glad you brought me new friends to play with." She turned to give him a kiss. "Will you play stones with us?"

"I think Gracie would rather play stones with you. Uncle Logan needs a rest after his long travels," he said, patting her back.

Gwyneth snorted but didn't say anything.

Quade raised his eyebrows as he peered at his brother. "Did you have a difficult journey, Logan?"

"Och, nay, just a different journey, as I was traveling with three lassies." He grinned at Gwyneth, earning a frown in response. He had kept his promise not to banter too much with her on the journey. Now that they were here, he was ready to tease her again. He continued to stare at her and she ignored him.

The servants brought out the apple and cherry pastries for the girls and set them on the table. Lily leaned down to Gracie and said, "Cook makes the best pastries here. Do you like apples or cherries better?"

Gracie nodded and Logan laughed. She probably hadn't enjoyed anything like a pastry in a long while.

"Which one?" Lily asked, waiting patiently for an answer.

Gracie finally pointed to a cherry tart made of oats with a honey glaze over it. Lily set it in front of her and said, "Here, I'll show you how to eat it." Lily filled her mouth and said, "Yum. Here, Gracie, you can eat the rest."

Sticking a wee finger in the tart, Gracie then plopped her finger in her mouth. Her eyes widened as she tasted the sweet delicacy inside and everyone at the table giggled.

Ashlyn said, "Is it that good, Gracie? Let me try."

The girls all fussed over the sweets, and Logan caught Gwyneth's gaze again. "Och, try a pastry, Gwyneth. Mayhap 'twill sweeten you up a touch."

Her gaze threw daggers his way and he laughed.

Alex said, "How could you hunt with all these lasses to guard, Logan? Couldn't have been easy."

Gwyneth answered, "He didn't hunt. I did. And I could beat him at hunting any day."

Logan jumped in, "She did well, Alex, but she was only competing against Neil and Gilroy. My job was to protect the lassies while the others hunted. Had I gone with her, I am sure I would have speared more rabbits than she did, though she did well and killed four the first night. And with my help, we caught the pheasant we brought back with us."

Gwyneth bounded out of her seat. "Take me to any range, any day, Ramsay, and we'll see who the best archer is." Apparently embarrassed by her fervor, she blushed and sat back down.

The whole table had quieted, awaiting Logan's answer. He glanced at Quade and saw the twinkle in his brother's eyes, challenging him to accept her offer.

Logan smiled and nodded. "Naught would give me greater pleasure than to accept your challenge, lass. Just promise me you won't get upset when you lose."

Gwyneth barked, "I won't lose." She glanced at Alex. "'Tis there a sound field nearby we could use in an hour or so, Laird Grant?"

Alex's chuckled. "Aye, I'll find one for you. Sounds like great entertainment for the afternoon." He smirked at Logan. "Just so you know, Ramsay, I'll be rooting for the lass."

Gwyneth directed her next comment to Alex. "Will you find an unbiased judge for our contest and come up with a fair target?"

Quade jumped up. "I would love to help set up a target for you, Gwyneth, but I probably shouldn't act as the judge since Logan is my brother. What say you that we find three judges, just to be fair?"

Logan and Gwyneth both nodded their agreement. "Then it's settled," Logan said. "You get one hour of practice before the start of the competition, Gwyneth."

"I don't need practice, Ramsay. You have no idea who you are up against."

Logan just winked at her for an answer.

As everyone got up to prepare for the challenge, Logan overheard Quade as he leaned over and whispered to his wife, "You're right. There will be some *real* sparks flying this afternoon on the field."

What in hell was that supposed to mean? Could it be that Gwyneth returned his interest? Had she said something to Brenna? He would have to do everything very carefully on the field this afternoon if he didn't want to push Gwyneth away. He didn't think she would like losing.

***

By the time Gwyneth walked out to the lists, a good sized crowd had gathered. The Grant had chosen a large meadow with several trees at the end to hang various rope targets for the contest. The trees were at different distances, but they both appeared to be good lengths for her. *Good, I will embarrass him even more with a crowd.* The crowd sat down the side of the meadow, with no one allowed at the end except the judges.

Gwyneth's entire family had practiced archery for fun. She had initially been taught by her father and her brother, Gordon. They had held many competitions, and it had been a long time until she was ever good enough to win a contest. After their deaths, her archery had taken on a different meaning for her and she had trained daily. Uncle Innis had worked with her until he was no longer able. Then Rab had trained her at the butts near the Kirk. She had been forced to cut back once she was employed by the Crown, but she still managed at least three trips a sennight to the butts.

Naught had driven her more than the thought of putting an arrow through the heart of Duff Erskine. Aye, she had an arrow saved for the man who'd tried to sell her as if she were an object. But her goal for today was to prove that women could be just as good as a man. Ramsay was about to eat crow.

It was a glorious day, with a slight breeze that swirled the fallen leaves around her feet. She waited, pacing occasionally to help gather her strength, while the clan gathered off to the sides.

A voice broke into her thoughts and she looked up in time to see an exuberant Loki leaping and running across the field. "I'm one of the judges. My laird chose me."

She couldn't help but smile at the lad. "Does that surprise you, Loki?"

He came to a quick halt in front of her, gasping in excitement. "Aye. I just became a Grant."

Gwyneth's brow furrowed as she stared at the lad. She had heard part of his story, but not everything.

"You see, I used to live in a crate behind the tavern

in Ayr, and Brodie Grant found me, and I helped him find missy angel, Celestina, and then we saved missy angel from the surly pig-nut—" his eyes grew wide as he swung his fist in the air, "—and we fought the mean Norse together, but I had to get my sire to the healer 'cause he was wounded." He paused to take a breath. "Then I went to tell my mama Brodie was wounded, but she wasn't my mama yet." He stopped to point at Celestina and gave her a huge grin. Tipping his head to the side, his hand came up to his mouth in thought. "I... helped her come here and...." He stopped, a scowl across his face as if he had missed something in his tale. His face lit up. "Then my laird had a 'ficial cereminny and made me a Grant. So now I have a sire, Brodie Grant, and a mama, and I am Loki Grant." He pounded his chest with a smile.

"After this contest, I'd like to hear more about that. Tell me, you don't have a problem with a lass beating a lad, do you, Loki Grant?" She smirked as he stared at her, his eyes wide.

"Nay, my lady. I will vote for whoever is best. I promise to be honest. 'Tis part of being in the Grant clan. I must always tell the truth."

Gwyneth ruffled his hair. "I trust you will, lad. Why don't you check the targets to make sure everything is set up properly?"

"I will, my lady." Loki yelled back over his shoulder as he took off down the field.

Alex came out onto the meadow carrying a chair over his head, which he set up on the side of the field. He disappeared again before returning with his wife, whom he settled in the chair with a fur over her lap.

Maddie raised both arms over her head and shouted, "Go, Gwyneth! Yay for lassies."

Gwyneth bowed to her and waved as the crowd continued to grow. Quade and Brenna settled in near Maddie with Gracie, Ashlyn, and the rest of the bairns—Jake, Jamie, Torrian, and Lily. Kyla and

Bethia had stayed inside with Alice, Maddie's maid.

Gracie and Ashlyn ran over to wish her luck, and the elder lass gave her a hug. "I hope you win, Gwyneth. I wish our mama was here to watch you. Will you teach me someday?"

Gwyneth gave her a kiss on her cheek. "Of course, I will."

The wee one tugged on her skirt, so she leaned over to pick Gracie up and sat her on her hip. Gracie kissed her and smiled. "My mama come soon."

"Aye, she'll be here before you know it. She misses you, I'm sure." She set her back down and the girls raced over to sit with Brenna.

Alex, Brodie, and Celestina joined her with Logan directly behind them. He bowed to her and flashed her a wide grin. "I can't wait to get started, lass."

Brodie addressed both of them in a voice loud enough for the crowd to hear. "I am in charge of the contest. Your judges are to be Alex, Celestina, and one more. Where is he?"

Barreling across the meadow with all his might, Loki shouted out, "Here I am. I'm a 'ficial judge." He stopped next to Alex, panting, and gazed up at his adoptive uncle. "Am I not right, my laird?"

"Aye, 'tis true, and we count on you to use your Grant honesty." He patted the lad on the shoulder and stepped back, signaling for Brodie to continue.

While Brodie explained the contest to the crowd, Gwyneth assessed her competition out of the corner of her eye. Logan Ramsay was a fine specimen of a man. His hair almost glittered in the sun, and his brown eyes sparkled with excitement. She was quite sure he was going to enjoy this as much as she was...that is, until he lost.

He stood a few inches taller than she did, which was rare. She could look many men in the eye. He flexed his hands as Brodie talked, sending his muscles rippling under the tight tunic he wore for the contest.

A warm glow spread across her belly and down to the juncture of her thighs. She swallowed, uncomfortably aware of her body's response to the nearness of this man. As if on cue, he turned and winked at her. She jerked her head away and focused on Brodie's words, but unable to erase Logan's image in her mind. She wondered how it would feel to have him hug her in a warm embrace, or run his hands down her body in a soft caress.

She returned her focus to the contest, still shocked that a man could distract her so. Two different distances, three shots each. Overall victory would go to the archer who achieved the greatest distance. Two large oak trees had been chosen for the targets, with very little to get in the way of either one.

She was to take the first shot. As she passed Logan on the way to the mark, he leaned over and whispered, "Lass, I'll let you win the shorter distance so no one will look poorly on you when I defeat you in the longer distance."

Gwyneth spun around and glared at Logan, fire in her eyes.

Brodie said, "No taunting allowed. This is to be a fair contest."

Logan held his hands up. "My apologies, lass."

Then he winked at her again—that infuriating gesture he always made.

Gwyneth's eyes narrowed. Now the contest was starting, and she would beat his arse but good.

CHAPTER NINE

Logan would wager he had the best seat in the meadow. He stood behind Gwyneth and a bit to her left, the perfect spot to watch her form as she prepared for her shot. More specifically, he watched her sweet bum; those tight leggings she wore concealed nothing, revealing even the flexing of her muscles. She shouldn't be allowed to wear such things. If he lost to her, it would only be because of how enticing she was in her warrior's clothing.

He imagined standing behind her and rubbing the soft surface of her bum as she drew her arrow, hearing her moan as he caressed her soft skin. She would have to remove those leggings. His next thought was of the two of them practicing with naught on. He wondered if she bound her breasts. They didn't get in the way, but did she flatten them or was she truly that thin?

Her first arrow flew and the crowd roared when she hit the coiled target made of matted straw. Hellfire, he squinted to look. She was almost dead center. Lucky Loki ran over and measured the distance with his hands and then turned to show the audience how far away her arrow had landed.

She swiveled around and winked at him, clearly proud of her accomplishment. God's teeth, she was a saucy wench. He had to clear his head or his bulging breeks would embarrass him in front of the crowd.

Brodie grinned at him as he walked up to the mark to take his turn. He glanced around the nearby crowd and noticed a sea of smirks that had not been there before. Gwyneth had surprised them with her skill. No problem, he could beat her. He pulled his bolt back and aimed. Unfortunately, right before he released it, a vision of Gwyneth nocking her arrow in the nude flew through his mind.

He was close to her arrow, but he couldn't tell for sure whose shot had flown true. Loki measured and turned to the crowd, showing the distance between his bolt and the center. The first round went to Gwyneth. Logan attempted to hide the shock on his face, but gave himself away as he heard his brother, Quade, chuckle over in the corner.

"Nice, brother, the lass beat you."

He turned to congratulate Gwyneth and stepped back, allowing her access to the mark as the crowd applauded her first win. "Nice job, Gwyneth." He moved back to his spot on her left, but then decided if he wanted a chance at winning this contest, he needed to move to her other side. Her sweet arse had the power to undo him and he couldn't let that happen. Not here. Not in front of his family and friends.

Hellfire, but she was fluid when she nocked her air and drew. He had to admit he had never seen anything like it. Somehow, she approached the sport with a grace a lad could never achieve.

Logan won the second arrow, redeeming himself, and he knew he could take the match if she wasn't so sinfully distracting. But then she drew her third arrow and marked it, releasing it to hit the target dead center, right on target.

The crowd roared to life when she won the third arrow, which gave her two to one and the win at the shorter distance. Now he was glad he had taunted her by telling her he would let her win the first round. Not that he had exactly planned to let her win, but he hoped he'd managed to get into her head. It might be his only chance for victory.

They took a short break and he grabbed some ale, hoping to boost his confidence. Quade ran over and laughed at him. "Finally found your match, eh, Logan? How I wish Micheil and mother were here to see this. I haven't been this entertained in years."

"Stop your mouth. I let her win. I told her before she nocked her first arrow that I would give her the win at the shorter distance."

Quade folded his arms across his chest. "She may fall for that, but I know you better. You wouldn't let anyone win, especially a lass. Unless…"

"Unless what?" Logan's chin came up a notch as he glared at his brother.

"Unless this lass means a bit more to you than any other. Are you smitten?" Quade's eyes widened. "You are, aren't you?" He grinned and slapped him on the back. "My wife said she sensed something between you two, and she was right. You want her bad enough to lose a match?"

"How the hell could I not want her? Have you seen her arse in those leggings?"

Brodie bellowed. "Next match. Ready yourselves."

Quade slapped him on the back. "Could you try and make me proud to be a Ramsay this time?" he asked, then ran off with a smirk.

Logan had first shot for this round. He grumbled and paced, knowing he had to ignore Gwyneth in order to win this contest. His brother's words echoed in his ear. Striding up to the mark, he set his bow to the ground, nocked his arrow, drew, aimed, and sent his bolt flying. Good hit, just off center. This was a much longer distance, so he knew she would struggle. A lass couldn't possibly have the strength to strike an arrow this far. In fact, he should have asked Alex to shorten it to be fair. He didn't want to embarrass her *too* much.

Gwyneth never glanced at him, but took her time and the crowd quieted for her. After she took her shot, it was too close to tell who'd come closest. Loki ran over to the target and held up his hands, declaring Logan the winner on this one. She walked to the side and Lily ran up to her. "Here, Gwyneth." She handed her a small stone. "This is a lucky stone for you. You just have to rub it." Gwyneth thanked her and rubbed it with a small smile before putting it in her pocket.

Logan marveled at how well his niece and nephew were doing now that their health problems had been cured. Lily's face lit up every room she entered. Still. He scowled. Where was his lucky stone? Lily should have given him the stone, not Gwyneth. After all, he was her favorite uncle.

The next round was just as close, but this time, Gwyneth won by a wee bit. He heard her sigh in relief. Hellfire, he had thought it would be over by now. God's teeth, but how had this happened? He was one arrow away from losing to a lass. Circling the area, he paced to clear his mind of a soft bum in leggings. He needed to focus or his reputation would be in tatters.

Brodie held his hands up to announce the final shot and reviewed the current standings, while Celestina and Alex moved to the target to verify Loki's judgments.

In the interim, Lily ran over to him and handed him a stone. "Here, Uncle Logan. I forgot to give you your lucky stone, too. I think you might need it." He took the stone from her and picked her up off the ground, squeezing her until she giggled. "Why did Gwyneth get hers first?" he asked as he tickled her sides. He noticed Gwyneth watching them with an expression he couldn't decipher. Was it longing? He guessed Gwyneth hadn't had much opportunity to deal with bairns living in a Kirk with the priests. He was beginning to understand why she was so serious all the time. He vowed to change that for Gwyneth.

Smiling, he set Lily down and she scampered back to Brenna's side, giggling all the way. As soon as they returned, Alex announced, "Contest stands as Loki has announced. One arrow each. Final shot to determine the winner."

The crowd hushed as Logan readied himself to make his last shot. He had to secure the win or he would never live it down, though if he had to lose to anyone, she would be the one. He had to admit she was a fantastic warrior. He would definitely want her on his side in a fight. He drew and shot. Direct hit to center. She couldn't beat him. His gut clenched in reaction, followed by a cloud of confusion. What kind of reaction was that? Shouldn't his chest be swelling with pride? Logan paced a small circle, trying to rationalize his reaction, but he couldn't.

He glanced at Gwyneth, but didn't gloat. Disappointment flooded her face, but then switched to determination. His attention was totally focused on her. Slud, but she was beautiful when she stood strong and proud. She stepped up to the mark with confidence. God's teeth, what was she thinking? She couldn't beat him, yet he had to admire her courage.

She took her time nocking and drawing, and making sure her position was correct. When she finally released her arrow, the crowd gasped, waiting for it to land. It hit the center of the target and fell to the ground. Her face fell, but she acted honorably and turned to congratulate him.

Somehow, he just couldn't gloat. His shoulders slumped as he saw the dejection on her face. Hellfire, he wanted this woman. Perhaps it wouldn't have hurt to lose to her just this once. Loki was yelling at the end of the field, trying to calm the cheering of the crowd. He didn't understand any of the lad's words until Alex let out a Grant war whoop and the crowd stilled and all turned to look at Loki. The boy motioned for the head judge, his sire Brodie, to come out to the target.

Gwyneth glanced at Logan in confusion. "What's it about, Ramsay?"

"I can't tell. I'm sure it's naught, Gwyneth."

Her hand waved at him. "Shush. I want to hear what Loki has to say."

Loki told Brodie that he wanted the other two judges to join him at the target to verify the win. Brodie beckoned to the others, and Logan decided to follow them to the target. It wasn't that Logan didn't trust the judges; he wanted to see for himself how close he had hit. Gwyneth fell in step behind him.

Brodie held his arm out to the two of them, obviously not wanting them to be privy to the judges' conversation. Gwyneth stepped ahead of him, but then stopped in her tracks. Logan took a step closer, breathing in her scent, and noticing how long her hair was in her plait. He wondered how it would feel to have her hair unbound, dancing across his chest as she rode him. As if on cue, she glanced over her shoulder at him, and he saw her tense, as if his nearness unsettled her.

Good, he wanted to unsettle her...right into his arms. He leaned a bit closer until his chest brushed her shoulder, hungering for any chance to touch her. Her breath hitched, but she didn't move, another good sign. He had a new goal in life. Someday, he would have her. For now, if he could just get her sweet arse to brush up against him, he would be a happy man, but that would probably be too much in front of all the spectators.

The crowd waited while the judges consulted together. After they had studied the target for a long moment, Alex turned around and held his arms up, commanding the crowd to quiet. Logan and Gwyneth exchanged a look—she appeared to be just as puzzled by this additional declaration as he was.

"The win goes to Gwyneth of the Cunninghams. Her arrow knocked Logan's off the target and took dead center."

The crowd exploded in excitement, everyone running over to see it. Logan's arrow was different than Gwyneth's, so there would be no way the two could be confused. Logan and Gwyneth arrived first, and they both stood and stared at the target. Gwyneth's arrow sat dead center, as Alex had described it, while Logan's was on the ground.

She had beaten him—both distances. The lass had beaten him fair and square, and he would never live it down, but some part of him felt pride in her accomplishment. Logan turned to her and said, "Well done, lass. Congratulations. I didn't think you could do it."

Gwyneth blushed and thanked him, her face beaming as the crowd rushed to her side.

Logan Ramsay had lost to a lass.

***

Gwyneth sat up on the parapets, enjoying the night air. She had been so happy to win, but the crowd that filled the great hall for the celebration was growing too rowdy for her. She needed the opportunity to clear her head.

For some reason, beating Logan hadn't been as satisfying as she'd expected and she didn't understand that. He had been a gentleman, not a sore loser, even going so far as to raise a toast to her abilities right before the evening meal. Every time she overheard one of Logan's friends or family ribbing him, she felt sorry for him. Why?

The door opened with a bang and Gwyneth jumped out of the spot where she sat. Logan stood in front of her, as if having stepped out of her thoughts, his hair whipped by the wind. His smug expression had disappeared, and in its place was a look she didn't understand. He walked forward until he was directly in front of her. Her stomach fluttered as he closed the distance between them, his gaze holding hers until heat spread through her. She wanted to reach out and touch him, but she was afraid, naïve about the ways of men and women. He didn't speak either, allowing a moment of tension and desire to spread through her. She didn't know what else it could be.

And then he did the most unexpected thing she could have imagined. He cupped her face in his hands and kissed her. She was so startled she jumped in place...but then she leaned into him. His lips were warm and he tasted of ale, but there was something intoxicating about it.

He pulled back and said, "I wanted to congratulate you proper."

He brushed his thumb across her bottom lip and she sighed. He dipped his head and kissed her again, and she parted her lips with another sigh. His tongue swept inside her mouth and she pressed her body to his, wrapping her arms around his neck as she tasted him in return, swirling her tongue inside his mouth until he groaned and tugged her closer. She never would have guessed that kissing a man could be so intoxicating and so frightening at the same time.

He angled his mouth over hers, deepening the kiss, devouring her until she trembled all over. His hands slid down her back and over her bottom, and he grabbed her bum to pull her closer. She felt his hardness against her belly and wanted to jerk away, but then decided she liked the fact that she had caused this excitement in him. Logan wanted her and she was finally willing to admit to herself that she wanted him, too. She ran her hands through his hair and sucked on his tongue as he moved one hand from her bottom and up her side until he found her breast. He searched for her nipple and froze.

"I had a suspicion you might bind your breasts. I like the idea." He stood back, a sly grin on his face. "Would love to see them unbound and free."

Suddenly aware of all that had taken place, she shoved at his hands. "Aye, 'tis the only way I can shoot. Keep your hands to yourself."

"A moment ago, you didn't mind my hands on you." He cocked his head as he gazed at her.

"Aye, well, now I do. We're done, Ramsay." She blushed and turned away from him.

"Suit yourself." With a soft shrug, he moved to go back inside, and before he closed the door behind him, he turned back to her and said, "I love the taste of you, lass. I want more." Then he left with a wink.

Gwyneth hugged herself, shivering, before she brought a finger up to brush her bottom lip, the taste of him still sweet. What exactly did he mean by his last sentence? Not having any experience with men, she didn't understand what had just happened, and it completely unnerved her.

She had just experienced her first kiss, and she'd liked it.

CHAPTER TEN

Two days after Logan kissed Gwyneth in the parapets, Caralyn and Robbie arrived safely at the Grant Keep, and the girls were ecstatic to have their mama home. There hadn't been a chance for him to find Gwyneth alone again, and he sensed she hid from him. Her surprised reaction had told him it could have been her first kiss. Perhaps he had gone too far, but the simple truth was he had enjoyed every minute of having Gwyneth in his arms. After her initial shock, she had turned into a passionate lass, and if she hadn't stopped him, he might not have been able to stop himself. Hellfire, but they were good together.

He was getting restless, and after another two days, he realized it was time to move on. Gwyneth had told Alex and Robbie she wanted to return to Glasgow, so he would lead her back through the Highlands to be sure she was safe. Then he could check on Micheil and his mother at their clan in Lothian. Brenna and Quade had agreed to stay in the Highlands until Maddie birthed her bairn.

Logan had looked for Gwyneth all day to no avail. At first he thought she must have been with her friend, but then he learned that Caralyn was shuttered with the Grants in Alex's solar. Hellfire, he had to find the woman. If she had headed back to Glasgow on her own without an escort, she would hear his bellow all the way from the castle.

After waiting patiently outside the door, he could tell the meeting was about to break up. Unable to wait any longer, he rushed in, stopping directly in front of Caralyn. "Where's Gwyneth?"

Caralyn shrugged her shoulders. "I'm not sure. I have not seen her this morn."

"Did she tell you she was leaving?" God's teeth, he had to know and now.

Caralyn nodded. "She said she planned to leave shortly."

"Where was she going?"

"In search of someone in Glasgow."

"Who?" Logan inched closer to Caralyn, towering over her.

Robbie jumped in front of him. "Stay away from her."

"She has information I need," Logan declared, hands on his hips.

"Then ask her politely and mayhap she will answer." Robbie glared at his friend.

"Slud. Have it your way, Grant. Caralyn, would you please tell me where Gwyneth has gone?" He tipped his head with a smirk, looking at her from over Robbie's shoulder.

Robbie nodded and stepped back; apparently satisfied Logan treated Caralyn with the respect she deserved.

"She has gone after the man who sold her, Duff Erskine."

"She left alone?"

"Aye. She has her bow and arrows, and her dagger, too." Caralyn glanced from Robbie to Logan. "Gwyneth always travels alone, except the time Duff caught her."

"And what is her purpose?"

Caralyn stared at her feet, nervously shuffling them.

Robbie stepped back in front of her and turned to face her. "Caralyn?"

"She's going to kill him."

Logan growled. "Foolish lass." He cursed a couple of times before he started to turn away.

Caralyn stopped him. "And Logan?"

"Aye?"

"She will not quit until he is dead."

It was enough to make Logan pivot and immediately run out the door. Quade came up just as Logan was leaving. "Now where are you going?"

"To find Gwyneth."

By the time the others stepped into the great hall after him, Logan had already grabbed another plaid, a loaf of bread, a chunk of cheese, and his satchel. He moved toward the door.

Quade yelled after him. "Good luck, aye? See you, brother."

"Och, aye," Logan yelled over his shoulder as he tore down the steps. All the while, he kept thinking of Gwyneth alone in the woods. The woman was daft, just plain daft. Just because she whipped him in some silly contest, she thought she could travel all the way back to Glasgow on her own safely, then find her target and kill him.

God's teeth, why in hell had he fallen for such a difficult woman? Stubborn, daft, foolish...what else could he add to her list of faults? A lass who did naught but needlework would have gone much easier on him. When he caught up with her, she would regret acting in such a brazen, overly hasty way.

***

Gwyneth had to admit she was a wee bit jumpy moving through the Highlands. Mayhap she should have waited for Ramsay to travel with her after all. She had considered it before leaving, but after the kiss they'd shared in the parapets the other night, she just didn't trust herself with him...particularly if it were just the two of them traveling alone.

Ramsay confused her. Part of her wanted to shove

him away and never see him again, yet another part of her wanted to fuse her body with his and never let go. Why? After all the disgusting things she knew and had heard about rutting, why did it suddenly sound so appealing? Late last night, she had awakened in a sweat, dreaming of Logan's bare skin pressed against hers, her breasts unbound and in his hands, his mouth. She had thought of other things she would never dare admit to another person. Shaking her head, she hoped to banish such thoughts from her mind. They were distracting, and traveling alone through the Highlands as she was, distraction was not something she could afford. Worse, something was rustling behind her and had been for some time as she made her way down the trail.

Gwyneth jumped off her horse and crept through the bushes, searching for the source of the noise. Her bow ready, she hoped she wasn't about to run into a group of wild boar. Hell have it, she shouldn't have headed out on her own. She had made it through one night, but there were many more to follow.

She rounded a bush and let her breath out in a rush, but she found nothing. Staring up at the treetops, she wished she didn't have an awful fear of heights. She could have climbed one to see where the bastards were. She could fire fast at one boar, but she might not be able to nock her second arrow fast enough if more than one was headed straight for her.

Sweat dripped down her forehead, even though the evening air was crisp. The dampness of her palms forced her to continuously swipe them on her tunic. The rustling sound stilled, but rather than feeling relief, she was more nervous than before. Her heartbeat pounded in her chest and echoed in her ears. She was too unfamiliar with the smells of the Highlands to know if aught was different here.

Not daring to move yet, she held her ground, peering in each direction. If she dared get back on her horse, she would gallop out of this area as fast as she could.

A fresh rustle to her left caught her attention. She turned her bow and readied herself to fire. A loud squealing wrenched the air just before a huge boar launched at her at full speed. She released her arrow and stopped him dead in his tracks, but not before a second and third beast came barreling out of the copse of trees, both headed for her. Grabbing another arrow, she sent it flying and connected with her target. The second boar went down, but she didn't know if she could shoot the third in time.

He gained on her as she reached in her quiver for another arrow, and she turned a few degrees to aim. The bastard was closer than she'd thought and he leaped straight at her, catching her in the chest with his hooves enough to knock her to the ground. *This is it. He's going to kill me. All this training will have been for naught. The boar is going to end my life in a second.*

His squealing continued, masking all other sounds of the night. As he aimed his tusks straight at her face, she grabbed her knife and was about to stab him anywhere she could. Just then, the pitch of his squeal changed and he fell to the side of her. Another squeal sounded close to her, reaching the same eerie pitch before cutting off.

Gwyneth panted in fear, not knowing what would happen next. Her heart was racing so fast, she was afraid to move. She pushed herself to a sitting position, just then noticing the warm blood trickling down her arm from a small wound. The loudest bellow she'd ever heard cut through the night and her eyes flew to the source. *Ramsay.*

"Gwyneth, have you no sense at all, you daft woman! Get up before another comes. They travel together. How the hell could a lass as smart as you leave on your own? You can't travel through the Highlands alone."

He reached her side as she started to sob, and pulled her to her feet. As soon as he saw her tears, he stopped his bellowing and reached for her.

She threw her arms around his neck, sobbing freely. She had only been this frightened a few times in her life, and she didn't like it. Thanking the Lord he had come along, she clung to Logan, swearing she would never let go.

He wrapped her tight in his embrace, but then pulled back to stare at her. "Lass, you're bleeding. Is it your blood or the beast's?"

CHAPTER ELEVEN

"'Tis just a scratch. Never mind that, just hold me," Gwyneth cried.

She couldn't let him go. Not having cried since the attack by the Norse, she didn't understand this need, but she had no control over it. She'd held in her pain for this long, so why had it forced its way out today? One thought overtook all others—Logan had come for her.

Frightened out of her mind, she pulled back and swiped at her tears. "Thank you, my thanks for following me. I was a dead woman. He would have killed me."

"Aye, he would have, especially with another on his heels. What were you thinking? These are the Highlands, not the Lowlands." He brushed the hair away from her face, wiping the tears from her cheeks as he held her.

Gwyneth could no longer deny what she wanted. She wanted Logan Ramsay. After that kiss on the parapets, she had thought of naught else. And he had cared enough to race after her. *He saved my life.*

Staring at his mouth, she gave serious thought to what she was about to do, but she didn't care. She wanted Logan Ramsay and she wanted him now. There had never been any foolish thoughts of marriage in her mind before, so what did it matter if she gave in to her desire. Her body told her what she needed from

Logan. She licked her lips as he gazed at her, following her tongue with his eyes.

Logan crushed her into his arms with a groan, capturing her lips with his. She fell against him and wrapped her arms around his waist parting her lips so he could invade her mouth with his tongue, teasing and tantalizing her with his hot desire. Boldly following his initiative, Gwyneth tasted him in return, only to find herself tugged closer to him, his hands encasing her bum and holding her tight enough for her to feel his hardness against her belly.

She pulled back, panting, barely able to speak. "Are we safe? Do you think we're safe?"

Watching Logan struggle to catch his breath as much as she did made her heady with power. He wanted her as much as she wanted him and she delighted in that realization. Her gaze caught his with a question.

"Aye, through here. I think we got all of them, but I want to be closer to Paz. He'll alert us to intruders."

Gwyneth followed him a short distance until they found a soft spot near the horses. Logan dropped his plaid and settled it on the ground. "Are you sure about this, lass?"

Gwyneth nodded and removed her tunic, flinging it off to the side along with her belt, her quiver and her leggings.

She began to unbind her breasts when Logan jumped, "Please, allow me."

After he was finished, she stood in front of him, waiting for him to do the same. Somehow, she had felt no shame standing in front of him this way, and the look in his eyes made her feel like a queen. She could tell how pleased he was with her just by the way he let his breath out.

"Lass, you're beautiful." Logan's gaze raked her body before he ripped off the rest of his own clothes.

Gwyneth blushed, but then smiled, happy that she

pleased him. He pulled her back to him and cupped her cheeks, kissing her tenderly this time, stroking her tongue with his until she thought her legs would buckle.

He helped her onto the soft plaid, and gazed into her eyes. "Do you know how much I want you?" His hand slid down her side, cupped her breast, then trailed down her hip until he found her hand and placed it on his hard length. "Can you see what you do to me, Gwyneth? You, just you."

Gwyneth was surprised at the feel of his hardness in her hand, which sent another thrill of power thrumming through her. She let him go and tugged him down for another kiss, letting him tease her with his tongue until she was crazed with need. Grinding her hips against him, she hoped to encourage him to speed things up. She wanted him.

"Relax, lass. We have no need to rush."

"Aye, we do. When I need something, I don't like to wait."

He chuckled as his lips followed her neckline and he cupped her breast in his hand, rubbing his thumb across her nipple until he brought it to a taut peak. His fingers trailed a slow path over one breast, then the other, finally shifting down across her belly and into the dense curls at her sex. He teased her folds and she spread her legs for him, allowing him access to her sheath. He smiled and he slid a finger in and out of her passage.

"Logan, please." Lord, but she couldn't understand all the sensations this man was causing her to feel. Her nipples ached, and the spot between her thighs throbbed with a need she didn't quite comprehend, forcing her to thrust forward in a most unladylike manner. Her entire body thrummed with a sensation completely new to her, but one she rather liked.

"Gwyneth, is this your first time?"

She nodded, and her breathing hitched as he

removed his hand from her core and returned it to her nipple, gently rubbing the sensitive tip until she wanted to scream.

"You know 'twill be painful your first time? I'll do my best to ease your pain."

She nodded again. Aye, she had heard it would hurt, but she was a warrior and could handle pain. "Get on with it, I can handle it."

"Lass, I have no doubt you can, but I wish to make this as pleasurable for you as I can. Relax and enjoy."

Gwyneth sighed in frustration and then her eyes widened as Logan lowered his head and took her nipple in his mouth. Lord, but she had never experienced such pleasure. He licked and suckled as she moaned in delight, squirming as his lips transferred from one breast to the other. While he continued his assault on her aching breasts, his hands found their way back down her belly, finding her core again and parting her folds with his finger. She moaned in sheer ecstasy as he plunged his finger inside her again and again, tormenting her with a sweet torture that reduced her to begging.

"Och, lass, you are so wet and hot for me. Do you know how that excites me?"

"Logan, please." She grasped his arms as she moved her pelvis back and forth in response to the pleasure building in her sex.

He brought his lips back to hers and kissed her deeply again. "Aye, lass, I want you as much as you want me." He settled himself on top of her, supporting his weight on his elbows. "I can't wait any longer, you make me wild with wanting you."

Logan teased her entrance a bit more with his shaft before he entered her just enough to cause her to spread her legs in welcome.

"Logan, aye, this is what I want. Please do it now." She grabbed his hips in an attempt to bring him closer, but he was too strong for her.

"Hang on, love." Logan paused to kiss her, then plunged inside her and broke through her barrier.

She gave a brief yelp at the sting, but stilled and gazed at Logan for guidance.

"I'm sorry, lass, but that was the worst of it. I won't move again until you tell me."

She noted the clenching in his jaw and the tension in his face as he held still, waiting for her. The pain subsided so she moved against him until the ache returned. She pushed ahead as need possessed her again. Logan moaned and pulled back before entering her again swiftly.

Gwyneth did the only thing that felt right, though her boldness embarrassed her. She bent her legs, hoping he could fill her more, get in deeper, and he growled in response.

Logan rammed her hard and she moaned in sheer ecstasy as he picked up his pace, rocking her, hitting her tender pearl just where she needed him. A force was building inside her, coiling with each push, growing as he stoked her to a frenzied peak, faster and harder, intensifying with every jolt against her until the release she had searched for finally let loose, catapulting her over the edge with a scream as she clenched Logan, yelling his name and convulsing with a pleasure she had never known.

Through her bliss, she heard Logan roar as he emptied his seed into her and she swallowed, trying to get her breathing under control so she could watch him as he shuddered against her.

When they had both reached a point where they could speak, Gwyneth met Logan's eyes and said, "Good Lord, Ramsay. I had no idea."

Logan grinned and kissed her. "We're fantastic together, lass."

CHAPTER TWELVE

Logan had to admit that it had been better than he expected. He kissed Gwyneth's cheek. "I pleased you, lass? The pain is not too much for you."

"What pain?" Gwyneth snorted.

Logan quirked an eyebrow at her.

She blushed. "Not a very ladylike sound is it. Rab used to tell me that. I guess it's a habit. Sorry."

"You have naught to apologize for. I'm more concerned about whether or not you are still hurting. Every moment was sweet."

"Nay, I'm fine. The pain was verra mild."

She gazed into his eyes until he caught the sparkle in them, followed by her sly grin. What was the lass thinking about? A few moments later, he found out.

"How often do you do this?"

Logan chuckled. "A man doesn't tell other women about his experiences. Why?"

"I don't care about your other experiences."

"Then why do you ask?"

"Because..." She hesitated before answering.

He kissed her forehead. "Because?"

"Because I wondered how long before we could do it again." Gwyneth averted her gaze and blushed, but then returned her gaze for his response.

He chuckled. "If you give me a few moments, I'll show you."

"Why do we have to wait a few moments?"

Logan chuckled and gathered her in his arms. "Saucy wench."

***

A few hours later, Logan rested on his side with Gwyneth cocooned in his arms. They had discussed their family and made love again, and he decided now was the time to broach the topic she didn't want to hear.

He whispered in her ear, "Do you wish to tell me why you left by yourself? Don't you think 'twas a wee bit foolish?"

"I can handle myself. You saw that in the archery contest."

He could tell her defenses had instantly gone up. "An archery contest is not the same thing as a trip alone. None of the Grants would have tried such a thing."

"You would have." She stared at him, quite sure of herself.

But other than her encounters with Duff Erskine, he was willing to bet Gwyneth had lived a sheltered life in the Kirk. Logan sighed. "Aye, but I have traveled these Highlands enough to know them a bit better than you do. Can you not admit you were almost in trouble by yourself?"

"Aye—" she bobbed her head, "—I should have climbed into the trees."

"Why didn't you?"

"Because." She glanced off into the distance, her voice barely a whisper.

Logan was baffled to see her this embarrassed. "I know you can climb; you must have climbed a tree to get all those apples for the lassies."

"Aye." She still avoided his gaze.

"And so, you didn't climb the tree because..."

She brought her gaze back to his, her eyes narrowed in a challenge. "Because. I'm afraid of heights. I can only climb the lowest branches as I did to retrieve the apples. I can't go any higher or I risk fainting. Does that please you?"

Now it made sense. The lass didn't want to admit to any sort of weakness. "Being afraid of heights isn't uncommon. There is no reason to be embarrassed. It *is* a reason to make sure you are not caught in such a situation again." He waited for her agreement, but none was forthcoming.

She changed the subject. "How far are you going?"

"However far you are going."

She sat up and turned to glare at him. "Why did you follow me?"

"When I found out you left alone, I had no choice," he said, sitting up and facing her. "I wasn't convinced you could make it alone in the Highlands. And I'm glad I came. I'll follow you to Glasgow."

"You don't need to follow me. Go back. I have a job to do, and I don't need your help."

"You mean killing Duff Erskine?"

"Aye. Who told you that?" She crossed her arms in front of her glorious breasts.

"Caralyn did. Is it a secret?" He reached over and grasped her hands to pull them away from her front. Slud, he liked looking at her.

"Nay!" She slapped his hands away and crossed her arms again.

"Then why are you upset?"

"I'm not upset." She turned her back on him and flounced back down on the ground.

"Aye, you are." Hellfire, she had spirit and he loved it. He fought to quell his grin or he suspected she would start swinging at him.

Logan allowed silence to settle between them again to give her time to sort out her thoughts. He ran his hand down her back in a soft caress, his fingertips just grazing her skin. After a few minutes, he started again. "Why don't you tell me everything about Duff Erskine?"

She sat up and turned back to face him. "Logan, I know you are trying to be helpful, but this is my battle. If you came in and killed him for me, I would be furious. He's mine to kill, and I can do it on my own. This has been my goal for the last seven years."

"But he put you on the boat not too long ago. Why seven years?" He needed to hear it all from her.

"Aye, he tried to sell me because he knows I'm after him. He's afraid of me because he knows I won't quit until he's dead. The only way he could control me was to have his men drug me." She crossed her legs and played with several leaves on the ground, staring at her hands as she spoke.

Logan tugged her onto his lap, turning her sideways so she could rest her head on his shoulder. He rubbed her arm and said, "Why? Why is he afraid of you?"

"Because he killed my father and my brother, and now I won't rest until he is dead." Her hand rested on his arm as if she needed something to steady her.

The fact that she reached for him instead of pushing him away was a good sign. He had to earn her trust. She shouldn't have to fight this battle on her own, but he knew he would have to convince her of it. "You know for a fact it was Erskine who killed your father and brother?"

"Aye, my younger brother and I saw it happen in front of us."

Logan's stomach clenched as he fought to hold back his gasp. He hadn't realized she had watched her own family die in front of her. God's teeth, he couldn't imagine a lass watching that. No wonder she had an edge and a mission. This changed everything. Vowing to help her carry this out, he waited, hoping the pause would bring forth the full explanation. He wanted every detail of the story.

Gwyneth cleared her throat. "I'll tell you everything, but you must understand that I'm doing so to make you understand what I must do. He is mine to kill and

I want you to promise me, here and now, that if you have the opportunity, you won't do it for me with the intent of helping me. 'Tis something I need to do for myself. Understood?" She sat up and gazed at him, awaiting his pledge.

What she asked went against his better judgment, but he didn't think she would budge on this request. Logan rubbed his eyes in thought and held his breath before releasing it in a whoosh. "Aye, unless the situation is the same as with the boars. It could be you or him. If it gets to that point, I'll kill him. Don't ever doubt that. I won't watch you die for your pride." He would probably live to regret this oath, but he could not deny her.

"My thanks." She settled herself back against his chest. "I grew up in Glasgow. My mama died a few days after she birthed my brother, Rab, when I was only a year old. I don't remember her. I had an older brother, Gordon, who was four summers my senior.

"After my mama died, my father raised the three of us as best he could. He taught us all how to use a bow to hunt, and we did so often. We never went anywhere without our bows except to the Kirk. Papa always said 'twas disrespectful to take a weapon to the Kirk." She played with the hair on his arm as if she needed a distraction to give her the strength to continue.

"My Uncle Innis was a priest at the Kirk in Glasgow. 'Twas one night after we left the Kirk when our nightmare happened. We had gone to pray and then stayed late for a visit with my uncle. We lived in a small cottage near the firth. As we neared our home, Papa heard someone crying, so we moved toward the sound, which came from near the river.

"When we got close enough, we found a couple of men loading women into a cart. My sire was a strong man who believed in right and wrong, so he yelled out to the men and asked them what they were about. It was verra dark, and I couldn't make out much of what they were doing, especially since I stood behind Da and Gordon."

Gwyneth sat up and turned to face Logan, tears misting in her eyes. "Logan, he pulled out his bow and killed my father and brother right in front of me. I was standing between the two, so I could see him undeniably clear. Duff stepped forward and fired without saying a word. I'll never forget that moment for as long as I live."

"Hell, Gwynie," he brushed back the strands of hair fluttering in front of her face. "I'm sorry, lass." He kissed the first tear as it slid down her cheek. He held her hand, brushing his thumb across the back, hoping to be some source of comfort.

Gwyneth stared up at the stars as tears rolled down her cheeks. "He fired two arrows fast, straight into their hearts and they crumpled to the ground. All I remember after that is falling on my da and screaming for him to wake up. He never moved again, and I was covered in his blood."

She swiped the tears off her cheeks and stared at her hands, her breath hitching as the painful memories ate at her. "The next thing I knew, Duff Erskine stood in front of me and stared at me. He wore a twisted grin and told me I was lucky he didn't do the same to me. Then he told me he would come for me in a few years and send me off on a boat, as he planned to do with the women on the cart."

"Where was your brother, Rab?"

"Rab thought faster than I did and ran for help as soon as he saw the arrows fly. I was frozen; I couldn't move at all. And the worst part? When the bastard stood over me laughing about my da and my brother, I didn't even try to hurt him. I didn't have my bow, so there was naught I could do, but I couldn't move at all, a huge force was keeping me pinned in my spot."

"Lass," he cupped her cheeks and brushed her tears away with his thumbs. "You had just watched your sire and your brother die in front of you. How could you have done anything? I wouldn't have been able to move either. 'Tis only natural."

Gwyneth shook her head so forcefully her plait swung back and forth on her head. "You would have done something, Logan Ramsay. I failed my family."

"How many summers were you? I think you're too hard on yourself."

"Ten and three. I was big enough to have swung at him or something. I could have yelled; I could have punched him. *Something*."

He kissed her forehead. "Gwyneth, at ten and three, I wouldn't have been able to do anything. You were too young, and you had just received the shock of your life."

Her hands latched onto his arms and her fingers dug into his flesh. "I should have done something! Do you know how many times that scene has played out in my head? Do you know how many different ways I have dreamed of hurting that bastard? He killed them for no reason. No reason!"

Logan understood. He could feel her entire body shake with emotion from reliving the tragic experience. He wanted to kill the bastard with his bare hands for what he had put Gwyneth through. The cold execution of her family members necessitated an extraordinary form of torture.

Duff Erskine was a dead man. He just needed to convince her to let him do it for her.

God's teeth, he had no idea how he could do that.

CHAPTER THIRTEEN

Logan reached for her and drew her in as close as he could. Gwyneth clung to him, wanting so much to be able to lean on him for support. It had been a long time since she had felt this comforted. Logan Ramsay was indeed an unusual man.

She cried in his arms for several minutes more before she was finally able to rein in her feelings. Settled on his lap, she rested her head on his shoulder while he rubbed her back, allowing her the time she needed to finish the story. After blowing her nose on a nearby leaf and wiping her face with another, she finally calmed enough to speak again.

Logan said, "No one came to help you?"

"Nay, 'twas too late at night," she hiccupped. "By the time Rab returned with my uncle, Duff was well down the trail of the firth with his packhorses. We picked up my father and brother and took them to our home to clean them up. I cried and cried and thought I would never be able to stop.

"Uncle Innis talked to the other priest and we were brought to live with him in a small room in the back of the Kirk. Eventually, they added two small chambers for sleeping. We helped clean, cooked, fished, and Uncle Innis taught us both to read. The Kirk had so many wonderful books that I read all the time.

"But the most important thing he did was help us practice with our bow. I became obsessed with it, and

Rab became obsessed with the church. We each had a different way of handling the tragedy. When Uncle Innis died last year, Rab took his place in the Kirk and became Father Rab. He had already gone for training with Uncle Innis." She pulled away and smiled at Logan, playing with his long hair. "I am so proud of my brother and I love him so much."

"How did you meet Caralyn and her daughters?" Logan asked.

"Father Rab travels to different Kirks sometimes. He is happy to go wherever he is needed, and he often takes me with him. We were at the Kirk in Ayr when I met Caralyn. I just fell in love with her sweet bairns, and I knew she was in a difficult situation, but I didn't know how to help her other than to be her friend. She was my only true friend because I spent all my time in two places."

"Two places?" Logan's brow furrowed. "Aye, the Kirk, but where else did you go?"

She smiled and kissed his cheek. "To the butts. My brother helped me find a suitable place to practice my shooting and a perfect target. He is an excellent natural archer. I never was that great at it until I had a goal. I practiced and practiced, and he gave me pointers on how to get better. My father taught the three of us, and we played around often, but I only became skilled after Uncle Innis and Rab worked with me.

"I vowed to improve until I could kill Duff Erskine, though my brother tries to talk me out of it, speaking about forgiveness and the teachings of the church. Still, I think he understands I am driven to do this."

"Your brother didn't see the arrows kill your father and brother, did he? If he ran, he saved himself from that memory. You do have that inside you, and I am sure 'tis a powerful beast to defeat."

"Aye, the memory never leaves me. Erskine will die at my hands."

***

Someone shook her arms. "Gwyneth, wake up. Come, love, you're having a nightmare."

Her eyes flew open with a start and stared directly into Logan's gaze. A nightmare. She panted, forcing herself to a sitting position, trying to bring her fear under control. Glancing down at the dirt, she heaved and reached for something, anything to ground her. Then she sought the only thing that promised to give her genuine comfort—she threw herself into Logan's embrace.

He wrapped his arms around her and whispered in her ear. "Lass, I'm here. Do you wish to tell me about it?"

Gwyneth sobbed as she clung to him. Duff Erskine had invaded her life once again. She had this dream frequently. Sometimes she dreamed about the experience on the boat, and other times it was the moment of her kidnapping. How she hated reliving the terror of having no control.

However, this was the first time she had ever had the comfort of a pair of large, warm arms around her. She was beginning to like having Logan Ramsay around.

Wiping her eyes, she leaned back and told him everything. Then she fell back against his chest and he held her, just held her until a wave of calm washed over her—a sense of renewed confidence and purpose. She would do this, and if by chance she needed help, Logan would help her.

Never, never would she be powerless again.

***

The next day, they rode through a meadow that was absolutely stunning, surrounded on both sides by tall craggy rocks. The air was still as they rode, the only sounds the birdsongs in the trees. Fortunately, there hadn't been any rain, and they hadn't run into any more boars either.

He glanced at Gwyneth and said, "Would you like a bath, sweeting? I know of a place not far from here we could use."

Gwyneth's face lit up. "Aye, please! I miss the Grant bathing room."

He spurred his horse into a gallop and yelled back over his shoulder, "Follow me."

As he was heading straight for a wall of rocks, Gwyneth swore he was daft before he reined in at the edge and pointed to a spot in the middle. When she pulled up next to him, a slow smile crept across her face as she noticed the slender opening. Just wide enough for a horse. They slipped through the crevice and Gwyneth sighed in pleasure at what she saw there.

"This is the most beautiful spot I have ever seen." Her gaze roamed over the ground covered in soft moss leading up to a deep pool. She dismounted and proceeded over to the stone edge, where water puddled in shallow crevices in the rock that led to a deeper pool in the middle. Bending over, she stuck her hand in the water and squealed in delight. "'Tis warm, Logan."

She turned around to gaze at him, her face beaming as she ripped off her clothes.

Logan quirked his brow. "Are you always this free to strip?"

"Aye, when there is warm water. You're coming with me?"

He chuckled. "Wouldn't be verra gentlemanly of me to allow you to explore on your own. Who knows what you will be up against?"

Gwyneth tiptoed across the rock until she came next to the spring. "Do you think it is verra deep?"

"Nay, you can stand up in it. Go ahead. There's no fish or aught else."

She lowered herself so she sat on the edge before dropping into the water with glee. She moaned and sighed in sheer delight as the warm water washed over her long limbs. Reaching up to her hair, she released the ties so it tumbled down on her shoulders and giggled as she swung her long mane back and forth, freeing it from its bindings.

Logan took one look at her with her hair down around her shoulders, jumped into the water and grabbed her, pulling her tight against him.

"Oh!" She glanced at his hardness against her belly. "That didn't take long, did it?" She grinned at him and grasped his erection, stroking him the way he liked.

"Hellfire, between your hair and your moaning, it took little more than a second. But now you have given me a challenge, for sure."

"What's that?"

He grinned as he picked her up by her waist and set her on the edge of the stone, spreading her legs wide for him. "'Tis a matter of my manly pride. I must make you moan more using only my tongue."

Gwyneth's puzzled expression made him grin and he set to proving his point. Within minutes, she groaned right before she clutched his hair and cried out his name loudly enough for it to echo inside the small chamber. She caught herself as she fell back on the rock and stared at him, watching him kiss his way up her belly.

"Did I keep my promise, lass?" He winked at her with the most wicked grin he could muster.

All Gwyneth could do was nod and whimper.

CHAPTER FOURTEEN

When they finally arrived in Glasgow, Gwyneth took him straight to the Kirk to meet her brother. She led him through the back door into a warm and inviting chamber behind the chapel. A table and chairs sat near the hearth, and a small area for food preparation was situated at the back of the room. He could see two rooms off the main chamber, probably for sleeping. Father Rab was a pleasant man, truly concerned about his sister.

"'Tis a pleasure to meet you, Father," Logan said.

"My pleasure, but please call me Rab. You don't need to address me as a priest in my home. You are here as a guest." His smile was genuine and warm when he turned his attention to his sister. "Gwyneth, come sit down and tell me about your trip to the Highlands."

The three of them settled at the table and Gwyneth shared the highlights of their journey with her brother. Logan could tell how much she loved and admired Rab. Her demeanor was often tough and cold, but not here. Only in the last few days had he noticed how beautiful her smile was, her white teeth glowing against her dark hair and the bronze color of her skin. It was more lovely for the fact that it had to be earned. Lord, but he had to admit that his protectiveness was growing stronger everyday with this lass.

Was it just the need to protect her or was it

something else?

Her face beamed as she told him about the Grant clan.

Rab winked at Logan. "I am glad to hear you enjoyed your journey. Mayhap it has given you something else to focus on for a while."

Gwyneth's face fell. "Nay, you know what I have to do, Rab. I can't let it go. He needs to pay for what he did."

Her brother's hand reached for her shoulder. "Are you still having nightmares?"

Logan nodded his head in unison with hers.

Rab's brow quirked, and his expression changed from friendly to fierce, as if he were finally piecing together something that disturbed him about their relationship.

"Please, Rab. Do not lecture me. Logan and I escorted the two wee lassies to safety along with four other guards. You know 'tis something I needed to do for my friend."

"Aye, but the trip back to Glasgow?" His hands moved to his hips as he glanced from Gwyneth to Logan. "Is there a need for me to perform a wedding right now?"

Gwyneth's reaction caused both men to jump. "Nay!" Her eyes widened as she stared at her brother. "No wedding! You know how I feel about that, Rab." She glanced at Logan and shook her head.

Logan's gaze pierced hers. "If she'll have me, I would be happy to marry her and call her my wife."

Saints above, where had that come from? He had shocked himself as much as anyone else. In the end it hadn't taken any thought at all. His sire would have expected him to make the offer since he had taken her maidenhead. Being out in the wilderness had made it all seem so natural, so right. He had enjoyed every moment they'd spent together in the Highlands. Now he had to do what was honorable. Besides, he did love her and would follow her forever if she chose to lead him. He *wanted* to wed her.

He turned to Gwyneth and took her hand in his, rubbing his thumb across her skin. "Gwyneth, naught would make me happier than for you to be my wife."

Gwyneth glanced at him, panic in her gaze. She shook her head and stared at her brother. "Nay, Logan 'tis not you. I told my brother I would never marry."

Rab interrupted. "Mayhap you could give us some time together alone, Logan? I have not talked to my sister in quite some time."

Logan nodded. "Certes. I have a couple of things I need to do. I shall return in a short while." He gathered his things and nodded to Gwyneth before departing.

After he mounted his horse in a fog, Logan flicked the reins, turning toward the center of town. Saints above, she had rejected him. The shock of that one word—nay—had just settled on him. All these years of running from the thought of marriage, and he had been rejected by the one woman he'd ever hoped to make his wife. What in hell was she thinking? Just because she had something she needed to finish didn't mean she couldn't marry him. Hellfire, she could be carrying their bairn. Mayhap she just needed time to think about it, since he had sprung it on her rather quickly. Father Rab would probably insist on the match.

He forced the incident from his mind. If that was her preference, then he had no choice but to honor it. His chin jutted out. As soon as he finished his errand, he would return to the Kirk, say his goodbyes and head straight to the Ramsay clan. His mother had stayed behind with his brother, Micheil, so he would visit with them first.

As soon as he reached at his destination, he tossed the reins to a stable lad and crossed the courtyard to the steps of the great hall. Once inside, he strode to the dais and greeted his host. "I came to advise you of my most recent journey."

"Aye, do tell. Then I have another assignment for you, and it's one that needs to be finished soon." Dougal Hamilton stood and strode to his solar, beckoning Logan to follow him inside.

Logan took a seat opposite Hamilton's desk, told his story, and then awaited his next assignment. Dougal Hamilton worked quietly according to the king and Dundonald's needs. Dundonald was the steward to King Alexander and it was his job to handle all the king's official business. Hamilton's job was to handle all the king's unofficial and covert business. Logan's habit of wandering had proven invaluable in assisting the Scots to obtain important information...and complete other special tasks. It was imperative that no one be aware of his job as a scout for the Scottish government. His brothers were the only ones aware of his secret missions.

Logan nodded, realizing that things had worked out for the best since Gwyneth had turned him down. He couldn't have completed another assignment if she'd agreed to wed him.

Hamilton continued. "I have a scout that has taken on the quest of destroying a particular piece of scum in Glasgow on their own for personal reasons, but the target needs to be taken out because of his threat to the Scots. This particular person started out as the usual criminal, but his activities have elevated over time to those of a heinous predator. I have new evidence of unspeakable crimes against women and I want him taken out. I need you to make sure this scout completes the mission without delay. I support the merchant's termination, but I am afraid my scout has a personal vendetta against the man that may interfere with the scout's ability to see the assignment through."

Logan said, "Then why not pull the scout from the

assignment and allow me to finish the task? I need something to occupy me at present, so it would work well."

Dougal clasped his hands together in his lap. "Because this particular spy is one of my best, and I think it would be in this person's best interest to complete the task on their own."

"Then how do I fit in?" Logan asked, confused.

"I want you to follow the scout without giving away your status. I fear the personal issue may cause this person to require assistance. I need you to ensure that the assignment is completed without any issues."

"Accepted. Who is the scout and where can I find him?"

Hamilton smiled. "*Her*. The spy is Gwyneth Cunningham. You are familiar enough with her after your trip to the Highlands?"

Logan couldn't hide his surprise. "Aye, I am. She is a skilled archer. I left her with her brother just now. Why did you not inform me of this before? I just traveled to the Highlands and back with her, as you are fully aware. And why did you not tell me she worked for you?"

Logan didn't know whether to be just shocked or furious, too. Gwyneth? A spy?

"Because you didn't need to know. I make the decisions, Ramsay, and it wasn't important enough at the time. I wanted you to get a sense of her skills on your own without my input. You agree with me that she is capable of completing the mission?"

"Aye, she is a strong archer and a warrior. But I don't know if she can complete this with all that has taken place previously. Set her aside and allow me to do it."

"Nay. This is her mission, and I will not deny her. It needs to take place, and I am guessing you are aware of the situation. Did she share her history with you?"

Logan stood, unable to keep his concerns in check.

"Aye, she did, and she is too close to this. Pull her out and allow me to go after Erskine. I'll see it finished." His voice grew louder as he continued to talk.

Dougal's expression changed to one of puzzlement. "Just how close to her are you? Is there more to this relationship that I need to be aware of? What exactly is she to you?"

Logan stopped and sat. He realized how this had to look to his supervisor. He had just held the woman in his arms for several days, but he couldn't let Hamilton know that, or he would be forced to step away from the situation.

He mulled over everything he had just heard and said, "There's naught more you need to know. I accept the mission and will see it through. Anything else I need to know about Erskine?"

Hamilton clasped his hands together on the desk and leaned toward Logan. "You need to be careful. He is no longer a small criminal. He controls many men, and much wealth. In fact, I want you to also see if you can find out who he controls in the government. Somehow, he has managed to evade any charges for all his previous crimes. He is a wealthy man. He must be paying someone to turn their head. I want to know who it is."

Logan thought again and nodded. "Agreed. I will move immediately. You must be aware of his most recent activity and what he did to Gwyneth."

Dougal's voice dropped to a whisper. "Aye, I am aware, and I had two scouts looking for him in your absence, but one of them is now dead. Hung by a rope in a tree by the firth, the buzzards picking on him when we found him. Find Duff Erskine, he is as elusive as ever. I want him dead for his most recent kidnapping attempt of the lasses and for killing one of my scouts. Find him before he kills another scout or attempts another shipment."

Logan nodded. Hellfire, he was still unable to speak.

He stood and headed to the door but stopped to turn around. "Gwyneth? One of your best?"

Hamilton nodded. "Aye, she is. She is clever, one hell of an archer, and no one suspects a lass."

And while Logan was still spinning with the shock of what he'd learned, none of that was a surprise at all.

Dougal's eyes bored into him. "Ramsay? Whatever it takes. Do it."

CHAPTER FIFTEEN

As soon as Logan left, Gwyneth lit into her brother. "Rab, I'm not marrying him, you need to stop. You know what I have to do and how I feel about marriage." She paced the room as she sputtered, still indignant at her brother's suggestion.

"Gwyneth, please calm down." Rab's voice lowered, in the fashion it always did when he sought to soothe her.

"I am calm, Rab, I just won't marry. I thought you understood." Under a man's control? Never. As much as she appreciated all Logan had done for her and her friend, she could not consider marriage, even with him. She thought of how her rejection must have sounded to Logan and sighed, yanking the end of her plait. He had to know it wasn't him, just the premise of such a strong, *permanent* commitment.

Rab stared at her for a few minutes before he ushered her over to a chair at the table and sat down beside her. "Gwyneth, I know what we dealt with when Da and Gordon were murdered was a burden heavier than what many children must bear. And I understand that you and I have chosen to deal with it in very different ways, but I worry about you."

Gwyneth stared at her brother. How she loved him, and how grateful she was that he had run for help on that fateful day. Elsewise she might have needed to bury him as well. Tears burned her eyes as she reached over and gripped his hands. "Rab, you know I must finish this."

Rab nodded, though she could tell her answer bothered him. "I do understand, though I've chosen a different path."

Gwyneth stared straight ahead and swiped at the tears on her cheeks.

Her brother continued. "Prayer has brought a wonderful peacefulness in my life that I wish I could share with you. Aye, I didn't see the arrows pierce Da and Gordon's skin as you did, and mayhap that is why the need for revenge has not consumed me, but this eats at your soul, Gwyneth. I wish you could let it go. I think Da would like to see you settled with a good man and bairns at your feet. This Logan seems like a good man, and he accepts you for who you are, leggings and all."

"Rab, you don't understand," she said, fighting the tears that threatened to fall yet again. "It wasn't just the arrows. I saw the life go out of Da's eyes. I am glad you didn't see it, but when I fell on him, he was still there. He stared at me with the worst look in his eyes, and then the light was gone. I watched as his soul left him. It was beyond horrible, and when I turned to look at Gordon, the very same thing happened." She gripped the bottom of her tunic with both hands, fighting for control. "Tell me one thing, Rab, and please be honest," she whispered. "Do you ever wish to see Duff Erskine dead?" She reached into her pocket and clutched the wee stone Lily had given to her, rubbing it furiously as she awaited his answer.

He blinked as his shoulders slumped. "Aye, but I pray for strength every day. I pray for forgiveness for my vile thoughts, for the hatred I sometimes still bear toward that man. Now I think about what Duff tried to do to you by throwing you on that boat, and I carry such anger that it haunts me. Every day I pray for strength. But mostly, I pray for you, Gwyneth, for I don't know if I could go on if I ever lost you. I pray for your happiness, for your deliverance from the hatred you carry inside."

"Resolution is close, Rab. Now that I am back, and the war has calmed, it's time for me to finish this. He won't haunt either of us again," she murmured.

"I know you need closure, but if you kill him, will you not be forced into another type of hell—that of guilt? Can you live with that on your conscience?"

"Aye. Erskine's death will give me peace to know I have finally found justice for the travesty that took place seven years ago. Think how many women I could be saving from a life of slavery, the life that was almost forced upon me."

"This is true," said Rab, his head bowed at the table. "I just wish the sheriff would take care of it, so you didn't feel forced to finish this."

"Duff is beyond the law. He lies. An investigation took place, but the right thing wasn't done. Something is afoot, and I need to find out what it is. He must pay quite a bit of money to one of the top officials. 'Tis up to me to uncover the truth, and then I vow to finish this."

"I know you will not rest until you do, but can you ask Logan to assist you? He could go with you."

"I don't need him. I can handle Duff on my own, Rab."

"For me, Gwyneth." Rab stood so fast that his chair almost fell over. "His men drugged and overpowered you before. Please. Agree to have Ramsay to help you. I would feel better if he was there watching over you."

Gwyneth smiled. "You don't trust the Lord to watch over me after all your praying?"

"Even the Lord takes all the help he can get." He wrapped his warm hands around Gwyneth's. "Please?"

Only her beloved brother could convince her not to go alone, and only for him would she concede. "I will speak to Logan when I see him again, but only for you.

I have already told him that I must deliver the killing blow myself."

Rab tipped his head back, rubbing his face in his hands. "Gwyneth, you worry me so."

Gwyneth stood and hastened over to kiss her brother on the cheek. "Relax, Rab. All will be well; you shall see."

He finally smiled. "I must admit I am hopeful. Whether you wish to accept his proposal or not, I believe you have feelings for Logan Ramsay, and naught would make me happier than for you two to wed. You have spent too much time in the Kirk and at the butts. There is more to life than vengeance. Please don't push him away."

Gwyneth tipped her head and peered at her brother. "He is a good man. I'll talk to him about helping me with Duff." How she loved her brother. Though it had surprised her a little when he turned to the church, she was pleased he'd found his vocation. Besides, even a lowlife like Duff Erskine would know better than to target a priest. The public outcry was more than he would be willing to face.

She wrapped her arms around him. "I love you, Rab."

"Where will you go?"

"'Tis time to finish this. I will find Logan, and then together we will go for Erskine." She turned and exited the church, her hand still rubbing her lucky stone.

Rab stared out the window after her, then bowed his head in prayer.

***

Logan rode back to Father Rab's Kirk, still trying to settle in his mind that Gwyneth Cunningham worked covertly for the Scots under the same man who supervised him. The thought of a woman operating in such a way had never entered his mind.

Well, he had known she was different all along. This was yet another sign of how special she was to him.

Good God, but she was a beautiful, clever lass who affected him in a way he'd never experienced before. The more the idea settled with him, the more he rather liked the thought of marrying her. 'Twas time to settle a bit, though he would never settle as his brother, Quade, had done. But Gwyneth loved the outdoors as much as he did. What would Dougal Hamilton think of his two agents marrying? He smiled when he thought of how surprised the man would be if it were ever to happen.

There would be time to settle that later; now he had a mission to complete. The truth was he would have followed Gwyneth whether or not Dougal had given him the order. Erskine was a bastard and needed to pay. With all the new information Hamilton had just given him, he had even more reason to see the scum dead. The man had no conscience. He would do what he needed to help Gwyneth accomplish her goal and put Duff's crimes to an end.

His only challenge would be to guarantee that Gwyneth was safe. Aye, she was strong, but he had to make sure her feelings wouldn't compromise the mission.

He dismounted and strolled to the back door of the Kirk, surprised to see that Gwyneth's horse was gone. If she had already left without him, there would be hell to pay. As he knocked, his gaze searched the area for any signs of her. There was nothing.

The door swung open and Father Rab stood in front of him, an expression of concern on his face. "Och, this can't be good."

"Father Rab? Gwyneth isn't here?"

"Nay, she left a short time ago. She told me she was going to find you, but since you stand in front of me, she must have gone after Erskine alone. The saints preserve us all, she promised she would seek your assistance first." He shook his head. "I will pray for her all night. My sister causes me such worry."

"Father, ease your mind. I will find her and protect her." Logan clasped the priest's shoulder.

"Many thanks, Logan."

"Erskine, I imagine he is oft found at the river's edge, but does he have a keep? And if so, where?"

"As far as I know, he has a couple of cottages he uses down near the water. He has a few men who work for him, and they often share huts. But no one knows where he lives, those are just his lackeys."

Logan said, "Don't worry, Father. I'll find her."

He bolted back out the door and jumped on Paz. Unfortunately, he now regretted the promise he had made to Gwyneth. The vision of a man swinging from a tree with his neck broken changed everything. If Erskine stood in front of him and Gwyneth was at his side, would he be able to step back and allow her the chance for vengeance?

He was no longer sure, but the lass had left without him. There was no time to waste.

CHAPTER SIXTEEN

Gwyneth left her horse well hidden in the trees when she neared the water. There were no docks yet in Glasgow, and the Firth of Clyde was well known for being too shallow for most boats near the shore. Now she had finally put together a key facet of Erskine's operation. She had seen enough to know he loaded women into a covered cart, then moved them by packhorses down river to a usable dock. She supposed it kept his entire operation more secretive.

What's more, from spying on him, she knew he could sometimes be found near the river, since he had so many lackeys around the firth. If she was patient, he would appear sooner or later.

And Gwyneth could be very patient. She settled into her favorite hiding spot in the bushes not far from the riverbank and waited, making sure she took note of everything around her.

She had already gone to see Hamilton and updated him on her whereabouts. He had given her the only assignment she was interested in—to kill Duff Erskine. Now was the time to complete it because the world would be a much better place without him. She felt a little guilty for lying to her brother about finding Logan Ramsay and taking him with her, but she hadn't been able to locate Ramsay, and now she was on assignment. She could function on her own.

A few hours later and nightfall was fast

approaching, but she wouldn't let that deter her. She had practiced shooting in the dark often enough to be skilled at it. No one approached her; no one appeared to notice her. This was one of the reasons she wore dark men's clothing. Besides covering against the brambles and dirt of the outdoors, it helped her to fade into the shadows. She used to hide her hair when she was younger, but no longer. People in Glasgow knew her, and most wouldn't bother with her.

Except for Duff Erskine. She focused all her energies on him.

She remembered everything about him the day he killed her loved ones. His brown hair was dirty and unkempt. He was always chewing on something and he often spit, brown disgusting fluid that she swore came from his heart. But there was one thing about the man that would never leave her—his stench. He smelled as if he hadn't bathed in weeks, and she couldn't rid her mind of that memory. No matter where she was, if she smelled strong body odor, it attacked her senses in more ways than one, often making her dizzy.

Over the years, Erskine had changed. His wealth bought him the best of finery, jewels on his fingers, and a different air about him. He believed he was above reproach, mostly because history had proven it to be true. Somehow, he escaped the sheriffs and magistrates of the royal burghs. He moved so fast from burgh to burgh that he was difficult to track, seemingly always progressing to a new location. But Gwyneth knew Glasgow is where he started, probably was his home. He was a flitting presence in other burghs, but not here. Glasgow was her best chance of finding him. Fragrant oils could cover up his stench, but not the rotting of his putrid soul.

Just thinking about the lousy cur caused her palms to dampen. She forced herself to focus on her surroundings. She had a limited view of the area, but she could hear. Taking a deep breath, she willed her body to calm so she could do what needed doing. A dog howled in the distance. The serenity of the night changed swiftly as the wind whipped through the trees. She lifted her nose to see if the aroma of an oncoming storm was in the air. Pausing to take in all the sounds of the town by the river, she had to accept that inclement weather was a possibility.

A shutter banged down the pathway, followed by the slam of a door. One set of heavy footsteps approached her and then passed by. A draft of wind told her who it was—Erskine. She peeked through the bushes just as his steps halted on the other side of her hiding spot. Had she been discovered?

The man took three steps back toward her and she held her breath, only to let it out as a man from the faraway cottage called his name and came running down the path toward him.

"Aye, Duff. I promise we'll have everything completed on your return."

Erskine stopped to speak to his henchman. "Good, see that you do," Duff answered. "If you don't, I have plenty of tree branches and rope to use for both of you. I have business elsewhere and I expect you to carry out my orders. If not, I have plenty to replace you." Duff pivoted and headed in the direction of the town stables. His steps were heavy and deliberate, a man who knew what he was doing at all times. Sure of his mission, he continued without hesitation while his lackey returned to the riverbank.

Gwyneth waited to see if his comrade would join him, but the two traipsed away in opposite directions. She stood and hid behind a nearby tree, waiting until her prey stepped inside the stables. She would have him cornered, right where she wanted him. If she timed it right, he would be at the far side of the large barn when she opened the door to the stables, and her arrow would find him easily. She had always thought to take him down outside, but if it happened inside the stables, he would have nowhere to run. No one had entered or exited the building since she had been here, so she thought him alone. Not many were out this late at night.

She and her father's murderer, her brother's murderer, and the man who had tried to sell her as a slave would finally meet on *her* terms.

The door to the stable creaked as he opened it, and banged shut behind him.

Now was her chance.

***

Logan stood in the center of town, trying to decide where to start looking for Gwyneth. Father Rab had suggested he might find her down by the cottages at the water's edge, so he headed there first.

He went on foot, his sword and daggers strapped to his person. The darkness of the evening crept over him just as the winds came up, threatening another Scottish autumn gale. The town was mostly devoid of people; they had apparently sensed the oncoming storm and tucked inside their cottages.

Traversing the area near the firth, he wondered what he would do if he saw the bastard before Gwyneth did. He wanted naught more than to put his sword directly into the blackguard's heart, but he had promised Gwyneth he wouldn't do it.

He reminded himself that even Hamilton had said to assist Gwyneth, not take the lead. But since Dougal had told him to kill Duff, he would have at least a partial justification for going against his word.

Nay, he couldn't do it. He had pledged not to interfere unless her life was in danger. Even so, he knew Gwyneth would hate him forever if it came to that. He couldn't let that happen. She would marry him once this was settled. She just didn't realize it yet.

He heard voices ahead, one voice clearly giving the other instructions. The unidentified male walked toward the stables, stopped, but then continued on his way. He waited in the shadows, hoping for a clue as to the men's identities. Eventually, another man followed the first, and gave him the information he needed. He called Duff by name.

There was only one Duff that he knew of, so it had to be Erskine. It would take all his self-control not to force the man to the ground so he could beat his face to a pulp, but he would.

Just as he moved in that direction, drops of rain started to fall around him and thunder boomed in the distance. Hellfire, he wished this was over.

Then there she was. He would know her lithe form anywhere. She glided across the grass without a sound, headed straight for the stables, her bow clutched in her hand. The rain molded every inch of her clothing to her curves. Never had he seen such beauty, but he forced his mind to focus on what was at stake.

He had been correct. Duff Erskine was inside those stables.

And Gwyneth was braced to kill.

CHAPTER SEVENTEEN

Gwyneth had waited a long time for this. Finally, retribution for her father and her brother was within her grasp. After a survey of the area again, she crept to the closed door and pressed her ear to the weather-worn wood. The soft rustling of boots moved through the straw, confirming her original impression—only one man moved inside, and he was hers.

Gwyneth readied her bow and waited just outside the door, fingering the lucky stone in her pocket one last time. She fidgeted with her arrows, reviewing the plan in her mind before she took the next step. Taking a deep breath, she reached for the rusty door handle.

Before her hand ever touched it, the door flew open with a bang.

Duff Erskine grinned at her.

Gwyneth was momentarily stunned, but she quickly recovered and arranged her bow.

"What, are you going to shoot me at this range? Go ahead and try. So you got lucky and were saved by the Norse. No matter. I'll still get my money for you someday. Truly, I could kill you, Cunningham, but you are worth much more to me alive, a beauty like you. Continue to follow me, you do not scare me. Worry not; we'll meet again on my terms."

His evil grin chilled her right to the bone, but he wouldn't win, not this time. She squared her shoulders. "Nay, you won't, Erskine. You are scum, and I intend to make you pay for killing my father and brother."

Erskine laughed and shoved past her. He stopped just outside the stable door and stared up at the thunder clouds above, then laughed. "You couldn't hit me on a good day, Gwyneth. With this rain, you won't have a prayer and you know it."

He turned his back to her and walked away, chuckling.

Gwyneth braced herself and aimed straight for his back. This was all wrong. She wanted to shoot him between the eyes or in his heart. She held for a moment, expecting him to turn around to try and goad her again. The rain ran down her face and over her hands, but she held strong.

"You couldn't hit the stables right now, Gwyneth. You'll never hit me," he called out over his shoulder, his voice careless.

Fury coursed through her veins. No matter if she shot him in the back. She let her arrow fly and waited.

Naught happened.

"Och, was that meant for me?" he guffawed. "You weren't even close. Didn't anyone tell you that you're a girl, lass? Lasses can't shoot. Whoever taught you did a terrible job, and he shouldn't have wasted his time." He continued to strut away.

"Turn around, Erskine, so I can see your face." She wanted to see the look in his eyes when she hit him with the killing bolt.

He turned around and stopped, staring her straight in the eyes. "You don't have what it takes to shoot me. Here you go." He held his arms up. "Here I am, kill me. You're a lass, and you aren't strong or smart enough to take me down. Give it up."

Gwyneth nocked another arrow, drew, and released it, but she missed him by two arms. The rain pelted her face, causing her vision to blur, and she swiped at her eyes. Unfortunately, tears now blurred her sight, his words hitting her harder than any she had ever heard.

"Ha!" His arms jerked up toward the sky as he spun around and walked away from her again. "You can't even hit a standing target. You'll never be able to hit me when I'm moving. Let it go, Gwyneth. Go to your brother's Kirk, get down on your knees and apologize to your father and brother for your failures."

She drew another arrow and let it fly, but her arm shook too much for her to control her aim. She was way off target. Her knees began to buckle, and she forced herself to lock them, drawing strength from her belly. She could not fail.

"Not a chance." His laughter echoed through the night. "Be careful that you don't hit the wildlife, would you, girl?"

Another arrow flew past him. "Say goodbye to your brother, by the way, because we'll be coming for you again in a sennight. This time the Norse won't be around to save you." He walked without breaking his pace, as if he had no fear.

Gwyneth clenched her jaw and sobbed in fury. How could she have missed him so many times, and at such close range? She didn't doubt her abilities with the bow—after all, she had won her contest against Ramsay fair and square only a few days ago. She stared after Erskine, who was still rambling along, taunting her as he went, so she noticed when he suddenly stopped short. She wiped the tears from her eyes and stared. Why was he no longer moving?

Logan.

As her vision cleared, she realized Logan Ramsay stood at the end of the path with his arm encasing Duff Erskine, a dagger at his throat.

"Nay!" she screamed. "You promised me, Ramsay. He's mine. Do not kill him. He is mine!" She tore down the path toward him, slipping and sliding in the mud, her arms flailing with urgency.

Logan did not budge. "Then do it," he said to her. "I'll hold him. Nock your arrow and kill him."

A bolt of lightning arched through the sky, freezing her in her place, lighting up Logan and Erskine in the blue of the night. For the first time in her life, she saw a touch of fear in Duff's eyes. She drew strength from Logan's gaze and reset herself because she was still a good distance away, nocking another arrow and pulling back. Tears still mixed with raindrops, and she was about to let the arrow fly when a rumble of thunder startled her. She couldn't do it.

She had sent countless arrows toward him and missed each time. And if she missed him this time? She could hit Logan—the man she…loved. It was not worth the risk.

She stood down, aiming her arrow at the ground, "Let him go."

Logan said, "Shoot him. And if you don't want to use your bow, come over and use my dagger."

"Nay, I have to kill him the same way he killed my da and brother." Gwyneth's entire body shook, as the realization that she had failed her father drove right to her core. Sobs echoed through the storm as she stared at the sky, the rain washing her tears away as she willed a bolt of lightning to strike her down. "Nay. Let him go, Ramsay. I'm a failure." Almost on key, the sky lit up as lightning struck a nearby tree, causing the ground to shake.

She fought to maintain her balance and covered her head while the roar of thunder echoed through the burgh. When she opened her eyes again, Erskine was gone.

***

Logan stood with the bastard in front of him, willing Gwyneth to shoot him, but she couldn't. A painful wail rent through the air and he watched as the strong woman he loved fell apart in front of him. He had a difficult choice to make. Gwyneth was too torn up with memories to finish the job. Could he do it? Should he do it? He could end the scum's life right now. One turn of his wrist and Erskine would take his last breath.

The haunted look in her gaze stopped him. If he did it for her, he would see that look in her eyes for the rest of their lives. Nay. A boom echoed as lightning struck nearby, shaking his grip. As if driven by an unknown force, he lowered the knife and shoved Erskine away from him. "Get your arse away from here. It won't take much to change my mind." Duff stalked off toward the water.

Gwyneth stood in the middle of the storm, utterly defeated by what had just happened. His heart ripped in two as he watched her stare at the sky, sobbing from her core over what she would view as complete failure. He ran to her and caught her just before she crumpled to the ground. He fell into the wet puddle beneath her and braced her fall, settling her on his lap as she continued to sob.

She held a death grip on his arms, and he let her sorrow leak from her. Lightning bounced around them, thunder echoing through the night, but not loud enough to drown out her pain. He continued to hold her, not knowing what else to do but cradle her in his arms and think of the thousand different ways he would kill Duff Erskine.

Tonight she needed him.

Erskine could wait until the morrow.

CHAPTER EIGHTEEN

The following morning, Logan and Father Rab sat in the room behind the Kirk, waiting for Gwyneth to arise. She knew that, yet she couldn't bring herself to get off the pallet after what she had done—*hadn't done*—the night before. The two carried on a whispered conversation, but she couldn't make out their words. She was glad of it, as she'd heard enough about her failings from Erskine. She didn't need to hear any more, particularly not from her loved ones.

No one knew better than she did about how badly she had failed. Finally pulling herself from the bed, she washed herself using the basin on the table and dressed in clean clothes before heading out into the room where her brother sat at the table with Logan.

She stepped into the doorway, and no matter how she tried, she couldn't right her slumped shoulders. Ramsay had held her for hours the previous night, just letting her release the pain of her failure. He was indeed a special man.

Both men stood as she entered the room, and she waved them back down into their seats. Not heeding her wordless request, Rab strode over and wrapped his arms around her.

She rested her head on his shoulder. "I'm sorry, Rab. I failed you and Da and Gordon. I'm sure Logan filled you in on everything."

"Gwyneth," Rab set her back and held her hands in

hers. "Bless you, but you could never fail me. I am glad you didn't kill him. Now I don't have to take you into the Kirk to pray for the Lord's forgiveness for your soul."

Her brother smiled and she couldn't help but return it. Of course, he wasn't disappointed in her. It didn't matter; she knew her failings well enough.

She glanced at Logan before sitting down at the table. "My thanks for standing by me last night and keeping your word." Her voice had dropped to a whisper and she couldn't look him in the eye, but she had said what she needed to say.

Rab set a bowl of porridge down in front of her, but she did little more than play with it, unable to eat just yet. "Logan tells me you were operating under verra difficult conditions last night. The storm was nasty. How could anyone possibly shoot in the dark and the rain? You are not a failure, Gwyneth."

Her brow furrowed as she peered at Logan. "Difficult conditions?" There hadn't been any difficult conditions. She'd finally been given several chances to kill the blackguard, and she'd squandered them all.

"Aye, the way the sky opened up as soon as you followed him to the stables. Rain, wind, and lightning can all affect your aim." Logan said as he glanced at Rab.

"I have practiced in the rain. It's never been a problem before." She shook her head to dismiss such thoughts.

"Gwyneth, that wasn't rain, it was a downpour. I don't know how you could see to make your aim straight. Plus the rain slows your arrows down when it's that heavy."

She hadn't given the possibility a thought. Aye, she had noticed the rain was blurring her vision, but her tears of frustration had not helped either. Could the rain really have changed the flight of her arrows?

"Aye," Rab said. "He tells it true."

"Fine, I accept that bad weather conditions affected me. I'll have to make sure the weather looks fine the next time I pursue him." She took a bite of her porridge and ignored the two men staring at her. The room had suddenly quieted.

Rab spoke first. "The next time? Gwyneth, please let it rest."

"Rab, I can't," she said, pausing to shove a spoonful of porridge into her mouth. "Besides, he said he was coming back for me, that he was going to put me on another boat. It's either Erskine or me." She glanced at Logan. "You heard him say it, did you not, Ramsay?"

Logan nodded. "Aye, I did. He said he would be back within a sennight."

"Well, you can't, Gwyneth. You had your chance. I won't hear of it happening again."

"Rab, I am sorry, but you can't stop me. I will train a bit more and go after him again. I will finish this. So the rain got in my way. I have to. You know that."

"Nay." Rab shoved his chair back and stood up. "Nay, I will not allow this to continue. Enough, Gwyneth. You must let it go."

Gwyneth stared at him, never having seen her brother this adamant before. She didn't know what to say, though she knew he couldn't stop her.

Logan stood and walked over to put a comforting arm across her brother's shoulders. "Father, I understand your concern, but she's right. He said he would come back for her and soon. Something must be done. You don't want to see your sister sold as a sexual slave in the East, do you?"

With that, her brother paled and grabbed the edge of the table. Logan helped him into his chair. "That is why he kidnaps women?" He took out a linen square and mopped his forehead. "'Tis heinous."

Logan sat down again. "Aye, he is a despicable man, and unless something is done, he will continue with his crimes and kidnap Gwyneth and others. Perhaps

Gwyneth would agree not to approach him without me next time." His gaze bore into her at his comment.

"Aye, Gwyneth, please do this for me. Promise me, sister. Although you promised before and left without him. Please. Take him with you. " Her brother's voice had reached an anxious pitch.

How she hated to upset him. Rab stared at her expectantly, and she wanted to promise him, but she didn't know if she could. She would pursue Erskine when the time was right, whether Logan was there or not.

"Father, would you be agreeable if I also committed to training her? You and your family have trained her and done a terrific job, but I think she needs someone to be a wee bit tougher on her."

Gwyneth jerked her head to stare at him. What was this game?

"Aye, I did train her, but I don't understand what further training she could need."

"Father, you're a man of the cloth, so I don't expect you to understand such things." He reached over to wrap his large hands around Gwyneth's, which rested on the table. He glanced at her when he spoke. "Don't be upset with me. I must speak my mind."

He returned his attention to Rab, still holding her hands, his touch imparting a welcome comfort. "She needs to be trained by someone who can be nasty, someone who can be hard on her."

Rab shook his head. "And you can do this? Why? I don't understand."

Logan's mouth set in a grim line as he rubbed his thumbs over the back of her hands. "It wasn't just the rain that got in her way last night... It wasn't even mostly the rain. He got in her head, Father."

"What?" Rab glanced back and forth between them.

Logan continued. "He got in her head, accusing her of weakness, of being a failure. He ruthlessly taunted her, knowing how his words would upset her. No matter how hard she trains, she is a woman, and women are more sensitive..."

Gwyneth wrenched her hands back and shoved so hard against the table that she knocked her chair over. "I am not, Ramsay."

"Gwyneth, would you please sit down and hear me out?"

Tears pricked her eyes as she met his gaze, the truth settling in her mind. She went over everything Duff had shouted at her as he walked away. He had used her weaknesses against her. Now she understood. Erskine had picked at her failings and twisted everything in her mind, making her believe what he said was true. She had made it true. Ramsay was right. She had never considered such a thing before. She set her chair to rights and sat down, staring at her hands in her lap.

Logan reached under the table for her closest hand and held it tight in his own. "'Tis well known that women are more sensitive than men, and much more likely to react to attacks of character. Sometimes bad men use this knowledge to control their wives or mistresses."

Gwyneth didn't look at him, but gripped his hand tightly. "How do you know this?" He was right; she knew it in her gut. She had fallen prey to Erskine's trickery.

"Some training I received a while ago. Doesn't matter where. What matters is that you need to train your mind against it. Recognize it for what it is and fight back. I believe I can help you with that, though you won't like me when I do."

Gwyneth raised her gaze to his. "How?"

"I'll get in your head like he did and pull at your weaknesses. We'll go to the butts and I'll train you to ignore me while you're shooting. And you *will* hate me." He said these last words with a sigh. "We'll start first thing tomorrow."

"Nay, today. I wish to start today." Gwyneth glanced at Logan and then at her brother. "I accept. Rab, if you give me your blessing to train with him, I'll agree to take him with me when I finish this."

Father Rab closed his eyes and nodded. Then he opened them and grasped Ramsay's hand in his and said, "Please protect my sister."

CHAPTER NINETEEN

A couple of hours later, they headed to the butts. Gwyneth grabbed an oatcake and followed Logan out into the misty morning. Mounting her horse, she shoved the food in her mouth and followed him down the lane to the butts. She planned to be there practicing all day.

When they arrived, Logan helped her dismount and kissed her cheek. Her body responded to his touch, just as it always did.

"What was that for?" she asked, still unsure of what they had between them.

His hand slid down the curve of her back, then rubbed her bum before he grinned and gave her a soft push toward the shooting area. She jumped at the contact, surprised at how one touch from this man could set off a bevy of responses across her skin that oft ended at the juncture of her thighs. This would not help her aim one bit.

She scowled but made her way over to the target area, awaiting his answer even though he didn't seem inclined to give her one.

"That was to remind you that I do have strong feelings for you, and that you can't take anything I say today to heart," he said, his gaze serious. "I know I will anger you and even hurt you, but 'tis for your own good. I will throw comments at you that are meant to upset you. Your job is to harden yourself and not allow what I say to change your focus and sense of purpose. Understood?"

"Aye." What could he possibly say to upset her that much? She would know he didn't mean it, so whatever he said would be easy to ignore. Insults coming from Logan would not upset her; she trusted him. Erskine was another story.

"Set yourself up. I'm going closer to the target and off to the side. I have seen how your shots go awry when you are upset. Promise not to shoot me, Gwyneth?" He winked at her as he crossed the field.

She ignored him. What a ridiculous question. Since she was quite sure she loved him, why would she ever shoot him? Hell, but the man conjured up dreams such as she'd never experienced before meeting him. Last night, she had woken up drenched in sweat, memories of a very hot tussle on the ground with him fresh in her mind. Nay, she'd never shoot him. Jump him? Yes. She couldn't stop the smile from spreading across her face at the thought of running over and wrapping her legs around his midsection, ripping off her top before thrusting her right nipple straight into his...

Logan's voice broke into her thoughts. "Gwyneth, I'd like your pledge on that. I'm not jesting. Do you promise not to shoot me?"

She stared at him. He meant it.

Logan chuckled from the middle of the field. "I must admit, I wish I could be in your mind presently to see what caused that sly grin on your face."

She scowled at him. "Aye, you have your promise. Now get on with it, Ramsay."

He stopped and faced her, his arms crossed in front of him. "I'm waiting for you. Or were you dreaming about me so much last night that you can't focus today? Take your shot."

"What? Dreaming about you?" She stopped in midsentence and caught his grin. He had already started playing with her. She got into stance and took her first shot, trying not to think about the dream, how he'd run his hands over her entire body before kissing her. The slow sensual assault had caused her to awaken moaning before she fell back asleep and finished their lovemaking. She released her first bolt.

"Saints above, you *were* dreaming about me. What a lousy shot, Cunningham."

Gwyneth stared wide-eyed at the target. Hellfire, he was right. She had missed it by an arm's length. After shooting him a glare, she set herself up again and let the arrow fly. She heard it land and knew she had done better.

Dead on. She smiled and placed one hand on her hip, strolling in a circle for emphasis before returning to her favorite shooting spot.

"One for two, Gwyneth. That's about what I expected from a lass."

She whirled until she faced him, fury seething from her pores. How dare he! But his smile caught her. *Ignore him. He warned you he would do this.*

Bull, but this was going to be more difficult than she'd thought.

"Aim at your target, woman. Can we not take all day at this?" Logan refused to meet her eyes.

She could handle this. Let him say what he wanted, she would continue. Taking stance again, she let another arrow fly, hitting a bit off center.

"Shooting like that, the only thing you'll take out is a bird flying by. I might as well sit down. 'Tis going to be a long day until you get your head straight."

Gwyneth ignored him and let three more arrows fly. Direct hits for all three. She gave Ramsay a smug look.

"Sheer luck, Gwyneth. Most women couldn't hit the broad side of the stables. Face it, you can't compete with men when it comes to something as difficult as archery. You ought to take up needlework."

That last comment struck a nerve. She snorted at the mere thought. Nocking and drawing again, her next mark was off-center. Curse it, she was letting him get to her despite herself. She raised her bow again, and her arm started to shake. *Forget the needlework comment. Concentrate.*

Logan walked over to her and held her arm steady. "Are you tired already? Have you not been practicing much lately?"

She jerked her arm away from his touch.

"Gwyneth, I told you this would not be easy. I do not mean what I say. You need to ignore me. That is what I am trying to teach you."

She fought the tears pricking her eyes. "I know. Go back. I can do this. Say what you need to say, make it more difficult. Make it as difficult as you can." She stared at the ground, already disappointed in herself for her reaction to Logan's barbs. She pulled on her bow and sent another arrow, forcing herself to keep her arm straight. Direct hit.

"Nice, sweeting." Logan winked.

They continued for hours. After a while, she finally found her inner spot, a place where she could go to ignore him and concentrate on her aim. In fact, she became so focused, she never heard half of the insults he sent her way. That is, until the end of the day came around. Perhaps it was because she was tired, but he got under her skin again.

Her arms were tiring and her last two shots had been off the target. Still, she knew she could do better.

"Face it, Gwyneth. You have done well today. You hit the target many times, but you have been off as much as you have been on. Do you really think you have what it takes?"

She ignored him, taking aim. She missed by quite a bit.

"You're too weak. A lass is too soft to compete with men. We have better aim, stronger limbs, but most of all, we have abler minds. You don't have the ability to ignore what I say. You're just like every other woman, too sensitive to insults. Aye, you can ignore some insults, but you know the truth.

"You are weak." He began a slow, meandering walk toward her. "You were weak that night, weren't you? You could have done something. Erskine killed your father right in front of you. Why didn't you do something to stop him?"

She heard that comment, all right. Truth be known, she not only heard it—it ripped right through all her defenses. The shield she held up daily to protect herself had just been yanked away. Now she was open for attack—wide open.

"You know you could have done something. But you're just a lass. Is that not right? A weak lass who can't even stop a man in front of her from killing her loved ones. Aye, I suppose you had no idea he was about to kill your father, so anyone would excuse you for that." Logan stepped closer, his voice dropping to a whisper.

Sweat dotted her brow as she listened, but she forced herself to fire another shot through her anguish. She could not let him beat her.

"But what about your brother?" His steps were soft, purposeful as he made his way closer to her. "You could have done something. Any *man* would have been able to stop that second killing. Any *man*..."

She dropped her bow and stared at him. He had just uttered the words that had torn out her heart every day for seven years.

"...could have done something. If you were a man, your brother would be still alive. If you were stronger, you could have thrown your dagger into Duff Erskine's heart. You could have pulled your sword and sliced his neck until his life's blood spurted from his body. You were close enough to take him out.

"But you didn't, did you? You poor, pathetic thing. No wonder it eats at you. 'Tis all your fault, isn't it? Say it." He stood right next to her as he delivered this final insult. "'Tis your fault your brother died, yours alone."

Gwyneth pulled her arm back and punched his jaw as hard as she could. His head swung back from impact, but she didn't let up. She shoved him in the chest. "Aye," she screamed. "You're right. Had I done anything, they might still be alive. But I didn't and now they're dead." She swung her fist and connected with his arm as he ducked. He stepped backward and she marched forward, still ranting. "'Tis all my fault. I could have prevented the entire thing." Tears streamed down her cheeks as her breath hitched.

"All of it," she whispered. "Instead I did naught and they died right in front of me. How bad does that make me?"

"Gwyneth," Logan said, reaching for her. "Nay, don't do this."

"Why not? You're right."

"I'm wrong, Gwyneth. It isn't your fault. I was trying to get in your head. Remember?" He grasped her hand and tugged her to him, reaching his other hand behind her head.

She gave up and let him pull her to him, grabbing at his tunic and pressing her face into his chest. "Something. I should have done something," she murmured.

"Nay, lass. Erskine knew what he was doing. He fired two arrows from his long bow before you could react. Did you have your bow with you?"

"Nay." Her hands still gripping his shirt, she sobbed into his chest.

"Then what could you have done?"

"I don't know…" She cried so hard, her entire body convulsed with pain. "I could have punched him. I could have thrown myself in front of the second arrow. I could have scratched his eyes out. Something." The level of her voice increased the more she talked. "Why didn't I do something for my own brother?" Her yell echoed through the trees. "'Tis all my fault Gordon is dead."

Logan supported her as her trembling body crumpled. "No, sweets, 'tis *not* your fault. I'm sorry, lass. I didn't mean to hurt you." Logan held her tight until she had no more tears.

Several minutes later when she was finally able to stop sobbing enough to speak, she said, "Help me, Logan. Please help me fix this."

CHAPTER TWENTY

Logan left Gwyneth with her brother and headed toward the tavern in Glasgow, in need of some libations. Hellfire, he hated this task. Aye, he wanted to make her stronger, but he hated to upset her. He hadn't realized how she would react when he taunted her today.

He left his horse at the stables and was walking over to the tavern when he heard his name bellowed from his left. He turned to see his brother, Micheil, galloping toward him.

"Micheil, what's wrong?" He instantly feared the worst. "Mother is fine? The bairns? Wee Bethia?"

Micheil waved his hand before he dismounted. "All are fine. Quade and Brenna should be home with Mother by now. The messenger from the Grants told me you would be in Glasgow, so I decided to track you down though I've been searching for hours. Besides, I've been home long enough. Now that the battle with the Norse has ended, I just had to get away and decided to search you out. What brought you here?"

Logan wanted to dodge the question, but his brother knew him too well to fall for such a tactic. "An assignment." He held open the tavern door and they stepped inside, locating a table and ordering two ales.

"How could you have received an assignment in the Highlands? According to Quade, you chased after a girl. I could hardly believe it."

"I left because a foolish lass I met was intent on killing someone. So I followed her to Glasgow, talked to my steward, who gave me a different assignment, and I have been busy completing my orders." Logan wasn't about to tell Micheil that the lass was his assignment...or offer up the truth of how much Gwyneth meant to him. While both his brothers knew he worked for the Scottish Crown, no one else was aware of his duties. And he never shared any specific information about his assignments. By keeping everything secretive, he didn't get asked too many questions. He liked it better that way.

"Who is this spitfire lass?" Micheil asked, a grin bursting out on his face. "I can see she's eating you up inside."

"Curse it, how could you know that?" He was usually much better at hiding his feelings. "Aye, I am focused on two different tasks at present. One is the lass I followed here, Gwyneth. The other is my assignment. I'm training her to improve her skills as an archer."

"A lass as an archer? I'd like to see that. You will allow me along on a training session?"

"Nay, but the fair will be in town and I plan to have her compete in the archery contest there. You can watch her win it. And as long as you're here, I have someone I want you to monitor when I'm with Gwyneth. I wish to make sure he's still in town." He wouldn't be able to follow Erskine if he was training Gwyneth. Micheil was someone he could trust to get the job done.

"Sure, no problem. Give me the details later. I want to hear about the female archer. You think she has a chance to win? She is that good?"

"Aye, she is. Her brother and uncle have trained her for years. The lass watched a blackguard kill her brother and father, so she seeks retribution. Working with her has been a challenge."

Micheil smirked. "I look forward to meeting the lass. She sounds perfect for you."

A lass brought their ales over, setting them down on the table. "Can I get you something to eat?" she asked with a bright smile.

Micheil turned to her, a wide smile spreading across his face as he checked her over from head to toe. "I can think of many things you could bring me to eat, sweet one, but we'll settle for two trenchers of stew, if you have it."

She giggled and blushed before running off to get their food.

Logan gave his brother an exasperated look. "Do you never stop?"

"What?" The smile left Micheil's face. "Just having a wee bit of fun with the lass. Besides, she liked it. Did you not hear her laugh?"

Logan's face darkened. "I'm warning you now. I know you enjoy the lassies, brother, but don't think of throwing your sweet talk at Gwyneth."

"So you do want her. I didn't think I'd ever see the day." A grin spread across Micheil's face as he stared at his brother.

"Just stay away from her." Logan's gaze narrowed as he saw the sheer look of delight dance across his brother's features. Hellfire, this was not going to be easy.

***

A few days later, Gwyneth sat at the breakfast table with Rab. It was the first day of the fair and she was excited to finally be able to see all the exhibits and contests. Logan had suggested she enter the archery contest, and she had agreed. She stuffed her mouth with porridge as fast as she could.

"Gwyneth, are you sure you wish to do this?" Rab asked.

"Aye. Logan says it will be good practice for me. He is sure there will be some spectators who will harass me because I am a woman in a man's contest."

"Perhaps they will not allow you to enter."

"Logan already checked the rules. It says naught about being a man. It just says 'the archer.'" She ate another spoonful of her breakfast.

"Probably because they don't expect any female archers. They could change their minds."

"They can't, he says. They can change the rules for next year, but they have to let me shoot. I plan to win." Gwyneth could barely contain her excitement at the prospect of beating men in front of an audience.

"Gwyneth, I need to speak to you about something else that is important to me."

Her spoon clattered on the table. "Rab, I don't like the expression on your face. What is it?"

"I know you won't like what I have to say, but I need to say it."

Gwyneth had no idea what her brother had in mind, but the look on his face pained her.

"'Tis about the way you dress."

She frowned. "What?"

"I would like you to dress differently for the fair." He shifted his gaze to his food after he made his statement.

Gwyneth glanced at the leggings she wore, the tunic pulled tight over her torso to allow free movement when shooting. "But why? I have always dressed this way. It helps me shoot better. I can't have clothing come in the way of my draw. Da never cared."

"Aye, because Da never knew where to find any skirts for you. Wearing Gordon's clothing was easier. You will be in front of everyone when you shoot, and most will stand behind you. Gwyneth, 'tis unseemly now that you are older."

"My skin is completely covered, Rab." Gwyneth fought the fury that threatened to break out of her, but she would not yell at Rab. Never at Rab. She couldn't understand what had brought this on so suddenly. "I never show my cleavage like some women. I bind myself to hide them." She turned her head from her brother to hide her blush.

"When you were wee, it didn't matter. You are a grown woman now. You need to act like one."

Gwyneth stood up, shocked that her brother felt this way. "What? This is who I am, brother, and I think you know that. Why now?"

Father Rab stood, taking a linen square from his pocket and mopping his brow. "Gwyneth, you don't understand. You are too naïve."

"Nay, I am not. I am choosing to live my life the way I want, not the way everyone else wants me to live."

Rab pressed both hands on the table and locked gazes with her. "You can't. You need to stop."

Aghast at her brother's outburst, Gwyneth had naught to say. She didn't know how to respond to him. He was asking her to change who she was. "But I am different, Rab, and you know it."

"I know you are, but do you realize how much attention you draw with the way you dress? Have you ever watched the men stare at you? 'Tis wrong. Please dress in skirts if you choose to make such a public display."

Gwyneth just stared at her brother as he blinked and mopped his eyes with his linen square before shoving it in his pocket.

Gwyneth walked over and wrapped her arms around her brother. "Rab, I'm sorry to put you through so much."

Rab had his breathing under control again. "Please, for me."

"I don't own any skirts. I could never find one in time for the contest."

"You must know someone who would be happy to lend you clothes."

She turned away from him and moved back to the other side of the table. The two of them just stared at each other for a long moment. She couldn't believe what he was asking of her, and she also couldn't believe she was thinking of denying him. She had never denied Rab anything.

She stood back and gathered her gear, ready to leave for the fair. "But 'twould not be me in those skirts, Rab."

She waited for him to speak, hoping he would rethink his stance. The young priest finally nodded his head, apparently accepting that he would not deter her.

"Then today, when you compete against the men in the archery contest, I want you to beat them."

Gwyneth kissed his cheek again before she headed for the door. "I will do that, just for you, Rab."

CHAPTER TWENTY-ONE

Logan met Gwyneth at her brother's Kirk to escort her to the fair. As they made their way around the booths and wares at the fair, Logan kept an eye out for the blackguard Erskine, just to be safe. Micheil had discovered he lived in a castle on the other side of town and had updated Logan last night, so Duff could show up anytime.

"Did you come to the fair often, Gwyneth?" Logan wanted to know more of her childhood, search out the good memories she held.

"Aye. Da always brought us here to eat, especially for the hog roast. Rab and I liked to search out the wares."

"And what are your favorite booths?"

"Rab loves the woodworkers. They carve such intricate designs. But I have always liked the weavers. Basket weaving is my favorite. Of course, you know I enjoy the blacksmith and the weapon booths, but Rab always tried to steer me away from them." She let out a long sigh. "Poor Rab tried to be a good brother and always brought me to look at the ribbons and the jewels, but they never held my interest. Sometimes, we did buy cloth."

"What about the minstrels?"

"I love to watch the weans follow the minstrels, and there are always some storytellers I love to listen to, but I liked the competitions the best. I loved the jousting and Rab hates it."

"So you must be looking forward to the archery contest."

Her face lit up. "Aye, I think I could win it. What do you think?"

He glanced into her bright eyes, unable to stop from returning her smile. "Agreed. You have an excellent chance to win."

"And do you wish to challenge me again, Ramsay?"

Logan grinned. "Nay. I need to watch your technique. I have only one goal right now, and that is to build your skills as an archer. I would rather cheer you on."

They made their way to the tent where she would need to sign up for the competition. When they finally found themselves at the head of the line, the man in charge handed Logan a piece of cloth with a number. "Competition starts in three hours. Wear this."

Logan handed it to Gwyneth, who pinned it to her tunic. The man stared at her. "What are you doing?"

"You said I had to wear the number on my tunic." Gwyneth tossed her plait back and put her hand on her hip.

"Nay, no' you. The one competing wears it." The man shook his head, as if he could not believe her foolishness, then took the number from her hand and returned it to Logan.

She reached over and took it back. "And I am the one competing, not him."

The man stared at her for a moment before speaking. "You're a lass. No women in the contest. You can't shoot."

"Aye, I can, and I'll beat you any day should you wish to challenge me." The man did not respond to her jibe and his jaw went slack as he returned her stare.

Logan decided he needed to get involved before there was trouble. "She's the one competing and she is a better archer than I am. Let her participate."

"But it says no women."

"Nay, it doesn't. And you can't change the rules today. The competition starts in a few hours." Logan crossed his arms in front of him, daring the fool to argue with him.

The man quickly scanned the rules and scowled. "You're right. It does no' say."

"Then she shoots. We'll be back later." Logan grabbed her hand and tugged her along behind him, not wanting to give the lout the chance to come up with another excuse to deny her. He pulled her up beside him. "Come, walk with me. I wish to buy you a gift."

"Why?"

"Because I want to." He tugged her down between the various booths selling ribbons, scarves, roasted chickens, and pastries. The woman he loved required a very special gift, he knew, not a ribbon or something to wear. When he finally reached the booth he had in mind, he put his arm around her waist and said, "Choose your favorite. I would like to purchase one for you."

Gwyneth's eyes widened as she perused all the goods displayed in the booth. He could tell by the look on her face there were more daggers and knives here than she had ever seen before. There were dark handles and ivory; simple designs and elaborate ones. Some were long, others were meant to be hidden in boots or clothing. She finally chose a small dagger with an ivory handle engraved with a bear. She rubbed her fingers down the smooth material, smiling.

"Many thanks, Logan. 'Tis beautiful." She brought her gaze to his and all he wanted to do was go somewhere private and make love to her.

Logan chose a few more and had them wrapped in a package. Once he paid for them, he turned to Gwyneth and handed her gift to her. "Use it wisely."

A loud voice shouting his name interrupted their

conversation. Before he could register the intrusion, Micheil stood beside him, running his gaze up and down Gwyneth's body.

Logan scowled and hissed at his brother. "Enough."

Grinning, Micheil brought his gaze up to Gwyneth's. "A pleasure to meet you. I am Logan's brother, Micheil." He held his hand out and took hers, whispering, "You look mighty fine in your leggings."

Logan grabbed his arm and pulled him away from Gwyneth, giving him a little shove. "I'll ask you to treat the lass kindly."

"Och, I would love to treat her kindly," his brother replied with a chuckle.

Gwyneth's confused expression only fueled Logan's fury. "Leave off, Micheil. Take your sweet charm elsewhere."

Micheil laughed and finally conceded. "Fine, I won't bother her. My lady, I can't wait to see you compete in the archery contest. I wish you well." He kissed the back of her hand and walked out of Logan's reach, his eyes twinkling all the while.

***

Gwyneth stood inside the archery area, awaiting her next turn. Logan stood not far away, his brother at his side. Thus far, she had beaten each of her opponents in the first three rounds, and the number of players in the competition was dwindling. Logan had been wonderful, supporting her whenever she shot. His discreet encouragement told her how much he believed in her, serving her very well.

All of a sudden, the man she was supposed to shoot against next demanded the attention of one of the judges. "This is illegal. My next opponent is a lass. I can't compete with her." He threw his arms up in the air as if he was being asked to do the impossible.

Gwyneth's eyes narrowed in on the lout causing the scene. She was about to speak up, but she noticed Logan was holding his palm out flat to her, asking her to stay out of the discussion.

She clamped her mouth shut, but she didn't understand why the man was so upset. None of the last three contestants had complained about her. As she awaited a decision, she overheard some of the observers outside the fence. They were heckling her opponent. "What's the problem, Glenn? Afraid the girl is going to beat you?"

"Och, won't that be a story to tell. Beaten by a skinny lass."

"Let her shoot. Are you that worried she'll win?"

She glanced at Logan for support as they waited. He beckoned her over to him, so she made her way over to the fence and leaned into him. "You've done great. Do you hear them getting in his head? They'll have him so upset that he'll be an easy win. But eventually, they will start working on you, too. You have to be strong. Some men have fun watching you, but not too many of them want a lass to win this contest. My guess is that most will be happy to see you win until the final round. Then they'll root for the man. All the Scots in the land will talk of you if you win. That will upset many archers. Be strong."

She nodded and stepped away as the verdict was finally announced. Glenn had lost his case.

"'Tis naught in the rules this year that says you have to be a lad to shoot," the judges announced. "So the lass shoots. We'll fix it for next year."

Glenn argued for a while, but no one paid him any heed.

The judge finally sent her to the target. "Your turn, lass."

Gwyneth squelched her grin and took her shot. As soon as she let the arrow fly, she knew she had made her mark. Direct hit, and the crowd went wild. Glenn shook his head. They had to make three shots each to win the round.

Gwyneth beat Glenn easily and the crowd started to

cheer her name. Glenn hung his head and stalked off the field.

She turned in time to see her brother arrive. He made his way over to Logan and nodded to her. This time she was determined make Rab proud, even though she hadn't changed into skirts as he'd asked. He was a priest, so he was bound to forgive her. She won the next two rounds, which put her in the final round. Her competitor was young and strong. He nodded to her and took his first shot, hitting near to center.

Gwyneth settled into her stance and was about to let her arrow loose when an unknown voice shouted out.

"Don't worry about her, Finley," he shouted to her opponent. "She can't hit the side of a stable, can you, lass?"

Gwyneth glanced at Logan and he nodded his head in encouragement. She set her stance and just as she let her arrow fly, the lad shouted, "Loser."

Some of the spectators booed him for his poor timing, but it didn't matter. She had missed the target and Finley had bested her in the first round. He took his second shot and it landed almost perfect.

Remembering her lessons with Logan, Gwyneth took her time before releasing her second bolt, managing to block out all the voices around her, even Logan's. When her arrow landed, the crowd roared. She won the second shot.

Finley made his third shot and it was good. Gwyneth readied herself for her final effort, and the heckler started in on her again.

"Finley, no worries, she can't handle the pressure. She always falls apart. You aren't really worried about a lass, are you? She's weak and foolish. No problem, no worries. She doesn't have what it takes to be a man."

Gwyneth dug deep to ignore him. She glanced over and caught Logan's gaze, soaking in strength. *He* believed in her, even if no one else did. Rab and Micheil stood next to him, their expressions hopeful.

She notched her arrow and aimed. This time she would wait for the heckler to yell something out and channel her fury at him into her arrow, just as Logan had taught her. She waited and waited, and sure enough, his mouth started.

"What, are you afraid, wee bairn?"

She let her arrow fly and hit the target dead center. The crowd erupted and Finley ran over to the target to check it for himself. She knew she had won.

Rab rushed in and pulled her into a hug as the crowd chanted her name. Logan sauntered over to her with a smug expression on his face. When Rab let her go, Logan patted her back, a bit leery of getting too close to her with Rab by her side.

He gazed at her and leaned in to whisper in her ear, "Well done, lass. I knew you had it in you all along."

She pulled back and stared at him. "Good, now can we go after Erskine?"

"Nay, not until night. I don't want witnesses to our deed."

Gwyneth was ready to scream, but she knew he was right. For now, she would bask in the fact that she had just beat seven men, with several witnesses.

She grinned from ear to ear. Tonight would be soon enough to chase Duff Erskine. Today was a day of glory. How she wished her father was there to see it.

CHAPTER TWENTY-TWO

The four of them made their way back to the entrance to the fair, even though they were frequently interrupted by well-wishers and congratulations. Gwyneth had to admit she enjoyed every minute.

A feminine voice interrupted her thoughts.

"Logan, my sweet. Here you are. I have been searching for you everywhere." A buxom redhead wrapped her arms around Logan and whispered into his ear, taking care to speak loud enough for all to hear.

Gwyneth hid her surprise. Rab glanced at her to see her reaction, but she didn't speak. Still uncertain about where their relationship was headed, she wanted to see what this woman had to say.

"My bed is as warm for you as ever it was," the woman stage whispered. She then turned to face Gwyneth and smiled at her, a wicked grin that made Gwyneth look away. As a young lass, she had never understood the friendships between girls. What was this woman implying? Had Logan turned to another because she had rejected him? Her heart pounded at even the slim possibility of losing Logan to another woman, a telling sign of her true feelings.

Logan reached behind his neck to loosen the woman's hold. "Iona, please stop spreading lies about me. Can you not see there is a priest at your side?"

"Och, Logan, my love. You are so shy. Anyone can

read your feelings for me." She gave him a coy look before glancing at Gwyneth again.

Iona was a voluptuous woman with long, flowing red curls. At one time, she may have possessed the kind of figure most men dreamed about, but to Gwyneth, she appeared too thick around the middle. Logan pushed her away, but not before Gwyneth caught the fury in his eyes. But why was he angry? Was it because he had been caught with another, or because the woman was lying?"

"Iona, I don't know what your game is, but you know there is naught between us. There was never anything between you and Quade either. You tried to destroy my brother's relationship with his new wife and you failed. Don't come to me next because your lies were discovered. Had it been up to me, you would have been banned from our clan long ago. Or is that what brings you to Glasgow? Have you finally been sent away?"

Tears formed in Iona's eyes as she grasped his shoulders. "Please, Logan. Don't be angry. You know how good we would be together. Come to me tonight."

She leaned over to kiss his cheek, but Logan shoved her away. "Stop your games, Iona. I don't want you and never have."

Molten fury flashed across her features, and her gaze caught his. "You fool. You would rather have this whore next to you, the one who dresses like a lad? She can never be half the woman I am." She turned her head sideways for another glance at Gwyneth, her haughty expression asking for a challenge.

Logan grabbed her arm and turned her away, marching her across the field, his stern voice streaming behind him, though his words were lost to the wind. Micheil stayed behind with Father Rab and Gwyneth. "Your pardon," he said, "she used to be a member of our clan. She is a little daft, I fear. There is no relationship between Logan and Iona."

Clearly uncomfortable, Rab cleared his throat and grabbed her elbow. "Gwyneth, shall we take our leave now?"

She didn't know what to say, so she just nodded her head. Hoping that Logan would return so she could hear his explanation, she hesitated and smiled at Micheil. "It would probably be best for us to move on." But before they could take more than a few steps away from him, Logan rushed back. He grasped Gwyneth's hand, but she pulled it away. "Gwyneth, don't believe a word she says. I have never had a relationship with the lass, though she has ever wished to be a Ramsay. She was always infatuated with my brother, but now that he is married and quite happy, I presume she has moved on to me. I have never been with her." He cast a sheepish look at Rab. "Your pardon, Father."

Gwyneth just listened quietly, then said, "Thank you for your guidance tonight. Rab and I will head back to the Kirk." She ducked her head and turned away, afraid she would betray her feelings.

As soon as they left, her brother said, "I believe Logan. The lass is not telling the truth."

"There is naught settled between Logan and me, Rab, so it doesn't matter. If he chooses her, 'tis his right. I have only one goal presently, and I have room for nae others."

The crowd thinned as they strolled down the path toward home, and finally they were alone. "Gwyneth, please," Rab said. "I know you feel something for the lad. I can see it in you when he is near. Please do not deny your feelings. 'Tis natural for you to take an interest in such an honorable man. And I do believe he is honorable, regardless of what that lass said."

"Rab, I am tired from the match. Can we go home now, please?"

Nodding, he led her on, but she noticed the slump in his shoulders. Apparently, Rab liked Logan as much as she did. But if Iona was the sort of woman who usually attracted him, what hope did she have of keeping his attention?

***

"God's teeth, Micheil. Could you not have warned me Iona is in town? What is she doing here in Glasgow anyway?"

"Och, I forgot to tell you. Mother sent her away. She caused so much trouble with some of the clan wives that mother told her it was time for her to move on."

"Hellfire, she has definitely lost her mind. And to say all that in front of Father Rab and Gwyneth? He'll never let me inside the Kirk again."

"Have no fear. Father Rab is a true man of the cloth. He'll forgive you whether he believes her or not. Admit it, you are more worried about what Gwyneth thinks."

"Aye, I am. I want to marry her, but I would like the time to pursue her first, get to know her better. I fear Iona did enough damage to cause her to distrust me. Gwyneth is naïve when it comes to men and nasty women. I don't know what she will think of this encounter."

"Iona lost a bit of her mind when Brenna stole Quade's heart. She never got over it. It seems she's still eager to take the name of Ramsay." Micheil grinned at his brother.

"If we weren't in the middle of a fair, I'd wipe that grin clear off your face. And I will as soon as I can get you in the lists again."

"I look forward to it, brother." Micheil slapped him on the back and walked over to the food booth to buy something to eat, winking at each fair lass he passed on the way.

"Hurry with your food, Micheil. I want to check on Erskine again."

***

Gwyneth couldn't sleep. Rain was forecast so Logan had postponed the mission until the next evening. It was well into the night, and she had tossed and turned for most of it. As soon as she shut her eyes, Duff Erskine's voice taunted her during the contest instead of the heckler's. She could not get it to stop. She threw the covers off her and sat up on her pallet. Enough. She didn't care what Logan thought—she was ready. It was time for Duff Erskine to die.

She dressed with purpose, carefully arranging her leggings, her wool socks and boots, even her tunic. Her weapons were sorted and arranged for quick retrieval, including the new dagger Logan had given her. Her lucky stone from Lily was still in her pocket. Glancing around the room, she wondered if she was forgetting anything, because she couldn't. This mission was too important for her to fail again.

This wasn't just her mission, but an assignment she'd been tasked with by the crown. Dougal Hamilton wanted Erskine's life to end. He still wanted to know if he had a partner, but the ending was always the same. Erskine needed to die, for the women and for the Crown.

She crept out through the main room and grabbed her bow and quiver. A soft sound interrupted her and she turned around. Rab. He stood behind her in his regular clothes instead of his priest's robes. "You're going after him, aren't you?"

"Aye, Rab, I have to. 'Tis time. I'm ready," she whispered.

"I know." He turned his head to the side, nodding while deep in thought. "Will you allow your foolish brother one small favor?"

"Of course, Rab. You know I love you." Her gaze caught his and she noticed the fear in his eyes. She couldn't blame him. How would she feel if their roles were reversed?

"Please allow me to say a blessing over you."

She nodded and bowed her head while he placed his hands on her crown and said the words that lived so strongly in his heart. When he finished, she peered at him through tear-stained lashes. "I'm sorry I have to put you through this."

Rab nodded. "Perhaps this time it will truly be finished. I wish there was another way. I am so afraid you will regret killing him with your own hands. The guilt, Gwynie, won't it get to you?" He paused for a moment, but then held his arms out to give her a hug. "Please come back to me, sister. I would be lost without you."

She gave her brother a kiss on his cheek and headed out the door.

The town was relatively quiet. She had thought it would be busy with the fair in town, but apparently the townspeople had tired easily and gone home. Deciding not to hurry, she thought over everything Logan had taught her with painstaking care. Tonight she could not fail. A slight breeze blew the strands of loose hair back from her face. A pack of dogs down the pathway fought over a piece of meat until someone threw a shoe at them. As she strolled toward the firth, the wind picked up with a howl and swept through the autumn night, rustling the leaves around her feet. Gwyneth tried to soak in all the details, certain she would wish to remember every detail of this night.

She made her way down to the water and was surprised to see a flurry of activity there. Hiding in the bushes again, she was able to make out Duff Erskine giving orders to three other men who were busy loading sacks into two wagons.

Perfect timing. She found her hiding place and waited.

CHAPTER TWENTY-THREE

This was it. This would be her night. Revenge would be hers and Erskine would know his death came at her hands. Finally, he would pay for all he had done. Thanks to Logan, she had the confidence she had never had before.

The men by the water continued to work without speaking to each other. Once their cargo was loaded into the carts, they mounted their horses and moved down the firth away from the town, several packhorses pulling their load.

Gwyneth stayed in her hiding spot until the men moved out of hearing distance. The path down to the river was bordered with plenty of trees and foliage that would keep her hidden. She wouldn't kill him until she found out his destination. Aye, he was within her range at the moment, but she hoped to discover his contact. This had all the markings of one of his larger operations, and there was a good chance that his protector would be here. Who covered for him?

Who were the men ahead of him, and what was inside the sacks on those carts? More women?

***

God's teeth, he knew it. Logan crept near the river and sure enough, there she was in her hiding spot in the bushes. The foolish lass was here on her own again, and after she had promised to take him with her.

Hellfire, Gwyneth was stubborn. He'd make sure to tell Hamilton that his best scout was overbearing, stubborn, and prone to taking unnecessary risks.

Unfortunately, daft Iona had shown up at the wrong time. He'd never had anything to do with the lass, but Iona seemed to enjoy setting her sights on the lads she couldn't have.

He hid in a tree and waited to see what Gwyneth's next move would be. Each time he saw the lass, memories of her sweet moans echoed through his mind, causing his usual discomfort in his breeks. The few times they'd made love had only fueled his hunger for her. He had been hopeful for another opportunity earlier tonight, but then Iona had found them. He could see the distrust in Gwyneth's eyes when Iona threw her arms around him.

Time would prove Iona wrong. Tonight, he needed to focus on Gwyneth and keep her out of harm's way. It was his duty and his desire.

***

An hour passed before they reached their final destination. Gwyneth had kept a good distance away, but stayed close enough to listen to what little conversation she could overhear. She thought she heard a moan or two coming from the carts, but she couldn't be sure.

Sure enough, when the men dismounted, she could see a longboat bobbing next to a dock. This far down the firth, the water had deepened enough for them to keep a boat. As she sat in her spot, she glanced up at the crescent moon, which was covered by fast-moving clouds. Slud, she hoped it wouldn't rain again tonight, though she could almost smell it in the air.

The men moved the sacks into the boat. An owl hooted in the distance, causing a slow ripple of fear to creep up her spine, the tendrils spreading into her belly. She pulled strength from her core to dismiss her fear, sharpening her focus on the men in front of her.

It was too late to regret her choice not to seek Ramsay's assistance. She had decided to come alone because she feared images of Iona with her arms around Logan would interfere with her concentration if he were with her. Tonight there could be no distractions.

"This is a good load, Clyde. You should bring me quite a bit of coin and some weapons in exchange." Erskine spoke to the man on the boat.

"How many this time?"

"Eight."

Clyde surveyed the area. "I only count seven sacks." The man peered over the carts as Duff's men unloaded the cargo and moved the sacks to the boat. "Take them out of the sacks once they're loaded on the boat. They'll have to eat eventually."

Women. Another cargo full of women was about to leave for the East. She would stop this one just as her father had tried to do years ago. But with one difference—she would be successful.

"There are only seven. I have one more coming."

"What? How could that be? One alone?"

"Doesn't matter, does it? Get the sacks of food and jugs of water on the boat. You need to leave soon."

"What's your hurry?"

"I have a bad feeling about tonight." Duff scanned the area, as if he were waiting for something. He wiped his face with his shirt sleeve, then strode away from the dock, turning to face his men before he left. "Just keep loading. I have one more thing to do."

Gwyneth made a mental note—there were two men by the carts, one on the boat. She wondered how many men would travel with the women. She had not one ounce of compassion for his crew, including the ones who had been thrown overboard be the Norse. Every last one of them deserved to be punished for their part in this travesty.

She followed Duff as he moved back toward town. A

lone man headed straight at him. Logan? But nay. The men conversed and she tried to determine who it was, but she was too far away.

Their conversation ended and Duff thanked the man before walking away. The man could be his boss, but she wasn't sure. Once Erskine came back toward the boat, he wandered aimlessly as if searching for something. Then it dawned on her. He was searching for *her*.

Her time was up. She needed to take action now or it could be too late. Raising herself up, she took aim at the men near the boat, knowing she had enough time before Erskine got closer. She fired her first arrow and struck the captain of the boat in his belly. Not a death blow, but it would certainly stop him. She fired the next arrow at the man who leaned over the cart and caught him square in his arse. He fell to the ground, cursing as he clutched his behind. Her third arrow struck the other man and he went down, too. When she turned to aim at Duff, he ran to his horse, she guessed for his bow.

"Stop or I'll shoot you through just as I did the others."

Gwyneth stepped out of her hiding spot, her arrow aimed for Erskine even though he was still a good distance away. Somehow, she was still hesitant to shoot him in the back. She wanted to look him in the eyes when she killed him.

"Turn around, Erskine. 'Tis time for you to pay for your crimes."

Duff turned around slowly, a sly grin on his face as he stared at her. "Och, and who is going to make me pay? You, Gwyneth?" He took a step toward her. "Do you think you can hit me today any better than you did the other day?"

Gwyneth held her breath and gathered all her strength and let her arrow fly.

She missed.

"No different than the last time is it? Well, it isn't raining yet, so you don't have that excuse." He turned away from her and headed back toward his horse. "Go ahead, you can't hit me. How many times have you tried?" His laughter echoed through the cold night air.

This couldn't be happening. She nocked another arrow and aimed right between his shoulder blades. Her stomach clenched in fear, so afraid she would fail again. The old familiar feeling of powerlessness crept up from her tailbone. She was useless against this man.

Nay, he would not beat her again. She thought of Logan and how he had taught her to ignore Duff's taunts and focus. She fired another arrow at him. His laughter told her all she needed to know. Tears flooded her eyes.

Nay, nay. This couldn't be happening again. She was a failure, an utter and complete failure. Her vision became so blurry with tears she decided to give up. One more bolt. She would shoot one more, and if she missed him, she would concede.

Blinking her tears away, she nocked her arrow, her left arm shaking, drew, and released it.

CHAPTER TWENTY-FOUR

The arrow just missed his head. Erskine guffawed, holding his belly. "Och, girl, you are far worse than I would ever have thought. Didn't I hear that you won the contest at the fair today?"

Erskine had reached his horse. He turned around with his dagger in his hand and started toward her. She closed her eyes in defeat. Naught mattered anymore. She was powerless again.

"That's right, give up, wee lassie. Climb on the boat and make this easy. I have a buyer for you and he's paying more than I would have ever guessed." He continued toward her with a big grin across his face.

Duff screamed. Her eyes flew open to see blood spurting from a wound in Erskine's arm, a knife protruding from his skin. A voice came over her shoulder. "Stay where you are, Erskine, or the next one goes between your eyes. Don't move, or I'll kill you." Erskine froze, dropping his dagger to remove the knife and clutch his arm.

Logan strode to her side. She had never been happier to see anyone, and there was naught she would rather do than throw herself into his arms. But it wasn't the moment.

She forced herself to return her focus to the business at hand. "Don't you kill him, Ramsay! He's mine. You promised not to interfere. Stay back." Gwyneth's words came out between sobs. She hadn't even realized she was crying.

Logan stood next to her, pointing to Erskine. Micheil came up from behind him and ran over to Duff, arranging himself behind him with his dagger at his throat.

Logan whispered, "I promised not to kill him, I never promised not to interfere. He was about to hurt you. You were going to let him hurt you."

"It doesn't matter. I am a failure. I missed him four times." She didn't dare look at him or she would throw herself into his arms for sure. Her knees threatened to buckle and her shoulders hung in defeat.

"Get yourself set." He stood off to the side, his eyes on Duff Erskine.

"What?"

"I'm not going to kill him. You are. Now get yourself set. Get another arrow nocked and set your aim. But don't release it until I tell you. Do you remember how we practiced?"

Gwyneth couldn't believe her ears. Logan was really going to help her kill him? She paused for a moment, took a deep breath, but then did as he instructed, getting ready to shoot Duff. Mayhap this was what she needed. With Logan here, the same as he had been in her training sessions, perhaps she would finally succeed in her goal.

"Where were you sending the lasses, Erskine?" Logan bellowed at him.

Erskine laughed. "I'll never tell you."

Micheil moved his dagger to the side just a bit and pierced his skin. Blood ran down his neck staining his fine neckcloth.

"Italy. The same place your woman is going when I finish with the three of you. They pay good money for female slaves there. Gwyneth will make a great one."

Micheil pulled his hold a little tighter. "Doesn't seem like you're in any position to make threats."

Logan turned to her. "Are you ready, lass?"

"I can't, Logan," she whispered. "I'm not strong enough." Her arms shook as she took aim again.

"Aye, you are." Logan walked over behind her and placed his arm under hers, lending support to her arm, then placed his leg behind her quivering one. "Where do you want to shoot him? Your choice."

She couldn't believe it, but with Logan behind her, supporting her body with his own, her tremors stopped. His strength seemed to flow into her blood, giving her a newfound drive to complete her goal. Gwyneth aimed for Duff's heart, but at the last minute, Rab popped into her mind. She lowered her arrow and let it go. It landed exactly where she had aimed it, at the juncture of his thighs.

Erskine screamed in pain, falling to the ground. Logan whispered in her ear. "Ouch. But well done."

Micheil kicked the fallen man and walked back toward the riverbank opposite them. "I'm going for the sheriff," he yelled over his shoulder as he broke into a run back toward town.

"Rab, all I could picture was Rab telling me not to murder him." She glanced at Logan, trying to explain why she had made this choice, expecting to see derision in his gaze. She didn't. She had done what she set out to do. She hadn't killed him, but he would never have relations again, she was quite sure of that. Smiling at Logan, she whispered, "My thanks." She dropped her bow and leaned into him just as raindrops started to fall.

A loud screech came from Erskine and they swiveled their heads in time to see him headed straight for them, hobbling, a knife in his hand intended for one of them.

Gwyneth grabbed her dagger and flung it at him. He dropped not twenty feet away from them. The sky opened up and a hard rainfall pelted them as they moved over to see if he still lived.

Gwyneth saw her dagger in his thigh. Why had the

scum fallen with just a dagger in his thigh? It wasn't a death blow. Her eyes moved up to his face to see his sightless eyes, but she stopped. Another dagger sat in his neck. She scanned the area for Micheil, but he was too far away. It couldn't have been Micheil's dagger. She and Logan had thrown at the same time.

Her enemy lay flat on his back with his arms spread wide, an arrow protruding from his male parts, a wound in his arm and her new dagger in his thigh, rain carrying his blood in rivers from his body. Or was it her new dagger in his neck? She wiped the water from her face to clear her vision, but she still couldn't detect which knife was hers. Glancing at the blood pooling under him, she reached for the two daggers. She pulled both of them out, holding them up in the rain to compare them.

"They're the same." She turned them over to be sure, but then glanced at Logan. "Your dagger is the same as mine."

"Aye, lass. I bought myself a matching one." He grinned at her.

"Then which one was mine? Where did you throw yours?"

Logan leaned over and kissed her cheek. "I couldn't be sure. Does it matter?"

"But whose dagger killed him?"

"We'll never know. It was raining and I couldn't tell for sure where mine landed." He shrugged his shoulders. "It was dark. He's dead, Gwyneth, and no matter what, you had a hand in it."

Satisfied with Logan's answer, she swiped her dagger and put it away, handing the other to Logan. Glancing at the ground one more time, she tried to absorb the memory of him lying there dead.

Duff Erskine was dead. She may have killed him.

Or maybe not.

***

Running over to the cart by the river, Gwyneth

untied the sacks and did her best to awaken the women while Logan checked on the men she'd hit with her bolts. Two of them had disappeared already, only one remained moaning on the ground. All the women were breathing, but they were still under the spell of whatever potion Erskine's men had fed them. Gwyneth covered them from the rain as best she could while Logan loaded the remaining man inside before he turned the packhorses around, leading them back down the river. As soon as they neared the town, they found the local sheriff shouting at one of his assistants on the ground, his hands tied behind his back.

The sheriff strode right over to Logan. "Good catch, Ramsay. Thanks for the alert before searching the riverbank. I suspected the fool about a moon ago, but catching him in the act is even better. I just sent your brother back to the castle to get more help, then he is going to Dundonald to inform him of the situation."

Good, she wouldn't have to run to Hamilton. Dundonald kept him abreast of everything. As soon as the sheriff had the situation under control, Logan walked over to put his arm around her waist and they headed back toward the Kirk. They passed a copse of trees in a deserted part of town, and Logan kissed her cheek. "Wait here a moment, lass." She watched as he strode over into the forest to check something while the rain and wind continued to batter them. Did he have in mind what she did?

"Ramsay!"

He turned around just in time to catch her as she launched herself into his arms. She almost felled him, but he managed to stay upright as she wrapped her legs around his waist. The rain continued to drench them and his feet slipped on the wet ground.

"I want you now, Logan." She kissed him and wrapped her arms around his neck, darting her tongue in to tease his.

He groaned, returning the kiss, tasting her

sweetness as he kissed her lips, her neck and nuzzled her ear.

She giggled, then tipped her head back and whooped at the night sky. "Make love to me, Logan Ramsay. Right now, right here."

Logan already had an erection begging to be set free, but he had to ask. "Right here, Gwyneth. In the mud?" He set her down for a moment. "I'm not strong enough to hold you without some support behind you. Somehow, I don't think you really mean for us to roll in the mud. I am happy to oblige you—" he took her hand and held it over his cock so she could feel his hardness, "—but I don't want to be halfway through and have to stop because it isn't working for you."

"Nay, let's not lay in the mud, but there has to be a way."

Logan grabbed her hand and led her into the trees, searching out a dry area. They found themselves underneath a group of pine trees that were so tall and dense they blocked out almost all the rain. He grinned. "This is exactly what I was hoping for, a little privacy out of the rain." He turned to her and tugged her close, "Does this suit you, princess? I hope so, because I can't go much longer without you in my arms again. You have been waving your tight wee bum at me for two days now, and the torture of not being able to touch you has made me daft."

Gwyneth laughed under the canopy of the pines, leaning against Logan as she stared up through the branches, transfixed by the beauty of the place. "Logan, 'tis amazing here." She tossed her bow down and removed her tunic before reaching for his brooch and dropping his plaid to the ground.

Logan stared at her breasts and said, "Unbind those beautiful mounds."

She giggled as he helped her free them and he cupped both in his hands, murmuring, "So lovely, Gwyneth."

He kissed her again, claiming her mouth with his, teasing her sweet lips until they parted. He growled when her tongue teased his and he deepened the kiss, so pleased to feel that her desire and her urgency were as strong his. She clung to him, pressing her breasts into his hard chest, tugging at his tunic until he helped her remove it and sighed with pleasure when his skin finally met hers.

Logan dipped his head to her breast and licked her nipple until it peaked. When he felt her fingers on his nipples, he suckled hers in return until she cried and ran her nails across his sensitive tips. He tugged her other nipple into his mouth, grazing it with his teeth. Needing no greater invitation, she reached down and took his hardness into her hand, wrapping her fingers around him and teasing him with a slow movement back and forth, up and down.

Before he unmanned himself and shot into her hand, he pulled away and threw his plaid down on the mostly dry ground. He settled her on the plaid and lay down on top of her, resting his weight on his elbows and placing his hand over her head. They both stilled instantly.

"Hellfire," he shouted.

"Logan? This isn't going to work."

"I know, I know. God's teeth, why didn't I think of the blasted pine needles? 'Tis autumn and they are dry and sharp." He stood up and looked around, driven by the sheer need of burying himself inside her, brushing the needles off her leggings. Thank goodness, her bare bum hadn't been on those needles.

"Do you trust me?"

"Aye. Please, we need to finish this."

He tugged her behind him, leading the way to a large set of rocks. After arranging his plaid on the flat part of the rocks, he tugged her leggings off and placed them on top of it.

Her puzzled expression told him he needed to

explain, so he told her what he wanted her to do. "Kneel down on the cloth." He took her hand and helped her into the position. "Trust me. If you don't like it, I promise to stop when you tell me."

He climbed behind her and tucked her into him, running his hands all down the front of her body, teasing her nipples, then skimming one hand down her belly and thigh until he found her curls. He groaned when he found her wetness, then plunged a finger inside her as she spread her legs to give him better access.

"Logan, I want you now, but I don't know what to do. Please."

He nibbled her neck and kissed her ear, whispering what he wanted to do, leaning her forward and showing her how to grab onto the rock for leverage. Running his hand down her bum, he caressed her soft skin before trailing his way back to her mound, parting her folds to help guide him in. "Lass, you are heavenly. I have waited to run my hands across your sweet bottom. Naught gives me more pleasure than calling you mine. You accept that?"

"Aye, just finish this," she moaned.

"When you agree to be mine, I'll finish this. I love you, Gwyneth. You will be my wife?"

"Aye. I love you, Logan Ramsay. Saints above, please."

Logan grinned. How he loved this woman, the only one who had ever been able to distract him from his purpose. He ran his cock back and forth over her entrance, teasing her until she begged him for more. "Logan, please. I need you in me now." He thrust inside her and she sighed at the invasion, then he pulled out slowly, just to tease her. Moaning, she spread wider to allow him better access, and he thrust in until he was completely buried inside her.

He leaned over and whispered in her ear. "Gwyneth, I'm not hurting you?"

"Nay!" she cried out as her muscles contracted on him, and she pushed herself back on him, encouraging him to speed up the pressure. "More, please more, Logan. Faster."

Logan grabbed her hips and thrust into her, increasing his rhythm as she writhed against him, driving his cock into her again and again, bringing them both to a peak that threatened to explode. He wanted it to last longer, so he plunged inside her wetness over and over, bringing them both to a desperate pitch, a voracious need tearing at him to make her scream his name in ecstasy.

"Gwyneth, you are mine."

"Aye, please, Logan."

He reached around and caressed her nub, still pounding into her female passage, finally sending her careening over the edge, contracting and milking him as she screamed his name.

And all he could think was, "Mine."

CHAPTER TWENTY-FIVE

Gwyneth sighed as she leaned back against Logan's chest, listening to the raindrops outside their small slice of heaven. "I had no idea you could do it that way." He had somehow been able to find a comfortable way to lean back against a tree while they sat on his plaid on a rock.

"Well, I thought it might be too fresh an idea for you, but hell," he kissed her cheek, "you had me wanting you in a verra bad way, and it seemed the best solution. Did I please you?"

"You could not tell? 'Tis a good thing we did it here. Had it been anywhere else, my screams would have woken up the neighborhood." She couldn't help but blush, though she wouldn't have changed any of it.

"And do you remember what you agreed to in the middle of our lovemaking?"

She pulled away from him so she could stare at him. "Aye, but you do not play fair by asking me when I am in such a raging need. Don't try that again."

He laughed, "I won't have to. You agreed to be mine. That is what I intend, you know. I will not do this again without marriage. Or I *will* have a talk with your brother."

Gwyneth tucked her head against his chest. "I agreed. Aye, I will marry you. But 'tis only because I love you so."

He brushed his thumb across her cheek. "I like the

sound of that. I hope you will learn to say it often."

She sat up and gazed into his eyes, his brown eyes flecked with gold and a bit of green. Clasping his hands in hers, she said, "I don't need to hear you say it. I know you love me. What more proof could I ever ask for than what you did for me back at the firth?"

"You are accepting of all that happened? No anger because I followed you? I promised your brother I would help you, you realize."

"I shouldn't have left without you. After seeing that ugly redhead..."

He grinned. "Ugly redhead?"

"Aye, she is ugly."

"Och, you are jealous. I like that, too." He snickered as he pulled himself up to a sitting position.

She gave him a playful slap on his arm. "Be quiet." Staring at her hands, she paused to gather her thoughts. "My thanks for following me, but most of all, for being a man of your word. When I couldn't hit him with my arrow, I felt totally defeated." Tears gathered on her lashes. "I don't know why he was able to upset me so."

"I do. He killed your father and brother. I would be more worried about you if he didn't upset you." He wrapped his arms around her and tucked her head under his chin. "But I knew you could do it, and I am proud of you for regaining control and finishing what you needed to do."

"I did," she smiled, "didn't I? I didn't think I could do it, but with your support, I did."

"He will never bother you again."

"Would you mind if we went to see Rab? I want to let him know what happened."

"Nay, I don't mind. I need to talk to him and make sure he knows of our pending marriage. I assume you would like him to marry us?" He helped her up and found her things. Fortunately, he had thought to hang her tunic on a tree branch, so it wasn't soaked. Her leggings weren't too bad either. Then he grabbed his tunic and pulled it over his head just before he picked up his plaid.

Gwyneth stared at his plaid, a grim line to her mouth. "Your plaid doesn't look well."

He held it up, trying to shake the wetness, pine needles, and mud from it. "Nay, it took a beating, didn't it?

She nodded. "Sorry, Logan."

He leaned over and kissed her lips. "'Twas worth every minute. Just remind me never to make you mad."

She glanced at him, puzzled. "What?"

"That was a hell of a place to shoot a man, wench. Well done."

***

It was almost dawn when they arrived back at the Kirk. When Gwyneth walked in the door, Rab blessed himself and rushed over, gathering her in his arms. "Thank God, thank you, Lord. Saints preserve us."

"'Tis over, Father." Logan didn't want to torture the poor man any more than they already had.

"What? You killed him, Gwyneth?" Rab's mouth fell open as he gaped at his sister.

"Well, not exactly," she cringed.

"What do you mean, not exactly? Is he dead or not?"

Logan held up his hand. "Father Rab, please sit down, and we'll explain."

Once Rab was settled in a chair at the table, Logan said "Gwyneth, why don't you go change your wet clothes. I can explain everything to Rab."

"Nay, please. I'll tell him quick, then go change."

Rab stared up at her expectantly, holding his breath.

"Rab, it was wonderful. I shot him with an arrow, but only to wound him. Then he charged us with a knife, and we each threw a dagger at him at the same exact time. One dagger landed in his thigh and one in his neck. So we don't really know who killed him. You don't have to pray for me, because I don't know if it was my dagger or not." She kissed her brother on the cheek and rushed into her chamber to change into dry clothes.

Rab stared at Logan, who was standing across from him. "I don't understand. You should have been able to tell who threw the killing dagger, Logan. I must know. There are special prayers I need to recite for the person responsible."

Logan nodded. "Normally, I would be able to tell, aye. But I bought Gwyneth a new dagger at the fair, and I bought myself the same exact one. Besides, if we had not killed him, he would have killed one of us with his knife. It was self-defense."

"He tried to kill my sister?"

"Aye, he rushed at us with his dagger bared. It was him or us, Father. Even the Lord believes in protecting oneself."

Rab was quiet for a moment, but then he broke into a smile, even as tears slid down his cheeks. "'Tis over? I don't have to pray for her soul for the next two years?"

"That's right, Father. 'Tis over." Logan sat down next to the priest and whispered, "There's naught wrong with your sister's soul, Father. She is a kind, caring person who has had to deal with some tough circumstances. Justice was served. He had loaded other women in the boat and was searching for Gwyneth when she confronted him. The lout had every intention of stealing her and throwing her onto the boat again. Now the women are all free. We sent the sheriff down there to take care of everything."

Rab seemed like he was about to say something, then he dropped his face into his hands and started to sob. Logan didn't know what to do other than to grasp his shoulder to let him know he was there.

Moments later, Gwyneth rushed back into the room,

having no doubt heard her brother. "Rab? Are you well?"

Rab stood and hugged her, weeping into her shoulder.

Not knowing what else to do, Logan decided to change the subject. "And we're getting married, Father."

Father Rab stood back and smiled. "Truly?"

Gwyneth nodded. "Rab, you will marry us, will you not?"

Rab beamed and hugged her again.

CHAPTER TWENTY-SIX

Gwyneth rode between Logan and her brother for the short journey to the Ramsay keep, Micheil behind them. She was still surprised that Rab had agreed to make the journey with them so they could be married with Logan's family present. He had located another priest to stay at the Kirk in his absence. The air was crisp and fresh since it had rained the day before. It wouldn't be long before the ground was covered in snow.

She could tell when they neared the family keep because Logan's posture straightened a bit and his face lit up. The Ramsay castle wasn't as large as the Grant keep, yet it was still quite majestic. Many cottages surrounded the walls and people emerged to greet them as they passed. She could see the questions on his clan members' faces as they continued on toward the portcullis. Once they reached the stables, voices behind them cried out more greetings, seasoned with children's laughter.

Gwyneth turned to see Lily and Torrian running toward them, several yards ahead of Quade, Brenna, and the babe. Father Rab was introduced to the group, but there was one person notably missing—Logan's mother. Her Highlander was fiercely loyal to his brothers, but even more so to his mother. She could see the pride in his face as they approached the outside steps to the keep. Aye, there his mother stood in her flowing skirts, a dark mantle over her shoulders, her arms crossed, awaiting her middle son.

"Greetings, Mother." Logan rushed forward to kiss his mother's cheek and she grasped his shoulders, drawing him in for a strong hug.

"Logan, you brought guests." She turned her radiant smile to Gwyneth and her brother. "Introduce us, please."

His gaze caught hers before he began, and she relaxed, empowered by the love she saw there.

"Mother, this is Gwyneth of the Cunninghams and her brother, Father Rab. I have asked Gwyneth to be my wife and Rab would like to perform the ceremony. This is my mother, Lady Arlene Ramsay."

Gwyneth said, "Lady Arlene, 'tis a pleasure to meet you." She dipped her head to the graceful woman who would be the closest thing she would ever have to a mother. Lady Ramsay was a beautiful woman, and she guessed a strong one as well. Brenna had spoken very highly of the woman. Gwyneth was hopeful of their relationship. Since she had no memories of her real mother, she wasn't quite sure how to act with Lady Arlene, but she so wanted all to go well. Hopefully, Lady Ramsay would accept her as a daughter.

Lady Arlene hugged her and said, "My thanks, my dear, for loving my son. I can see it in your eyes—the both of you."

Gwyneth didn't know how to answer that, so she just smiled. Logan's mother greeted Rab before returning her gaze to Gwyneth. Somehow, she knew what the older woman was thinking. Never before had she felt the need to apologize for being herself, but suddenly she did.

Seeming to sense her discomfort, Logan rested his hand on the small of her back. Empowered by his touch, she said what she thought would be proper. "My lady, my apologies for not dressing appropriately. I grew up in a family of lads, and this is how I am most comfortable, especially atop a horse." She dropped her gaze, praying the woman would not chastise her.

Lady Ramsay clasped Gwyneth's hands in hers and waited until everyone was quiet. "My dear, he is my son and he is verra special. I knew it would take a special lass to love him. Never apologize for who you are, and do not change for anyone but yourself. Though I'm sure you'll wear a skirt when you marry, won't you, dear?"

Gwyneth liked everything she said except the last sentence, but she decided it would be best if she didn't tell Lady Ramsay right out that she didn't plan to ever wear a skirt.

They all moved inside and Lady Ramsay called for food for the guests. As soon as they entered the great hall and sat down, Quade got after his brother. "Logan, you cost me. Brenna said you were taken with her enough to settle down, but I just couldn't believe it. Now I owe a boon to my wife, thanks to you." He said to Gwyneth, "Welcome to the Ramsay family, lass. I only jest with him. I am happy my brother has chosen well."

Brenna beamed. "Of course, he was besotted. He chased her from the Highlands all the way to Glasgow. How could you not see it, husband?"

Avelina joined them, and they all sat around the table. When Logan bragged about Gwyneth's prowess as an archer, telling the story of her win at the fair, Avelina's eyes glowed with excitement. "Gwyneth, will you teach me?"

She nodded, unable to speak for fear she would shed tears in front of her new family. They were every bit as wonderful as the Grants, but they were a smaller group. How content she felt here, with Logan next to her, his arm around her waist, watching as he conversed with his family. She peered down the table and saw Rab chatting with Lady Ramsay. She hoped her brother was as happy to be here as she was. They were finally going to be part of a large family again, though she would be broken-hearted when Rab returned to Glasgow.

As soon as they sat down, Brenna had gone to the kitchens to check on the food for the travelers. The food hadn't been brought out yet when wee Bethia took her tiny fist and banged it repeatedly on the table before shoving it back into her mouth. The entire family burst into gales of laughter at the bairn's antics, and her response was to break into a huge grin, her two teeth protruding from her bottom gum and her chubby legs bouncing with excitement. Logan reached over and pulled her from Brenna's lap and tossed her into the air over his head, causing her to erupt in another fit of giggles. He continued to play with Bethia and Lily until trenchers of mutton stew were placed on the table along with special bowls of vegetables and meat for Quade's older children.

Gwyneth watched him with a smile on her face, in awe at how wonderful her husband-to-be was with weans. She remembered how he had been with Ashlyn and Gracie. How could she not love a braw man who handled bairns so well? She had softened to him long ago; she just had been too busy with everything else in her life to notice.

Lady Arlene, who sat next to her, leaned over and kissed her cheek and said, "My thanks for bringing my son home. I missed him badly."

Gwyneth finally had a mother.

***

The next day, the hall bustled with activity as the clan tried to decide on wedding plans. Logan's mother, Brenna, and Father Rab sat at the main table with her, discussing details about the ceremony. The conversation mostly took place between Lady Ramsay and Rab. Gwyneth had little to say, though Brenna tried to draw her in on occasion. When they decided on the date and the location, Gwyneth had nodded in agreement. Lady Ramsay had volunteered to handle the decorating and Gwyneth had been quick to grant her that privilege, only suggesting that she would like to see some natural greenery and pine cones inside the chapel, not caring anything about big bows and ribbons.

Brenna then offered her suggestion on food, based on their current stores and what they could hunt. Not feeling she could contribute much more to the conversation, Gwyneth broke away and headed to the kitchens to grab a chunk of bread to gnaw on. As she was about to push the door open, she heard her name and stopped. Two voices could be heard through the door.

"Can you believe Logan is marrying that lass he brought home?"

"Och, it won't last long."

"What do you mean?"

Gwyneth found herself leaning in toward the door.

"Look at the daft woman he chose. She runs around in men's clothing, and she's flat-chested and slim in the hips. Men want real curves in their women."

Gwyneth backed up in surprise. Were these women right? What did she know about what men wanted? She'd only ever been in a relationship with Logan. She heard a creak behind her, but she was too absorbed in the conversation in the kitchens to take notice.

"But Logan brought her home, so she is his choice."

"Not for long. He may marry her, but I'll be in his bed in no time. He loved to bed me before that witch came here."

Gwyneth jumped as Brenna flew by her and strode through the door.

"Take yourself out of my kitchens, Agnes. I will not have you talking about my family that way. I'll find another to replace you."

"But my lady…"

"Don't even make an attempt to defend yourself. I

heard what you said about my husband's brother and his soon-to-be wife. Get out now."

The door flew open and an irate servant stepped through it. Even with her golden hair all pinned up, she was a pretty woman full of ripe curves. The woman stopped in front of Gwyneth and glared at her before continuing on her way.

Brenna came back through the door and clasped Gwyneth's hands in hers. "I came looking for you and overheard her words. I'm sorry you had to hear them. Agnes will not be welcomed in the keep again. In fact, I'll speak to Quade about asking her to leave the clan. We don't need people like her around."

Gwyneth just stared, still stunned by what had happened.

"You haven't met many nasty women before, have you?" Brenna said.

Gwyneth shook her head. "I knew verra few women before coming to the Grant Keep. My mama died when I was young and I grew up around my father, brothers, and uncle, along with the priests at the Kirk."

"Well, not all women are like that. Please remember we are thrilled to have you in the family. Don't pay any attention to her. Logan is fiercely loyal to his family, and I'm sure that will hold to you as well."

After pulling Gwyneth in for a hug, Brenna returned to the table, sitting once again by Quade's side, and Gwyneth retrieved her bread from the kitchen. When she stepped out, she peered at the group, looking for any sign that Brenna had told them about Agnes, but they didn't act any different, so she made her way back to the table. Though Gwyneth had little experience with women, she was excited Brenna and Avelina would be her sisters. They had both been wonderful to her.

Logan returned from their morning hunt and came over to her side to greet her. "Confused, sweeting?" He sat down beside her and took her hands in his.

She decided not to mention the servant since they were among others. "Logan, I know naught about planning a wedding."

"You don't know what you'd like to do for the ceremony?"

She stared into his eyes. "I don't know anything about this. I have never been to a wedding."

"You never attended one at the Kirk? Your brother must have married many couples."

"Rab oft married people, but I was never interested. It seemed silly to me at the time. Now I wish I had been more attentive."

"Well, if the details are of little import to you, then we can make haste." He grinned and whispered in her ear. "I would be happy to have you in my bed this night."

"May I ask you a question?" She moved over to the hearth, tugging him behind her, where they could talk. Though she'd intended to keep quiet about the incident in the kitchens, she decided to find out if there were any truths in the lass's claims. There would be no lies in their marriage.

"Of course."

"Do you have a mistress now, or do you plan to ever have a mistress after we marry."

"What? A mistress? Nay. I love you and I do not want any other. You are the one I want in my bed." The last sentence he whispered as he stroked her cheek.

"Even though I don't wear skirts and gowns? It does not bother you? Will you seek out another in skirts?"

"Nay. Who have you been talking to?" Logan asked with a frown. He glanced around the hall as if searching for the person who'd instilled her with doubt.

"I just need to know if you are displeased with my appearance." She stared at her boots because she was afraid for him to see the expression on his face. "Why do you love me when I don't look like the other lasses?"

"I love you for what is inside, not for the clothing you wear. I love you because you don't mind being different and you love the outdoors just as I do. I am happy with you as you are."

Brenna hustled over to them, and leaned down to address Logan so only he and Gwyneth could hear. "She overheard Agnes talking about you, that's the problem. Agnes thinks she'll find her way into your bed after your marriage because the woman you chose wears warrior's clothing. She bragged about it to her friends in the kitchens, but I have sent her home. I'll straighten the rest of them out in case anyone else has a similar notion, though I doubt it. Agnes is *special*." With that, she turned and headed toward the kitchens with a purposeful step.

Logan's reaction was swift as he turned to Gwyneth. "Agnes? Nay, I have no interest in her. She is way too plump for my taste and she's nasty besides. I am quite happy with you just the way you are, Gwyneth. Though I would love to talk you out of binding your beautiful breasts." He nuzzled her neck with his last comment.

"Are you sure, Logan? I don't want to get married if you are interested in another." Gwyneth thought about what she had said, wondering what kind of curves Logan preferred, but not willing to ask.

Logan stopped and gazed into her eyes as he held her chin in his hand. "Gwyneth, I could have chosen any of these women here or in Glasgow. I choose you."

He kissed her and she blushed, embarrassed that she had asked him such a thing.

His mother was still seated close by, as was Rab, so he sensed her hesitation. "Come," he held his hand out to her. "'Tis a lovely day. Shall we go for a walk?"

Logan grabbed her hand, excused their absence to the others, and crept up the steps and out the front door of the great hall. He ran through the courtyard, tugging her behind him. "We'll find somewhere in the forests to walk." He wiggled his eyebrows at her. "Someplace verra private?"

"Och, aye." She gave him a wee shove from behind, encouraging him toward the stables.

As soon as they mounted their horses, they made their way out the gate. Gwyneth sighed, basking in the fresh outdoor air. "You know I am more comfortable out here."

"Aye, 'tis one of the reasons I love you so."

She gave him a sly look. "Mayhap you would accept a challenge, Logan? Do you think you could beat me on horseback?"

He grinned, an evil look flashing across his features. "Lass, I would enjoy challenging you at anything."

**

They were about to leave when a desperate voice interrupted their playful spirit. Logan turned to find the source and saw Torrian running after him and screaming. The sensation was as painful as a fist to his gut, and it threatened to take his air away. "What is it, Torrian?"

"Lily." Torrian yelled. "She's gone. We were playing, but then someone hit me over the head. When I woke up, she was gone."

Logan squelched the urge to vomit. His wee Lily? Someone had kidnapped her? How had this happened? The children were always accompanied by guards when they played away from the keep. The others needed to know what had happened, but first he needed more information. He reached down and pulled Torrian onto his lap at the same time he let out his Ramsay whoop, alerting his guards they were needed. "Show me."

They headed out to the meadow where the bairns had been playing. He glanced over his shoulder to make sure Gwyneth still followed, and saw she was directly behind him, Torrian's faithful dog Growley running alongside her. As soon as they arrived, Logan rode over to the one remaining guard in the area.

Logan reined his horse next to the guard. "Ewan? What happened?"

He waited for the guard, who was shaking his head, to speak "'Tis all my fault, Logan. Three lasses came flying into the field on horseback, two of them with naught on and big..." he glanced at Torrian, "...well, you know what I mean. We all took our eyes off the bairns. We chased the women on the horses. The two went one direction and the third went in the opposite direction."

"And?" Logan was going to choke the man if he didn't speak up.

"We all followed the two with naught on. They left the meadow after a while and when we returned, Torrian was on the ground and Lily was missing."

"Where are the others?"

"I sent them to search for a trail. Lyell said he would head to the keep for more guards once they found a sign of where she went. I never saw Torrian get up, I was talking to Lyell. Then I was afraid we had lost Torrian as well."

"The third woman. What did she look like?" Logan barked, losing his patience with the fool. There would be hell to pay. These guards had the most important job at the keep—protecting the laird's heirs. How could they have made such a mistake?

"She was flame-haired. Lyell thought it was Iona, but I didn't see her clear enough."

Iona. A dead weight fell into the pit of his stomach. Iona was not right minded, and that frightened him more than anything. Visions of Lily tied up and held captive made his blood boil.

He turned to Gwyneth. "Gwyneth, take Torrian back and fill Quade in on what's happened. Tell him everything." He handed the wee lad over to Gwyneth.

"Logan, take me with you. I can help."

"Nay, Gwyneth. Protect Torrian. I need someone I can count on to protect him." He gave Ewan a pointed look before spurring his horse on. "This is between Iona and me."

CHAPTER TWENTY-SEVEN

Iona paced in the small cabin, staring at her captive.

"Why are you doing this, Iona? Why do you hate me so?" Lily sat on a stool at the table, her hands tied behind her back, her little feet tied together, too.

"Because, you little fool, my rightful place is at the head of the Ramsay clan with my husband. Your father should have married me, but nay, he had to marry the Grant lass. Fine, he can have the cow. 'Tis too late for him, but 'tis not too late for Logan. Logan is mine."

"But Logan is in love with Gwyneth. He's going to marry her."

Iona marched over and yelled at Lily. "Keep your mouth shut. I don't want to hear anything you have to say."

Lily burst into tears and tugged at her bindings. "Stop yelling at me."

"All you ever do is whine, whine, whine, Lily. Well, I do not want to hear it, and I have the perfect solution…"

Lily's eyes widened as she stared at Iona, ceasing her wails for the moment.

"Here." Iona pulled up a stool next to Lily and set a loaf of brown bread in front of her. "Eat."

"Nay. I can't eat that. It will make me sick. Mama says I can't eat any bread at all. I'll toss it back up, I will."

Iona screamed. "I said eat it."

"Nay, I don't want to be sick again. It hurts my belly. Please don't make me eat it." Lily's voice had dropped to a whimper.

She'd have to make the lass sick. It would be the only way she could tolerate being around the whiny wean. If Lily became sick, she'd probably stop talking. Iona ripped off a piece of the bread and held it in front of Lily's mouth. "Eat."

Lily locked her lips closed and shook her head back and forth.

Iona pinched the girl's nose until she was forced to open her mouth to breathe, and then shoved the bread into her mouth. "There, you little witch. Now eat it."

Lily glared at her and promptly spit the bread out on the floor.

"You'll eat this or I'll beat you over and over again."

Lily opened her mouth with a sob, chewing the piece of bread Iona put inside as slowly as she could.

Iona smiled and stood up to pace the room, her hands twisting in glee. "I have found the perfect spot for you. No one will ever find you and Logan will be mine." She stopped a moment to stare out the window.

Her brow furrowed when she turned back to Lily. "Finished that piece, aye? Good, here's another." She forced another piece into the girl's mouth. "I tried to talk sense into him, I did. I followed him to Glasgow, and when I saw him at the fair, I was sure he would follow me. But he had the lass in warrior's clothing with him. There was no other way, Lily. But he loves you so. I knew I could use you as bait. I know he'll come for you. Once I get him out here alone, he'll see that he wants me. Then we'll make our plans to marry and take over the keep. I'm sure he would love to be laird once I get rid of Quade."

Lily cried, "That's my da. Please don't hurt my da."

"Och, be quiet, Lily. Soon I'll send you to your

hiding place. It took me a while to get your spot arranged for you, my dear, but I am sure no one will think to look there. Then Logan will love me." She returned to the window, her gaze crossing the landscape. "I wonder what color dress I shall wear for our wedding. Mayhap I will wear my hair up."

She turned to Lily, who was still chewing. "And you know what else? Once I am living at the castle, I'll take care of your stepmother and your father... Then Logan will be head of the clan, with me at his side." Her eyes stared at the ceiling as her arms crossed in front of her chest.

"A few moons later, I'll have to kill your grandmamma, too." Her lower lip pushed out in a pout as she glanced at Lily and shook her head. "She doesn't like me, which won't do at all." Her hand went to her face as she settled on a stool. "I'll have to think about this. I will have to kill them in two different ways, so no one will suspect me. Poison will work verra well for one of them, but what about the rest?"

Iona moved around the cabin, lost in thought as she tried to decide what she would do next. Then she gathered her things together and threw them in a sack. Grabbing Lily by the arms, she hauled her out the door and tossed her up on the horse, mounting behind her.

Iona spurred the horse and said, "No one will ever find you, Lily. I'm sorry, but I must do this. After all, I had to get Logan out to my cottage somehow. But we don't need you here with us. We wish to be alone. I'm afraid the wild animals will have you for their dinner tomorrow. You've done your job, wee one."

Lily squealed and Iona yanked on her hair.

Leaning over the side of the horse, the wee lass said, "I don't feel so good."

Iona smiled. "Perfect, absolutely perfect timing."

***

Logan tracked Iona easily until he came to a small

creek. God's teeth, but he lost her in the creek. He searched the entire area on the other side of the small river, but found naught. He couldn't pin down any horses hooves, horse dung, anything. She had disappeared.

He couldn't give up, not now. Not ever.

He ran his hand down his face and closed his eyes, willing a solution to come to him. He needed his tracker's instincts to kick in, but it just wasn't working today. His shoulders slumped, defeated by the thought of his wee niece in the clutches of a blackguard like Iona. Every minute mattered.

He was having trouble getting it together, but he had to regain control for Lily's sake. His wee niece, whom he adored, was out there scared and probably hungry. He would find her, and Iona would never return to traumatize his family ever again. Spurring his horse, he moved on, though he was unsure of which way to go. Reaching in his sporran, he pulled out the lucky stone Lily had given him, smiling at the memory of her cheerful face, so serious about how lucky the pebble would be for him. He dutifully rubbed his fingers over the cool stone and whispered, "Which way, Lily? Which way?"

He followed his gut and took off in that direction. About an hour later, he came to a cabin and reined his horse in before he came too close. He stared at the cabin, unable to recall who lived there. Perhaps it had been deserted for a long time.

After dismounting, he crept around the back of the cottage and listened for a moment, hoping to find out if Lily was inside. He didn't hear any sounds, so made his way to the front and opened the door.

Empty. No one was there, but his gut told him they had been here. On the table, he found a fresh loaf of brown bread, and something on the floor. He leaned over to finger the clump.

Aye, right, Lily had been here. Iona had forced her

to eat bread, and Lily had spit it out. *That's my girl, Lily. Fight.*

CHAPTER TWENTY-EIGHT

Gwyneth brought Torrian back to the keep and informed Quade of everything she knew. It took a few moments for Torrian to repeat his story, then Quade turned and disappeared, but not before Gwyneth noticed his clenched jaw and his hands balled into fists at his sides. There would be hell to pay for those guards, she knew that. How could they have been so lax? All over two nude women? Men were fools.

She walked away from the group talking in the great hall and returned to her chamber, collecting everything she would need to find the wee lass. Logan was too attached to think rationally. He may be the best tracker in all of Scotland, but not when his family was involved. She would find Lily on her own. He needed back up, though he would never admit it. Fine. She would help him…just as he'd help her when there had been a need.

As she crept down the staircase into the great hall, no one paid any attention to her. She slipped over to the door and let herself out, thinking she was alone.

She wasn't. Lady Arlene Ramsay exited the door behind her. Turning Gwyneth to face her, she cupped her cheeks and stared into her eyes. "Please find them. My son says none are any better than you in the wild. He says you are an expert marksman, too. My question to you is, are you capable of killing another if need be?"

Gwyneth noted the fear and worry in the lady's

gaze. Answering her truthfully, she nodded her head and stared at her feet. "Aye, I can and I will, if 'tis necessary."

Logan's mother grabbed her hands. "Find her and end this. Please. Then find Logan and bring him back with Lily." She kissed Gwyneth's cheek and pushed her away.

Gwyneth glanced over her shoulder at her. "I will, I promise."

The look in Lady Ramsay's eyes spoke of her belief in her. "Thank you. Godspeed."

***

Iona bustled around the small cabin, humming a perky tune as she puttered with the food and the candles inside. She wanted everything to be just right. Soon her fiancé would be here, he would tell her how much he loved her, and they would live happily ever after.

She sighed as she imagined how the scene would play out when he found her. First, he would throw the door open and run to her because she was so beautiful.

"Och, Logan. I have been waiting for you. What took you so long?"

With his hand over his chest, he would declare his love for her. "It doesn't matter. I am here now. I love you, Iona. Now we can finally be together without any interference."

Iona clapped her hands with glee. "We will live a wonderful life together. I will give you many bairns and we can move to the keep."

He rushed to her side, grasped her hand in his, and fell on one knee in front of her. "My sweet, will you marry me? I cannot live without you by my side for one more day."

"Aye, of course, Logan. We can marry and I will give you a special gift for a wedding present."

His eyes shone with love for her as he stood and wrapped his arms around her waist. "What, love? Tell me now. You know the suspense will be too much for me. And we must marry right away."

She giggled and hid her face in his chest.

"Tell me," he grinned. "No secrets. What gift have you? Where is it so I can open it?"

"Oh, husband. 'Tis not something you can open. My plan is to get rid of Quade and Brenna so you can be laird. Wouldn't you love to be laird of the castle, with me as your wife by your side?"

"You would do that for me?"

"Aye."

Logan would be so pleased that he would pick her up and spin her in a circle. "I love you, Iona. We will run the Ramsay clan better than Quade, you'll see. How will you do it?"

"I'll wait just a couple of moons before I set my plan in place. And no one will know."

Iona stared into space, imagining the kiss Logan would give her once she agreed to be his wife. Someday, the minstrels would sing songs about how beautiful and clever she was, and how much her husband adored her.

Suddenly wrested from her dream by a noise outside the cottage, she stilled and listened. Someone was out there. She grabbed her knife and hid it in the folds of her skirt. Whoever it was would die soon.

***

Logan had tracked Iona to another cabin, a good distance from the first one. Why she moved around, he wasn't sure. He crept up to the window and peeked inside. Iona was alone. Where was Lily? He didn't like the looks of this, so he didn't waste any time in confronting the daft woman.

He strode over to the front door and threw it open.

Iona jumped, but then calmed, a slow grin creeping across her face. "There you are. I have been waiting for you, my love."

"I'm here, but I'm not your love. Where is Lily?" He

filled the doorway with his warrior stance; his feet braced apart, his hand near his sword, ready to draw at the least provocation.

"Lily? Why do you ask me?"

"Lily. You kidnapped her from the meadow where she was playing with Torrian and Growley."

"Nay, I did not." Iona's hands fisted at her hips.

Logan reached her in a second, grabbing her gown in the front and pulling her close. "Aye, you did. Now where is she? Iona, don't play with me. If I have to beat it out of you, I will."

She shoved at him, but he didn't release her. Her sneer told him she had the girl hidden somewhere. "The little brat is far away from here. You'll never see her again."

"Iona, where is she?"

"I'll never tell. I don't want that whiny brat around us. You love me, Logan. Admit it. We'll marry and I'll kill Quade so you can be laird and I'll be lady of the castle. You'll see." Her voice wavered and she reached for his face.

"Do not touch me, you daft woman."

"Daft? I'm not daft. You are." She tried to scratch him with her nails. "You're the fool who can't see how good we could be together. Give up that female warrior. Why would you want a woman who walks around in men's clothing?"

"Because she is clever, compassionate, and kind. Unlike you. You treat everyone as if they owe you for something."

"They do. You do. You owe me. My mother said I would marry noble blood someday. Why can't you see it? I belong in the laird's castle. I promised my mama when she died that I would fight to be the laird's wife. Now I am ready to make her proud."

Logan thought he would lose his mind talking to this daft woman. She talked in circles and she revealed nothing. He had to find Lily, he just had to.

The thought of her alone out here with the wild boars and pigs made him ill.

"Marry me, Logan, and you'll see how good we'll be together."

"It'll never happen. Now, where is my niece? You'll be hung for murder if you don't tell me."

"Well, I almost did murder the little brat. She argued with me about everything. She wouldn't do what she was told, and I wanted to kill her right then."

"What did you do to her?" He grabbed her gown and lifted her off the floor. "Did you hurt her?"

Iona tried to loosen his hands, but to no avail. "She wouldn't do as she was told. I had to shut her up."

"What did you do?"

"I made her eat bread, that's all. Then I knew she would stop her whining."

Logan let her go, tossing her back so she had to catch herself to keep from falling. He didn't know what to do. He paced in a circle, wanting to drive his sword through her black heart, but then he still wouldn't be able to find wee Lily. "Iona, please. I'm sure there is a man out there who would love to marry you. Tell me where Lily is."

"I don't want another man. I want you, Logan Ramsay. And I won't tell you where Lily is until you marry me." She sat in a chair and crossed her arms.

Logan placed his hands on the table across from her and bellowed at her. "Tell me where she is! I'll never marry you. How can I marry you when you have been banned by my mother and my laird from my clan? Iona, it cannot be."

Iona's lower lip trembled and she turned her head to stare out the window. Her voice dropped to a whisper as the tears slid down her cheeks. "You don't love me, do you?"

"Nay, Iona." Logan sat in the chair opposite her. "Please. You have risked the life of a bairn. Do the right thing. Tell me where she is."

"I can't."

Logan's blood boiled, but he forced himself to remain calm. "Why not?"

"I can't name the place. I would have to show you." She stared at the floor in a trance.

"Then I'm begging you. Show me where she is."

"If that's what you wish, I'll show you." She nodded before she stood, glancing at him.

"You're doing the right thing. Show me."

She shrugged her shoulders and sighed, walking out the door.

CHAPTER TWENTY-NINE

Logan helped Iona mount her horse, then followed her into the woods. They rode for some time when he shouted to her. "How much farther is it?"

Iona grinned at him and spurred her horse to go faster. She flew away from him, a wicked laugh echoing through the forest.

Logan had a bad feeling. He didn't think she had any intention of bringing him to Lily. He prayed she wasn't so daft that she didn't remember where she was, and he prayed even harder that she was still alive. If Lily was out there, he would find her.

Iona raced at a frantic pace. He took off after her, dodging branches and tree limbs along her path. They came into a small clearing and she laughed harder, pushing her horse even more. Logan could tell her horse had tired. She probably never thought to feed the poor beast.

At the edge of the clearing, a downed tree limb came out of nowhere and Iona didn't see it in time. The horse either had to stop in its tracks or it had to leap over it. Doing the latter, he almost made it over, but his hind leg caught on the tree and the horse fell hard, tossing Iona off its back into the soft grass.

She would have been fine but the horse collapsed on a broken leg, forcing it to the ground. He couldn't land solid and ended up rolling. Unfortunately, the horse rolled over Iona's legs. The scream was one of agony, and Logan expected to find her dead when he got to her. The horse still flailed and kicked, managing to catch her in her side once before he was able to stand and move away, collapsing on the other side of the meadow.

Logan dismounted and ran to her side. He was almost sickened by what he saw. Her legs were both broken and twisted, one at a grotesque angle.

She screamed and screamed, her pain clearly unbearable. Logan fell on his knees next to her, but he knew there was naught he could do.

"Logan, help me, please."

"Your legs are badly broken. There is naught I can do for you."

Her breathing became irregular and her eyes took on a glassy look as she searched the area for something, but he knew not what. She screamed again in agony. "Do something, Logan, please." Logan scanned the area for her horse, but he was nowhere to be seen.

The only thing that would help her was to drive his dagger into her heart and take her out of her misery, but even he couldn't do that.

"Logan, I'm sorry. You don't have to marry me. I was only trying to make my mother proud. Please. There must be something you can do. Help me. Get the healer." As she continued to talk, her voice weakened.

Logan had seen injuries like this before. The horse had crushed her insides, maybe even with the kick to her side. She wouldn't live for long. He had to get her to tell him where Lily was before she lost consciousness.

"Please tell me where Lily is."

"She's..." Her eyes fluttered shut.

"Iona!" Logan yelled at her.

Her eyelids opened again, and she stared at him.

"Tell me where Lily is. Do the right thing before you die."

She nodded her head and closed her eyes.

"Iona!"

Her eyes opened for a second and mumbled, but he couldn't understand a word she said.

He dropped his ear next to her lips.

"What?"

"In the trees."

Iona took her last breath.

Logan stood up and bellowed like he had never done before.

Where the hell was 'in the trees?'

***

Gwyneth had ridden her horse for hours, but without finding any sign of Lily. At one point, she had met up with several Ramsay guards, and they'd informed her Iona was dead, but no one knew where the wee lassie was.

Dismounting, she decided she needed to rest her bum and move her legs. Growley had followed her and stayed with her, but though he used his nose often, he hadn't found anything more than she had. They were moving through a rather thick part of the forest when Growley suddenly barked, his nose pressing to the ground.

Gwyneth halted as a distinctive odor reached her nose. Growley barked several times before she recognized the smell as vomit. Walking in a circle, she managed to determine where the odor was the strongest. Growley sat at a different spot, his tail wagging as he stared at her. She moved over to the spot and there it was—vomit on the ground.

Hadn't Logan told her how sickly Lily had been before Brenna's treatment plan?

She scanned the area but didn't notice anything unusual. She yelled Lily's name several times until she heard a faint whimpering.

"Lily?" she shouted.

A cry and a weak, "Here."

Gwyneth moved through the area, but couldn't find anything. "Keep talking, Lily, so I can find you."

"Here."

A faint whimper echoed through the trees, but it wasn't loud enough.

"Up here."

Up? Gwyneth looked up through the glorious tree tops, many leaves still clinging to their boughs, hanging on until a swift wind would come along to drop them to the ground. Sure enough, a large wooden board sat amid the branches, to the right of the tree trunk.

"Lily?" She stood directly under the board. "Are you in the trees?"

"Aye."

"Climb down. I'll catch you."

"I can't."

"Why not?" When she asked the question, a chill ran up her spine. Please God, nay. *Don't make me. I can't climb up there. Please help me find another way.*

"She tied my hands to the tree. I can't move. And Iona made me eat bread so I'm sick. I don't know if I could climb down."

"Lass, are you hurt anywhere besides your belly?"

"Nay, but I want my mama. Please come get me, Gwyneth."

"'Tis fine, Lily. I'll get you down. Give me a few minutes to figure out a way."

"Hurry. Please Gwyneth. I want to get down. Is Iona there?"

"Nay, sweetie, she won't hurt you again." Gwyneth's gaze searched the area as if something would jump out at her. Finally, she walked over to Growley and petted his head. "Go, Growley, go find Logan. He can climb up there. Go get him."

Growley stared at her, his tail wagging. Gwyneth scowled at him. "Some help you are." She glanced up through the branches again. It seemed like an easy climb, as long as she didn't look down.

Precisely the problem. If only she could climb without looking down. Sweat broke out across her forehead at the mere thought of how high the board was off the ground. She paced in a small circle, willing herself to overcome her fear.

"Gwyneth, please. I have to go in the bushes."

Hellfire, why did she let her fears eat at her so? She was once again completely powerless. She had sworn to herself Duff's death would secure her freedom, but it had not. Fear held her captive.

Growley brushed her side and nuzzled her hand, giving her a little push. Tears threatened to spill down her cheeks, but she swiped them away. *Change your thinking.* That's what Rab had taught her.

Taking a deep breath, she stared up through the tree limbs. "Lily, you hang on. I'm coming for you." She began to recite a litany of prayers Rab had taught her and set her bow down before placing her foot on the first branch and tugging herself up.

"Lily, talk to me, honey. I need to hear your voice." She would draw strength from the lass. Visions of Lily fighting to survive when she was too weak to lift her head from her bed, of Gracie and Ashlyn staying strong in the hands of the vile brutes who'd held them captive, flooded her mind. Three verra strong lassies battling unbelievable adversity drove her forward—one hand over the other and her feet would follow.

A quick glance below told her she was moving up, but her stomach roiled and her foot slipped. Heights made her dizzy. *Don't look down.* Her father had told her that very thing when she was younger.

"Gwyneth, where are you?"

A feeble voice beckoned her. "I'm on my way, sweet. Keep talking." She closed her eyes until the dizziness stopped. She could do this. Another deep breath. The pounding of her heart thundered in her ears. She glanced up to see how much further she had to go. Not much.

She leaned her head against the rough bark of the tree and thought of Logan, of how much he loved Lily. The thought of him made her stronger. She envisioned his leg under hers and his arm under hers, the same way he had helped her with Duff Erskine. Lily needed her.

Tiny sobs reached her ears, and she squared her shoulders and stared up at the board a short distance away. One hand reached up and grabbed the next branch; her other hand and her feet followed.

Before she knew it, her head was level with the board and she peered at Lily.

The lass peeked at her and said, "I love you, Gwyneth."

She grabbed the next branch and propelled herself so she sat next to Lily. She made it with a thud and said a quick prayer of thanks.

CHAPTER THIRTY

Logan rode his horse for a mile before he caught up with his brother.

"Quade," he yelled to the group of guards.

His brother whistled, stopping the ten guards with him. He glanced at Logan with such a hopeful expression, but he couldn't give his brother what he wanted, not yet. "Iona's dead, Quade. Her horse fell on her after a jump and killed her."

"And? She took you to Lily or told you where she was?"

Logan shook his head. "Nay. I tried to get the information from her, but the only thing she told me was 'in the trees.'"

"Then Lily is alive somewhere. But what did she mean by that?" He stared at the sky, lost in thought. "I don't understand that. I don't picture her putting Lily in a tree somewhere. At least we know she is alive. That's something. We'll find her."

Logan hung his head, upset that he couldn't give his brother better news.

"Logan, we'll find her. You're the best tracker in the Lowlands, if not among all the Scots. We'll find her. My Lily is strong, and whatever has happened to her, Brenna will fix her." He divided his guards up and gave directions for their search. "Meet back here at dusk." His gaze searched his guards. "When you find her, bring her back to my wife first. Then come for me.

I want you in pairs." He sent them in different directions except for two he held back to stay with him.

Before riding off himself, he stared at Logan, who was still sitting motionless on his horse. "What is it?"

"I failed you, brother. I'm sorry."

"Nay, you didn't. You found Iona. If she had killed Lily, she would have gloated. My daughter is still out there."

"I don't know if I can find her."

"God's teeth, you're giving up?"

Logan shrugged. "I feel the same way I did when they were sickly. I don't know what to do. I have no control over this situation. Iona was in my hands and I handled it all wrong."

"My daughter is counting on you. Are you just going to walk away?"

Logan paused for a few moments before shaking his head. He knew what he had to do, but the threat of failure or the possibility of finding his niece dead felt like more than he could handle.

"Logan, get control of yourself. I've never seen you like this. Be strong." He glared at his brother, but his gaze softened after a moment. "I need you, Logan. Together, we'll find her, but I can't do it without you."

He ran his hand down his face. Quade was right. He couldn't give in to his worries. He had to stay strong for his wee niece. "Nay, I'll track her."

"Good. If we're lucky, Gwyneth has already found her."

Logan stilled. "Gwyneth? I sent her back to the keep to protect Torrian."

"She's out there with Growley, hoping the dog will pick up her scent. Don't be upset. Mother encouraged her to go."

God's teeth, Gwyneth was out there, too? A fist punched him square in his gut. He had two people to find. "Then let's move. It'll be dark soon, and our chances of finding her in the dark are slim. The fact that Growley is with Gwyneth gives me hope." There were two people he loved out in the forests. It was time to find them.

Quade agreed. "Lily is afraid of the dark. I want her found before that. Let's split. I'll send one guard with you and keep one with me."

"Nay. I travel alone, Quade." He grinned, feeling a bit like his old self. "You should know that by now." He grabbed Paz's reins and took off.

***

Gwyneth scooted over next to Lily, but the board moved underneath the lassie. She stilled, waiting until it stabilized. "Lily, we're going to have to move fast. I don't trust this board."

As soon as she was able, she slid close to Lily, leaned down, and gave her a kiss on her forehead. "You are unhurt, my dear?"

Lily's tears slid down her cheeks. "Aye, but I keep heaving. I don't feel well. How will you get me down?"

"One step at a time, lass." Gwyneth leaned over and cut the bindings on the wean's hands. A dark fury grew inside her belly when she saw the raw marks around Lily's wrists. She took a deep breath and peeked over the side of the board, then shut her eyes tight. This was going to be much more difficult than she had anticipated, but she had no choice. Aye, it was a long way down, but the only way out was down.

She helped Lily sit up and move her limbs. "Can you hang onto me, Lily?" The poor thing had dark circles under her eyes and cracked lips from all her heaving. Gwyneth brushed her hair back. Oh, how she wanted to hug her tight, but she didn't trust the board to stay in place.

"I think so, but I am verra tired. 'Tis not so far down, is it?"

Gwyneth grabbed her hand and tugged her close. "Don't look down. It won't help." She helped the girl crawl to the edge of the board, inch by inch. "I think I'll have you climb on my back. You can hang onto my shoulders and wrap your legs around my waist. Then you'll have two places you can hold on."

"I'll try, Gwyneth. Just get me down. I want my mama and papa."

"I'll get you to them. Are you ready?" She gave Lily a big smile, hoping the wee lass wouldn't detect her fear.

"Aye." Lily got behind Gwyneth and grasped her shoulders.

"Here, lass. Let me grab hold of the tree and you can rest on the edge of the board to wrap your legs around me." Gwyneth stepped on a branch and made the mistake of looking down. A wave of nausea roiled through her and she swallowed and squeezed her eyes shut.

"What's wrong, Gwyneth?"

"Naught." She opened her eyes, feeling resolve harden inside her. She had to do this. Finding the two branches she would use, she placed her feet and leaned toward Lily. "Go ahead. Climb on and wrap your legs around me."

As soon as Lily put all her weight on the end of the board, the piece of wood teetered and Lily screamed.

"Grab onto me, Lily!"

Lily got a good grip on her just as the board tipped sideways in the branches. Clinging to Gwyneth, the lassie buried her face into her shoulder.

"Lily, ease up. Grab my shoulders, not my neck," Gwyneth gasped. As soon as she could breathe, she glanced at the board, still dangling from the branches close to them and decided she needed to move as fast as possible. "That's better, Lily. Now hang on. We're going down fast."

"Watch out for the board. It might hit us.'"

"I know. I'll be careful."

Gwyneth struggled to find her next footing since her

view was blocked, but she found it and moved down the tree. She said another prayer and thought of Logan and Rab, and continued down the trunk, sweat dripping down her face as she moved. *Keep going, keep going.* She thought she would heave, and prayed the sensation would hold off until she was on solid ground again.

"Hurry, Gwyneth, I don't know how much longer I can hang on."

"Lass, you're doing great. Keep your legs tight around me." Down they went, slow but steady until they neared the bottom. A crash above them echoed in the air and Gwyneth looked up in time to see the board hurtling toward them.

Lily screamed and Gwyneth clutched at the wean's hand and leaned to the left side of the tree in a last ditch effort to keep the board from colliding with them. Lily's legs fell away from Gwyneth's waist and she screamed again, swinging to the left of the tree while still managing to hang onto Gwyneth's shoulders. A sharp pain shot through Gwyneth's right leg as the board caught her on its way down, but she wouldn't let go.

"You're bleeding, Gwyneth. It hit you," Lily cried.

"We'll be fine, we're almost there." She gritted her teeth as the pain in her leg grew, but she managed to straighten on the tree again. Her leg hurt, but at least it had missed both their heads. "Wrap your legs around me again, lass."

Once Lily was in position again, she continued down the tree. When they finally reached the bottom, Lily collapsed as soon as her feet hit the ground, and Gwyneth lowered herself to the ground next to her. She grabbed the lassie and hugged her tight. "We made it. We made it."

Tears of joy fell as she realized what she had accomplished. Lily was here, safe, and she had faced her biggest fear. She laughed as she patted Lily on the back. Growley joined them and licked Lily's face.

"Gwyneth, look. You're bleeding." Lily moved back to gaze at Gwyneth's leg, Growley's nose sniffing her wound.

When Gwyneth saw the amount of blood pouring from her leg, she ripped part of her tunic and tied it around the wound. A wave of dizziness assaulted her, so she scooted over to lean against the tree trunk, trying to calm her breathing. Wiping the sweat from her brow, she pressed the bandage against her wound, trying to slow the bleeding.

Gwyneth glanced at Lily. Now that they were no longer at risk of falling from the tree, she noticed how weak Lily was, her wee hands trembling as she petted Growley. "Lily, go to my horse and get something to drink. I might have an oatcake for you."

Unfortunately, her horse was grazing a good distance away. Lily tried to walk, but she stumbled twice, finally crumpling to the ground with tears in her eyes. Gwyneth pushed herself to a standing position, but was shocked by how badly her body trembled when she tried to move. She made it over to Lily, but fell down beside her.

She sighed as she tugged Lily onto her lap and wrapped her arms around her. The temperature was dropping and Lily's wee body shivered.

Lily glanced up at her and said, "Gwyneth, I'm cold. What are we going to do?"

Gwyneth glanced up at the treetops. It wouldn't be much longer until the sun dropped completely. She sighed and kissed Lily's cheek. "We wait. Uncle Logan and your da will find us." She hugged Lily as tight as she could, trying to give her what little warmth she had left in her body, but she knew she didn't have much left of her own. "Growley, come." She patted next to them and Growley sat. Lily snuggled up to Growley's heat and Gwyneth covered her with her arms, covering her as much as she could.

She hoped they would be here soon, because she was tired, very tired. Her head dipped onto Lily, but the wee one had already fallen fast asleep.

CHAPTER THIRTY-ONE

Logan's frustration had only grown in intensity by the time he ran into Quade again. "Anything?"

"Nay, naught. We have searched everywhere. I am ready to tear every single strand out of my head. Where the hell could she be?"

"We don't have much time. 'Tis almost dark." Logan hadn't told Quade about the bread he had found in the cottage. Eating it would have made Lily violently ill again, and would sap her strength as well. Nay, Quade didn't need to know that. He scanned the area again, thinking, then dismounted and studied the ground. "This way. The area is so dense, I did not check it thoroughly, and it was a while ago." He pointed to a spot in the brush. "Now I see evidence of a horse here. Let's walk." Quade motioned for the other guards to stay behind and search in a different area.

Quade followed him deep into the forest, each of the brothers pulling his horse behind him. They had traveled a short distance more when Logan halted.

"What is it?" Quade stopped directly behind him.

"Did you hear that?" Logan leaned in one direction.

"Nay."

"Shhh." He held his breath, praying to hear the sound again. Quade stared at him, the hopeful expression in his eyes forcing Logan to look away.

They listened and Logan burst into a grin. "Lily. I heard her scream." Leaving his horse in the brush, he tore off in the direction of Lily's voice, Quade following.

God's teeth, he had prayed before, but he hadn't prayed this hard in a long time. Lily had to be well, and how he hoped Gwyneth was with her. Growley barked and came running at them through the dense brush. "Where, Growley? Show me," he yelled. As if understanding the question word for word, the big dog turned around and led the way. Finally, Growley halted ahead of him and sat down next to Gwyneth in the clearing in the middle of a copse of trees, her horse not far away.

Exhilaration flooded Logan's body, but then a fist punched him right in his gut. Gwyneth sat holding something in her arms, her head listing over whatever she held. Nay, not his wee Lily. She had to be alive.

He yelled his approach and Gwyneth's head shot up. A split second later, Lily's pale smiling face rose up next to Gwyneth's.

"Papa! Uncle Logan!"

Logan's walk slowed as Quade rushed past him to grab Lily into his arms. A huge rush of relief engulfed Logan's body; he had never been so happy to see two people in his life. He wondered why Gwyneth remained on the ground, but when he finally reached her side, he saw the blood pooled around her leg, the pallor in her features, and the trembling in her hands.

"Logan." She shook her head. "I'm sorry."

"Sorry? For what?" He knelt down beside her. "You saved my niece. You're hurt." He cupped her face with his hand and was shocked to see how cool her skin was. It was only then that he noticed that her eyes were glazed and her lips held a dusky color he didn't like.

"I couldn't get on my horse. I tried, but I couldn't...make it. Lily is weak, and she hasn't eaten, and I couldn't get her back. I'm so sorry."

Quade asked, "Is she well? What's wrong, Logan? Do you need my help?"

Logan leaned down, his eyes misting as he stared down at the woman he loved. "You're safe. I'll get you back." After checking to make sure the bleeding from her leg wound had slowed, he kissed her cheek and whispered, "I love you. My thanks for rescuing my beloved niece, but you are not leaving me. Neither of you are ever leaving me again." He loosened the tourniquet on her leg and tore off a piece of his plaid to apply more pressure to the wound.

Quade overheard him. "Well, if that's going to happen, you're going to have to settle down."

"We will. We're getting married and will live in Lothian. And no one is leaving again." He scooped her up into his arms and hugged her tight. He turned to his brother, who held Lily with her head on his chest, and kissed his wee niece on the cheek. He glanced at Quade's face, where he saw the same concern he felt. Neither of the lasses looked good.

Quade whispered. "We need to get them to Brenna."

"Aye." He moved over to his horse and set Gwyneth down so she could lean against his brother while he mounted his horse. Then Quade handed her up to him and he settled her in front of him. The two guards they'd left behind joined them and soon they were headed back to the keep, Growley in pursuit.

He was so happy to have Gwyneth in his arms again. He kissed her forehead and smiled at her, but she didn't respond. Had she fallen asleep...or had she passed out?

"Gwyneth?" Logan shook her, but she didn't awaken. He needed to get her back to the keep and fast.

***

Gwyneth was running through a meadow chasing someone. Nay, she was chasing two people. Her brother, Rab, ran in one direction beckoning to her, while Logan called to her from his horse in another direction.

She would have to choose, and she didn't know how she could possibly do it.

Someone caressed her arm and her eyes flew open. Logan sat in a chair at her bedside, concern in his gaze. When she stared at him, a slow smile crept across his features. His eyes sparkled while he leaned over to kiss her cheek. She tried to push herself up in bed, but fell back against the pillow because she didn't have the strength.

"Stay there, love. You are in nae condition to move."

She tried to remember where she was, but the cloud in her mind wouldn't clear. "Something to drink?"

Logan jumped out of his seat and filled a goblet for her, then yelled out the door for Brenna before he returned to her side, helping her sit up and sip the ale he brought her. The room filled in a hurry, first with Brenna and Quade, then Lily, Torrian, and Lady Ramsay.

She couldn't understand why they all stared at her so. It was unusual for so many people to come to a bed chamber, wasn't it? Finally, Rab walked in the door and she could read the relief in his eyes when he looked at her. He carried a cross in his hand and his bible. What was going on?

Lily popped up on the bed beside her and kissed her cheek. "My thanks for rescuing me, Aunt Gwyneth. May I call you that now? Uncle Logan says you are getting married right away."

Rescuing her? She nodded at Lily in answer to her question, then glanced at Logan in the hopes he would help her clear the fog from her brain, but he never said a word.

Brenna set Lily back on the floor and sent her out the door.

Torrian, who'd been standing next to his parents, came up to her next and said, "Thank you, Aunt Gwyneth."

From his position next to the wee lad, Quade leaned

down and kissed her forehead. "Nice to see you awake again. Many thanks to you." He stepped out of the room with Torrian, following Lily.

Rab still stood by the door, tears in his eyes as he gripped his bible to his chest. "You are well, sister?"

She could only shrug.

Brenna sat on the side of the bed and checked her wound briefly before standing and patting her hand. "I think you are on the mend. I'll let you spend some time with your brother, then I shall return with some broth for you. You are still weak, so I don't want you getting out of bed. Logan, keep her here." She stood to leave.

Before turning to join her, Lady Ramsay grasped Gwyneth's hand in hers and said, "You have my undying devotion, my dear." Then the two of them stepped out of the room.

Rab and Logan were the only remaining visitors.

"I'll leave you with your brother for a minute," Logan said, glancing between the siblings. "Then I'll return." He clasped Father Rab's shoulder before he left, closing the door behind him.

"Rab? What has happened?" She peered at her brother, hoping he could help her remember.

Pulling a chair up to her bedside, Rab sat and held her hands, first offering a prayer of thanks with his eyes closed, then a blessing.

"Rab?"

He kissed his cross and said, "You don't recall? You saved Lily on your own. According to Lily, you climbed up a verra tall tree to rescue her from her bonds and carried her down on your back."

Gwyneth rubbed her forehead as the memories returned to her. "Aye, now I recall. The board and the trees. It was terrible, Rab. I was so frightened."

"But you conquered your fear of heights. Lily said you even dodged the board when it came hurtling down through the branches, and that if you hadn't swung the two of you to the side of the tree, you would both have been hit in the head."

Gwyneth groaned when she tried to lift her leg. "Aye, I have a wee gash on my leg. I was bleeding..."

"Wee gash? Hardly. You bled and bled, 'tis why you are still so weak. Brenna was worried about you, but no more so than Logan and I. But you are better, I think."

"Aye, I am still tired, but I will be fine. You are well?"

"Other than the two years of my life you have frightened off me, I am fine. Gwyneth, Logan does love you. I was able to see just how much over these last few days. You still wish to marry him?"

"Aye, I do, Rab. But will you ever be able to forgive me for leaving you? I like it here. I don't want to be in Glasgow anymore, with all the reminders of *before*. His family is wonderful, his clan members are wonderful. I think I would like to stay."

"I certainly will support you in whatever you want, and I must tell you that Quade and Lady Ramsay have invited me to stay and be the priest for his clan. They have a lovely small chapel, and Logan, Micheil and Quade have promised to build a small room on the back for me to live in. If you agree, I would like to accept. Mayhap someday I will have a niece or nephew to love." He smiled, awaiting her answer.

She reached for her brother and gave him a hug. "Aye, Rab. Naught would make me happier than to have you here with me. I think 'twill be good for both of us."

Rab chuckled and kissed her cheek. He stood up and said, "I love you, Gwyneth. You have made me verra proud and happy. I will take my leave. I know Lady Ramsay would like to speak with you in private."

Gwyneth's brow furrowed, and all she could think was, *What have I done wrong?*

CHAPTER THIRTY-TWO

Lady Ramsay strode into her chamber. Her head held high, she sat on the chair next to Gwyneth's bed, adjusting her skirts just so before folding her hands in her lap.

Gwyneth had no idea what to expect from the woman.

"My dear, I hope you do not mind that I asked to speak with you alone. This is not something I would say in front of my sons, so I hope you will keep my confidence." She cleared her throat before meeting Gwyneth's eyes.

Gwyneth nodded, not knowing what else to say.

"When you first came here, I was happy to have you in our lives because of the light you have brought to my son. I have always worried about Logan. He is a strong man, aye, but I know that his heart is often soft. As his mother, I knew why he wandered, and I didn't think he would ever be able to stop.

"Logan was overjoyed to be an uncle to both Torrian and Lily. When Torrian took ill, Logan took it verra hard. He adored his nephew and wanted to make him well again. He struggled with his inability to help the bairn. Then Lily came along and fell ill to the same sickness." She glanced at her hands as she struggled to control her breathing. Gwyneth guessed she was close to tears.

"Along came Brenna Grant, who gave me my

grandchildren back. How I have enjoyed them since she has conquered their sickness. Aye, they can become ill occasionally, but never in the way they did before. And Brenna pulled my firstborn back from a verra low place. I will always thank her for that.

"Enter a new terror, Iona, who ripped all of our hearts again by kidnapping our precious Lilykins." She paused to wipe a tear from her face. "I am here to thank you for what you did, because I don't think you exactly realize what you did."

Gwyneth stared at her, confusion keeping her from speaking.

"When everyone returned," Lady Ramsay continued. "I heard the same thing from both of my sons and from many of our guards. They had given up, believing they'd searched every area where Lily could possibly be hidden. Aye, Logan had dealt with Iona, but he had not found his niece.

"But not you. Gwyneth of the Cunninghams continued on where all the men had failed. Only you, a lass, were clever enough to find my granddaughter. And Logan and your brother say that you have a debilitating fear of heights... I am amazed at what you have accomplished."

Tears slid down her cheeks and she pulled a linen square from the folds of her skirt to mop the dampness from her cheeks. "I was going to fight you about marrying my son in your leggings and your tunics. I thought I could convince you to dress appropriately, at least for the wedding. But no more."

She stood from her chair abruptly. "If anyone has anything to say about how you dress, they will have to deal with me."

Gwyneth stared at her soon-to-be mother, shocked, but didn't dare interrupt her.

"For I know, if it had not been for you, we may have lost our darling Lily. If you had not been dressed as you were, you would not have been able to scale that tree or carry my granddaughter down. You would not have been able to cut her free or pull her out of the way of that board when it fell. Truth is," she stared at the ceiling, fighting the tears that threatened to overflow and slow her voice, "Had you not come along when you did, Lily says she would have catapulted to the ground...or been left to hang there with her hand still tied to the tree." The woman broke into a sob.

Gwyneth felt she needed to say something. "Lady Ramsay, you do not need to continue. What happened, happened."

She jerked her head up to stare at Gwyneth. "Oh, but I do. Had it not been for you, my granddaughter would be dead. My sons would not have made it in time. Even Brenna says she was close to death when they brought her here.

"So I pledge to you, my new soon-to-be daughter, that I will never again question your judgment. Wear a tunic, dress as you will. You have made all of us verra happy, especially my son. Welcome to my family, and may God bless you."

She collected herself before leaning over to place both hands on Gwyneth's cheeks. "I thank you for being who you are, and I am pleased we have found a new priest to stay with us and bless our clan." With that, she kissed Gwyneth's forehead and spun around, closing the door behind her.

**

Logan paced the corridor while his mother spoke to Gwyneth. He didn't know why his mother had asked to speak to her alone, but he trusted her to do what was right. That wasn't what caused him to pace.

He paced because he had something to do, and he needed to do it soon. He felt he needed to be honest with his wife to be, and he would let her decide whether or not she still wanted to marry him. Aye, he loved Gwyneth, but could he handle what life could bring to his loved ones?

He had always been able to control most of his life until wee Torrian had become ill. How he loved his family. Watching Quade and his mother be ripped apart by Torrian's illness upset him beyond belief. And when Lily had come down with the same thing? He had been so low, he hadn't known if he could pull himself out. So he had run away.

He ran and ran whenever he couldn't control a situation—just like he had felt in the middle of the forest when Iona had died without telling him where Lily was. All the guards in his clan hadn't been able to find Lily, and after all his efforts, he had been ready to give up.

He was willing to give up on his niece, the wee lass that had a smile that could light up an entire room had needed him and he had given up. Did he have the right to marry someone? How could he protect his wife and his own bairns if he was a quitter?

The door flung open and his mother strode out with a red face, swollen eyes, and a linen square in her hand. She hugged him without saying a word and left.

Logan put a smile on his face and headed into Gwyneth's chamber. He kissed her cheek and sat on the chair next to the bed. "All went well with my mother?"

"Aye." She glanced at him and said, "What's wrong?"

He stretched his smile wider. "Naught. May I ask you something?"

Her brow furrowed and she said, "Of course."

"How did you do it? How did you fight off one of your biggest fears?"

"I don't understand."

"Your fear of heights. You are petrified of climbing trees. How did you climb up and get Lily down when the doing of it must have made you ill?" He had to know.

"I had no choice. There was a wee voice whimpering in a tree begging me to climb up and get her. She was tethered to the tree. The only way she could get down was if I went up."

"But what made you come to that decision, that you were the only answer?"

"Well, I did try something else. I told Growley to go find you, because I knew you could climb up there without any problem."

"And?"

"Big help he was," she snorted. "All he did was stare at me and wag his tail every time Lily spoke."

"That's it? Growley wouldn't leave, so you climbed the tree? There must have been something else driving you." He leaned forward, awaiting her answer.

"Nay, Logan. Lily begged me. What else could I do?"

"How difficult was it? You must have done it quickly."

"Nay, I was not as fast as I should have been. I had my moments of nausea and dizziness where I wanted to go back down the tree, but there was no alternative. I did what Da taught me long ago. I took the first step, trusting the rest would follow. He was right. I knew Lily was too weak to come down on her own even if she hadn't been tethered. I could hear it in her voice."

He leaned over and cupped her face, then brought his lips to hers and kissed her deeply. When he pulled back, she gave him a confused look.

"Are you having second thoughts?" she asked.

"I'm doubting myself, not you." He settled back in his chair. "I just don't know if I would make a good husband and father."

CHAPTER THIRTY-THREE

"Why?" Gwyneth stared at him in shock.

He paused to gather his thoughts and then hung his head. "I gave up. After Iona died, I gave up. I was totally defeated because the whole situation was out of my control. I sat in the forest and bellowed my frustration and I was ready to quit when I caught up with Quade."

"You did?"

"Aye. I didn't find Lily, you did. I should have been the one to rescue her. I have the reputation for being the best tracker in the land, but I couldn't find my own niece. Had it not been for you, we would never have found her in time."

Gwyneth sighed. "Logan, first of all, when your family is involved, I think your mind does not work in the same way. Look at what happened to me when I confronted Duff. I could shoot an arrow to win a contest, but not around that man."

"True, but you managed to do it in the end."

Her voice dropped to a whisper. "Aye, but so did you."

Logan scowled. "Nay, I didn't. I quit. What kind of father would I make if I quit so easily?"

"You didn't quit."

"You weren't inside my head. I was ready to give up. Had Quade not pushed me on to continue, I would have gone home."

"And I would have let Duff kill me or put me on that boat, but you came along."

He stared at her, processing her words.

"And you did find us. I was the one who had quit. I knew I could go no further. All I could do was settle myself on the ground and wrap my arms around Lily to try and warm her. But I do recall my last words to her."

"What?"

"I said, don't worry, Uncle Logan and your da will find us. And you did. *You didn't quit.* If you had, Lily and I would probably still be out there."

As he pondered her words, a slow smile crept across his face.

"What is it?" She cocked her head at him.

He grasped her hands in his and kissed the back of each one. "My thanks for helping me make sense of everything in my mind. I do believe we complement each other verra well."

"That's what I have been trying to tell you, you stubborn man. Together, we will protect our family well. It's not just on your shoulders; it's on mine and on the rest of your family, too. I can think of no better man for me. I love you so and couldn't handle it if you left me now. I am so excited to become part of a larger family, and so is Rab. We won't be alone anymore."

Aye, she was right. They were wonderful together—and with their forces united, they could fight anything. He stood up and started to climb into bed with her, but then stopped. "Wait. One more thing I need answered."

"Go ahead."

"Did you really cut off a man's sac and throw it into the firth?"

Gwyneth burst out laughing and reached for his hand, tugging him so he fell on top of the bed next to her.

"That worries you a wee bit, does it?" she prodded him.

"Aye." He rearranged his breeks. "The thought does make me cringe, or at least makes me anxious to protect my private area. I saw where you shot your enemy."

"I didn't exactly cut his sac off."

"What did you do?"

"When I was on the boat, drugged, the Norse pulled a galley up next to our boat, as I already told you."

Logan could see she was going back to a bad place, so he wrapped his arms around her and held her close.

"One filthy Norseman jumped on me, ripped my clothing, and tried to rut at me. Somehow, through the cloud of the drug, I managed to find my dagger and stab him between his legs. From where he grabbed himself, I can only assume I found my mark, and there was a lot of blood."

"You are one strong lass, my love." He kissed her forehead.

"So I twisted the truth a bit. I never actually cut it off, but I did stab him where it hurt. Had I the chance, I would have cut it off and thrown it, but another ship came along and the Norse fled."

"Our paths may never have crossed had that not happened, but I still wish it hadn't. It must have been a horrible experience for you."

"Aye, but truth is, I was so drugged that my memories of it are fleeting."

A knock on the door interrupted them, and Father Rab popped his head in. His eyes widened at the sight of the couple in the bed together. "Gwyneth!"

"Rab, he is on top of the bed holding me. Stop. We are getting married."

"Aye, and in no less than a sennight. I insist! And you will not argue me. 'Tis time you do things proper."

Logan climbed back out of her bed and sat on the chair. "Aye, Father."

Gwyneth laughed, and Rab chuckled as he walked back out the door.

CHAPTER THIRTY-FOUR

Logan had insisted that Gwyneth come down for the midday meal. He seated her at their table on the dais and the servants brought serving platters of mutton stew, pheasant, baked apples and berries covered with a cooked oats and honey topping—Lily's favorite—along with crusty dark bread.

The only reason he'd needed to be stubborn in his insistence was that Gwyneth couldn't walk much yet, at least not enough to handle the stairway. Brenna had stitched her leg, and she still suffered much pain. He'd needed to carry her down the steps.

Gwyneth couldn't manage any of the rich food, but Brenna brought her a thin broth with carrots and turnips. She ate no more than half a bowl. She leaned back in the chair Logan had insisted she sit in, grateful for the extra support. He had covered her with his plaid, and she'd gratefully wrapped herself in it.

At the end of the meal, the table full of Ramsays, along with Rab, of course, all quieted, staring at her.

"Aunt Gwyneth, we need to ask you a question," Lily said.

Quade nodded. "The suspense has been too much for us. No one can guess."

She looked at their expectant faces before speaking. "Guess what?"

"How did you find me?" Lily asked.

Logan added, "Aye, we had gone through that area

before without noticing anything astray. How did you think to look up? I never would have guessed to find her in the trees before Iona had told me."

She grinned. "I don't know if I should say. Growley and I both figured it out at about the same time."

"Why not? We need to know. 'Tis a learning experience." Quade glanced around the table. "Naught you could say would upset us."

Gwyneth turned to Lily. "Were you sick when you were in the trees?"

"Aye. I kept heaving." She nodded her head as she held tight to Brenna's hand.

"Where did you heave?"

Lily gave her a puzzled look, then her face lit up. "Over the side."

"Aye."

"You saw where I heaved?" Lily's eyes grew wide at the thought.

Gwyneth shook her head and waited for them to understand.

"Nay, Lily," Brenna said, catching on first. "'Twas the odor."

Gwyneth nodded.

"And Growley smelled it, too. Am I right, Aunt Gwyneth? Growley has a good nose." Torrian jumped out of his seat to pet his dog, who licked him in the face.

"Aye." Gwyneth grinned. "When I noticed the odor, I turned in a circle and searched the area. Growley sat in one spot with his tail wagging."

"Why?" Torrian asked.

A room full of faces stared at her, all of them curious to hear her response.

"Growley sat directly underneath Lily, right next to the spot where she had heaved."

Torrian laughed and hugged his beloved pet.

Pushing his chair back from the table, Quade yelled, "Growley, come." He patted his lap. Needing no greater invitation, Growley leapt over to his side. "Sit." As soon as the deerhound did as commanded, Quade handed him a big piece of mutton, which Growley devoured in seconds.

Logan's booming voice interrupted the festivities. "There is something we must ask Torrian and Lily."

Wee Lily jumped off Brenna's lap and scooted up onto her uncle's lap. "What is it, Uncle Logan?"

"Gwyneth and I wondered if you would walk with her to the chapel, and if Torrian would walk with me."

Both bairns clapped their hands in excitement, and they turned to stare at Quade for his approval.

"I think that's a wonderful idea." Quade said, looking to Brenna, who nodded and smiled.

Rab said, "I can't stand with my sister, since I will be at the head of the chapel, so I think that is a lovely idea."

"And Uncle Logan," Lily patted his chest as she peered up at him. "I know why you and Gwyneth found me."

"Why is that, sweetie?" Logan asked.

"Because you both still have my lucky stones."

"Of course, I should have known," he chuckled.

"Uncle Logan, listen." The lass was so serious the table hushed to hear her next words. "Did you compare your stones? I chose them carefully."

"Nay." He reached into his sporran and pulled out his stone, setting it on the table in front of him.

Gwyneth gasped. "'Tis the same." She reached into her pocket and pulled out her own stone, setting it next to Logan's. "They are exactly the same stone."

Lily beamed. "Aye, the stone broke in half when I found it, and I knew it would bring you two together." Then she ran over to Gwyneth and placed her hands on her knees. "I wanted you to be my aunt, Aunt Gwyneth. See? It worked."

Logan and Gwyneth just stared at each other.

***

The following day, Lady Ramsay, Brenna, and Lily joined Gwyneth in the great hall with bolts of fabric to choose for the wedding.

Lily chimed in first. "Aunt Gwyneth, what are we wearing? Can we both wear the same thing?"

Gwyneth hadn't given it a thought. She had considered making a new tunic, but what of Lily? "I'm not sure, lass."

Lady Ramsay and Brenna both stared at her.

"Please? I want to be dressed just like you."

Gwyneth scowled, unsure of what to do next. While her future mother-in-law had given her blessing for Gwyneth to wear what she wanted, that didn't mean she'd be fine with Lily doing the same. And besides, her wedding day was special, and she thought of Rab, so perhaps...

Lady Ramsay said, "I will support your decision, Gwyneth. I said it before, and I won't go back on my word."

Gwyneth glanced at Brenna, who nodded in agreement. After she gave it some thought, she announced her choice.

***

The expression on her brother's face told her all she needed to know about whether or not she had made the right decision. She had been thinking of his distress at the fair, and that she would be in the House of the Lord, so decided to do it for one day.

"Gwyneth?" He strode over and stood in front of her in his black robes, holding his bible in one hand.

"Aye, Rab. I am wearing skirts like a proper lady, but just for today." She gave her brother a sheepish look, hoping he wouldn't make light of it. She was surprised by how beautiful she felt in the unfamiliar clothes.

"You are lovely. How I wish Mama and Da could see you today." He kissed her cheek. "But why? I didn't expect you to give up your leggings."

"Lily. She told me that she wanted to dress just like me. So I decided mayhap I could dress as a lady for one day, for both you and Lily."

Lily smiled at Father Rab. "Isn't she beautiful?"

"Aye, she is, and so are you, Miss Lily." Rab took Gwyneth's hand in his. "I am so happy for you, Gwyneth."

They made their way to the door, getting ready to leave the great hall and walk to the chapel. They would meet Logan in front of the small church, which Rab would enter through the back. The others would be waiting inside for them. She straightened her skirts, not sure she would walk well in them, but she had practiced with Brenna and Lily.

Gwyneth was dressed in a dark green outer gown and a pale green kirtle, with a gold chain belt adorning her thin hips. The colors had been selected by Lily, who'd insisted they look like the forest. Gwyneth's over gown had long bell sleeves, and her kirtle was the same pastel green as Lily's gown. They both wore circlets on their heads. Her hair was free flowing, falling in waves down her back with flowers and ribbons interwoven with the darks strands.

Lily's hair was golden as sunbeams, but it was decorated the same. The color had come back into her cheeks and she lit up the room with her infectious smile.

Gwyneth offered Lily her hands. "Are you ready, my sweet?"

Lily nodded, giggling as the three of them emerged on to the steps of the great hall. Two horses awaited them, and Rab helped Gwyneth mount and straighten her skirts, before assisting Lily.

When they arrived in front of the chapel, she blushed at the shocked look on Logan's face. She hoped he wasn't upset she had decided to wear a skirt and wear her hair down. Her heart pounded as he approached her horse to help her down, Micheil assisting Lily. He grasped her waist and she placed her hands on his shoulders, afraid to look him in the eye until her feet touched the ground.

"Gwyneth," he whispered.

"Aye?" She brought her gaze up to meet his, hoping to see that he was pleased with her decision. She could describe his expression as none other than stunned, which didn't help her decide how he felt.

"Lass, you take my breath away."

Gwyneth blushed and asked, "You are not upset that I'm not in my leggings?"

"Nay." He held his hand out to her. "You are beautiful. Come, 'tis time for me to marry the love of my life."

Logan wore a white leine and his Ramsay plaid wrapped around his waist and over his shoulder. A large blue stone brooch held it in place. The Ramsay plaid was beautiful in shades of blue, black, and green. Aye, she had seen it before, but today the colors his family wore were rich and strong, not made to blend into the outdoors. She noticed Lady Ramsay with a linen square in her hand, sitting beside Avelina, Quade, Brenna, and Micheil. She was amazed at how quickly she had come to love her new family.

Rab performed a beautiful ceremony, and Gwyneth saw the tears in his eyes when he finally told Logan to kiss his bride. She grinned and wrapped her arms around her new husband as he lifted her off the ground and kissed her deeply, only stopping when Lily's giggle interrupted them.

As he set Gwyneth back on her feet, Lily said, "Wait, Uncle Logan."

They turned to see what the lass wanted and she stood there, her outstretched fists holding the stones she had given them. "You have to keep these. You left them on the table, but they are to be your lucky stones forever."

They each took their stone and hugged Lily between

them, then gestured for Torrian to join them in the embrace. After a moment, Logan stood and held his hand out to her, "Come, love. We must go into the great hall to greet the rest of our guests."

Gwyneth had enjoyed every minute of the ceremony, but she was overwhelmed with the revelry inside the great hall. The area was packed full and minstrels kept everyone entertained. She had never attended such a feast in her life. Trenchers of pork, pheasant, and boar were plentiful, along with numerous vegetables and fruit tarts.

Logan's family had been wonderful, but she had a sinking feeling in the pit of her stomach. Tonight, she and Logan would lie together as husband and wife, something she was looking forward to, but the thought of doing it in the keep with everyone around made her very nervous.

"Why are you so unsettled, wife?" He leaned over and kissed her cheek as they sat at the dais, in the middle of the exuberant celebration.

Gwyneth blushed, embarrassed that he could so easily read her mind. "I look forward to being alone with you, but..."

"But what?"

"I am afraid to sleep with you here. You know how loud I can be." She peeked at him through her lashes, doing her best to whisper so no one could overhear.

He grinned. "That I do. And I hope to make you moan louder than ever tonight."

"That's what I'm afraid of, Logan. Not here where your mother can overhear us. She's just down the passageway from our chamber."

"Nay, she isn't."

"Aye, she is. Besides, I heard there is to be a bedding ceremony and I don't want to do that. Can we not take part in that tradition? I would surely die of embarrassment."

Logan winked at her. "I have taken care of

everything."

***

Logan had guessed how Gwyneth would feel, and he wanted their wedding night to be special. He held his hand out to her. "Come, we're running away."

Though she looked puzzled, she placed her hand in his. The evidence of her trust like a warm ember inside him, he nodded to Quade to go ahead with their plan. After nodding back, his brother moved over to the main doorway of the great hall and started to make an announcement.

As soon as everyone turned to see what Quade was about, Logan and Gwyneth ducked into the kitchens.

"Logan? Where are we going?"

He hustled her along behind him, hoping they wouldn't get caught. They wouldn't be missed for a few minutes, but that was probably all the time they had.

"Away," he said over his shoulder. "We're going to our own private place."

"But can I not get my leggings first? I would like to get out of this gown."

"Wife, learn to trust your husband and follow me."

Logan tugged her out into the crisp night air where a horse awaited them. He lifted her up into the saddle and then mounted behind her.

"Logan, where are we going?"

"Shush. You must trust me. This is my wedding gift to you and it's a surprise." He tugged her back against him and spurred his horse through the bailey and the gates. The two guards at the portcullis waved them on and finally they were free.

He set his horse to a gallop and nuzzled Gwyneth's neck as they took off into the moonlit night, a light mist clinging to the earth. A short time later, he pulled on the reins and slowed Paz down as they neared a copse of trees. When he came to a halt, he helped Gwyneth down and they crept through the wooded area hand in hand.

Finally he stopped and held his arm out to her. "Our wedding chamber, my love. Just for you."

Gwyneth gasped as she took in everything in front of her. A dense cluster of trees concealed a small clearing, just large enough for the size of a large bed. Fronds and pine boughs had been interwoven in the tree branches above to create a canopy over the clearing, and the ground was covered with bedrolls, furs, plump pillows, and several plaids. Several baskets of food sat on either side of the clearing, hanging from the tree limbs.

"Logan, I love it."

He tugged her through the trees at the side to find a small creek that wound behind the area, hidden by some large rocks. "The water is a bit cold, but 'tis private."

She threw her arms around his neck and kissed him soundly.

He growled and pulled back. "Time for us to get you out of that gown."

Returning to their makeshift bed, he helped her with the ties in the back.

She said, "The only thing that would have made this perfect is if I had thought to pack my leggings for the morrow."

Before she dropped her skirts to the ground, he reached down behind the pillows and picked up a wrapped package. The surprise on her face when he handed it to her was worth every minute of his effort.

She tore off the ties and folded the material back. Inside sat a dark green tunic and new leggings to match. "Logan, many thanks." She ran her hands over the soft cloth before clutching them to her chest. "You have indeed thought of everything."

She dropped her gift onto the furs and cupped his face in her hands. "I do love you so. This place is the best gift you could have ever given me." She kissed him, teasing him with her tongue, before pulling back to ask, "How did you know?"

He shrugged his shoulders. "Because I love you. Now, about that gown..."

EPILOGUE

Gwyneth had to admit she had never been so happy in her life. She glanced at Logan's beaming face as he jested with his brothers, all of them sitting in chairs around the hearth in the great hall. How she loved him. They had taken a large amount of ribbing over their disappearance on the night of the wedding, but all was forgiven.

Rab had almost cried when they returned hand in hand, but he'd managed to hold everything together. She was so pleased he would be staying on as the priest. Rather than losing the one remaining member of her family to join this new family, she would have everyone she loved with her.

Quade and Micheil and Logan were so close, which was another reason it felt right to settle here. The brothers would build a new cottage for Logan and Gwyneth, and they had chosen a spot in the forest. They would stay in the keep as winter came upon them, then move in the new year. Logan promised her they would sneak off to their hideaway once in a while, just to be alone, and because she loved the spot.

Lady Ramsay was a constant source of support and inspiration, and she'd offered to teach Gwyneth to cook so they wouldn't have to come up to the keep for all their meals once they moved.

She only had one issue left to settle, and she couldn't decide how to go about it. She needed to get in touch with her supervisor. But having pledged to keep her affiliation with the crown secret, she couldn't tell her husband...and he was unlikely to understand if she disappeared to Glasgow for a day.

All of a sudden, Logan stood and held his hand out to her. "Come, wife, I have someone I want you to see." Logan kissed her cheek and tugged her over to Quade's solar.

She had no idea who she would find inside.

When she stepped through the door, a tall man stood facing the window, his back to them. As soon as they entered, he spun around and smiled at them. Logan strode over to greet him, his arm still around Gwyneth.

She gasped when she realized who it was. Dougal Hamilton settled his hands on his hips as he stared at the newly married couple. "Why, Gwyneth, I see marriage agrees with you. You are glowing, though the shocked expression on your face isn't becoming. Logan kept our secret, I see."

She turned to her husband and said, "You knew?"

Logan kissed her cheek. "Aye."

"You didn't tell me?"

"Och, I couldn't, love. Dougal wouldn't allow me."

"Gwyneth." Dougal came over and stood in front of her. "Don't blame your husband. He was sworn to secrecy just as you were."

"When? When did you find out?" she asked Logan.

Dougal spoke up. "It was all my doing. I was worried about you with Erskine, so I assigned him to follow you."

Gwyneth took a step back, pushing away from her husband. He had only followed her because she had been his assignment? She glared at Logan as she tried to process the news that threatened to tear apart her world.

"Whoa, whoa, Gwyneth, nay. I know what you're thinking. I followed you down from the Highlands on my own, and I was already in love with you when I met with Dougal." He covered her hands with his, rubbing the back of them with his thumbs.

Gwyneth collapsed in a chair, unsure of what to believe. Finally she managed to look up and meet Dougal's gaze. "Logan's right," he said. "He was already besotted when he came to me. I could see it in his eyes. In fact, the reason I assigned him to you was because I knew he cared. I wanted you to have someone there for you, so the situation with Duff Erskine would be wrapped up well."

Gwyneth reviewed the sequence of events in her head. "When did you assign him to me?"

"Not until the day you returned from the Highlands. He had just left the Kirk to come see me," Dougal answered.

"After I proposed marriage to you and you turned me down." Logan still held her hands as he spoke.

"She turned you down?" Dougal asked, then turned to Gwyneth. "You turned him down?"

"Aye, I was confused at the time, and only focused on one thing." She paused to consider the situation, and decided Logan had told the truth. He'd proposed as soon as they returned from the Highlands. "I accept your explanation. Then why are you here?"

"For one thing, to congratulate my two best spies on their marriage. I think your union will be a verra happy one."

"And?" Gwyneth asked. "You aren't taking him away from me, are you?"

"Nay. I will leave you alone for now. You need to get to know each other. But come spring, I hope you will both consider returning to work for me."

"Doing what exactly, Hamilton? I don't wish to be worried about my wife going off on her own somewhere."

"Nay, of course not. I wouldn't send her anywhere without you."

Logan and Gwyneth turned to look at Dougal, then at each other.

"Together?" Logan asked. "You'll let us work together?"

"Aye. Imagine how strong you two will be if I assign you to work together."

"Truly?" Gwyneth asked, lighting up at the suggestion.

Logan grinned, wrapping his arm around her waist.

Dougal strode over to the door. "Time for me to move on." He reached for the handle, but stopped and turned to them. "For now, you only have one assignment."

"What's that?" Logan asked.

"Make a bairn. I don't care whether it's a lad or a lassie." He stared at the ceiling. "Imagine the abilities of a wean from the loins of you two." He chuckled. "What an intriguing thought."

THE END

Dear Reader,

Thank you so much for reading *Highland Sparks*! I am so excited to have published this fifth novel in my Highlander Series. I really enjoyed telling Logan and Gwyneth's story.

I love to hear from my readers and I also value your opinions. Please share your thoughts with me. There are several ways you can let me know what you think:

1. **Write a review on Amazon or Goodreads:** Please consider leaving a review. They can really help an author, particularly one who is self-published as I am. I don't have a marketing department or an advertising team backing me. Any reviews are appreciated, and yes, I do read them all. If you didn't like the novel, then please offer constructive criticism so I can improve. Angry responses do not help me and I ignore them. You do not need to use your real name for Amazon, Barnes and Noble, or Goodreads. These reviews are also helpful for other readers.

2. **Send me an email at keiramontclair@gmail.com.** I promise to respond!

3. **Go to my Facebook page and 'like' me:** You will get updates on any new novels, book signings, and giveaways. Here is the link: https://www.facebook.com/KeiraMontclair

4. **Visit my website: www.keiramontclair.com:** Another way to contact me is through my website. Don't forget to sign up for my newsletter while you're there.

5. **Stop by my Pinterest page:**
   http://www.pinterest.com/KeiraMontclair/
You'll see how I envision Logan, Gwyneth, and the others.

The next Clan Grant series novel will center around Micheil Ramsay and a member of the Grant Clan you have never met.

Keep reading!
Keira Montclair

ABOUT THE AUTHOR

Keira Montclair is the pen name of an author who lives in Florida with her husband. She loves to write fast-paced, emotional historical romance, especially with children as secondary characters in her stories. In her spare time, she is a voracious reader, especially historical romance! She also loves to take ballet classes. She has worked as a registered nurse in pediatrics and recovery room nursing. Teaching is another of her loves, as she has taught high school Mathematics, Medical Assisting, and Practical Nursing.

Her Highlander Clan Grant Series is a reader favorite and she has many other stories planned. Her next endeavor will be a contemporary romance. She loves to hear from readers. If you send her an email through her website, she promises to respond.

Made in the USA
Coppell, TX
12 June 2023